Once Upon A Winter
By Melyssa Williams

Red Team Ink
DBA of Zealot Solutions, Idaho LLC
5447 Kendall St.
Boise, ID 83706
Copyright© 2016 by Red Team Ink

For permission requests or information about discounts for special bulk purchases please contact: redteamink@gmail.com. Substantial discounts on bulk orders are available to corporations, professional associations, and small businesses.

Printed in The United States of America

Library of Congress Control Number: 2017930054
ISBN: 978-0-9982349-3-9

Title: Once Upon A Winter
Description: First Edition

For ballet dancers everywhere, from the sheep to the mice to the nut-crackers to the sugar plum fairies.

And to my mom. Thanks for all the ballets and books.

Cast of Characters

Marie (Ree) Stahlbaum – A fifteen-year-old clockmaker's apprentice and young lady of quality.

Dr. and Mrs. Stahlbaum – Marie's parents.

Fritz – Marie's older brother who's a soldier.

Louise – Marie's older sister and an eighteen-year-old spinster.

Jessa Pratt – Ree's closest friend.

Herr Christian Drosselmeier – Ree's godfather, clock maker, Justice of the Peace, and mysterious inventor.

Hoffman – The robotic butler.

Melisande – The Stahlbaum's maid.

Nikolai – A mechanical nutcracker brought to life by Drosselmeier.

China – A clockwork doll with a mind of her own.

Cullen Souris – A villain with an army of mechanical rats.

Faith and Hope – Half reindeer-half girl creatures in the forests of the Bavarian Alps.

Georgie, Anastasia, and Pork Chop – Members of the Angels—resident pickpockets of the town of Sea Level, and boarders at Miss Ginger's School for (Gifted) Young Criminals.

Ginger – Sea Level's proprietress of Miss Ginger's School for Young Criminals, and an infamous stage actress.

Winter – The Snow Queen.

Sylvie – A faerie.

Captain Fennimore and Crew - The captain and crew of the pirate airship, The Suddenly Surrendered.

ACT I
The Party Scene

Chapter One
A Dangerous Christmas Eve

Later, the party goers would comment on the delicacy of the cakes, the frivolity of the entertainment, and the becoming headwear of the ladies, but as polite society at all times behaved appropriately, they never mentioned the deaths. This was of great comfort to the host and hostess.

* * *

Ree Stahlbaum entered the parlor tentatively. She was not tentative due to the lack of lighting, but due to the fact that she had misplaced her Hair Decoration and Toilette Robotic again and didn't want to tread upon it once she located it. Sure enough, two steps into the parlor and not only did the missing robotic whir at her with a ferocious (yet cheerful) noise, but at the very same instant, she heard the piercing voice of her elder sister, Louise. The combination of the two elicited a yelp from Ree that bounced off the walls of the parlor.

"It is mere moments before the guests begin arriving, Marie, and you know how dreadfully long it takes to make your hair presentable. Longer than moments." Louise Stahlbaum was angry, and when she was angry, her lovely face blotched, which made her even angrier because her peaches and cream complexion was something she was proud of. The cook used to complain they needed their own cow to keep up with the demands for buttermilk, which Louise used as moisturizer. She took a deep breath, and approaching Ree from where she had materialized a moment before, she lifted a lock of Ree's cherry red hair and attempted to tuck it back up behind a strand of fraying ribbon. It fell out promptly, and Louise glared at it. Three years older, Louise took it personally that Ree had not grown up to be everything she had hoped and mentored her to be. Their mother had always been slightly absent, and Louise's mother hen tendencies had been strained to the breaking point with her little sister. Ree never could sit still, show up on time for anything, or be trusted with items of importance, such as fetching things, and reflecting well upon her older sister.

"I know, Lou, I'm starting now, I really am. It's just that I misplaced everything and I lost track of time. Melisande will fix it in no time, and look – I'm at least dressed in a punctual manner." Ree twirled a bit for her sister. Twirling was an action she normally refused to stoop to, but she knew when she needed to grease some wheels, so to speak. Ree's gown of peacock blue with green trim had been, at first, eyed critically by both Louise and Mrs. Stahlbaum, but then embraced when the same unusual color combination had been spotted on a very fashionable French woman just last week.

"At least no one will be looking at your hair." Louise sighed. "Not with a dress like that. And Melisande is a maid, not a miracle worker. Nevertheless, I expect to see you in place momentarily, young lady. Now, hurry up!" She had taken to calling Ree 'young lady' in a manner that was maddening and insulting to Ree and made her feel as though she were six years old again and not allowed in the Grand Parlor under any circumstances.

Nevertheless, Ree obediently seized the silver handle of the hip height steel basket that was capable of organizing and color coding various ribbons, hats, gloves, and other items, and also capable of coming alongside during shopping trips. Ree had come up with the idea and fashioned it herself after one too many shopping expeditions with her sister where she had been laden down with so many bolts of fabrics and squares of lace that her arms had ached for a week. The robotic had charmed her mother nicely, and even Lou could see the value of it, but the same couldn't be said for Dr. Stahlbaum, who wasn't amused that shopping was now even easier and more pleasurable for the women in his household. Ree had been approached by many eager young ladies who desired a self-propelled shopping robotic of their own, but Dr. Stahlbaum had staunchly refused to entertain the notion of his youngest daughter going into business like a common street urchin. Peddling wares was not something a Stahlbaum did. The list of things Stahlbaums did not do was rather extensive, and if you asked Ree, rather annoying.

The Stahlbaums were wealthy, a fact that, while Ree could appreciate the wealth in its simplest form, also annoyed her greatly. It seemed to her that while she was naturally grateful for her hard working papa and a pleasant enough upbringing, being a young lady of stature and virtue was something she was never going to quite live up to, nor did she particularly want to. Louise was more suited to her life of leisure and pomp, and was every inch the lady, at least when she wasn't shouting across the house at Ree. Their male sibling, Fritz, was also suited to the life he was born to – he wore it like he wore his leather gloves - and it seemed Ree's mechanical tendencies and urges to throw ladylike behavior out the window (not to mention her hair accessories) was a bit of a drain on the sympathies of her family. Ree was pretty convinced she was doomed to a life of comfortable obscurity, thanks to her riches and a loving family. Secretly, she thought it unfair and only in recent years had ceased daydreaming of being a runaway, penniless orphan. Or at the very least, an urchin. Adventure never found wealthy girls. It couldn't even penetrate the brick walls, or scale the rose covered fences. It was Ree's sad lot in life to be pampered and loved all her days, which were sure to be long since she could afford excellent medical care. She sighed just thinking of it.

"Yes, Mother." Ree kissed her long suffering sister, fondly, and exited the dark parlor. "Though Melisande could do a more proper job with my hair if all of you would only allow the gas lighting."

Louise didn't favor the prodding with a response. Though gas lighting was all the rage, she didn't trust it, and neither did the other Stahlbaums. If the imagery of her wayward sister's hairstyle being adequately tamed didn't sway her, nothing would. Ree made a disappointed face at the lack of a rejoinder and stubbed her toe on the robotic as they moved down the hall. *Feeling my way*, she thought in annoyance, her toe throbbing. *In the pitch blackness. Like a coal miner. A wealthy coal miner. How droll.*

Melisande did the best she could in the time allowed for Ree's hair – pinning and swirling and tucking until Ree squirmed and begged for release – and firmly anchored a new hairpiece over the streak of white. Ree's hair had already been a thing of eye catching color, with its strands of fiery red and copper, but after a misuse and mis-measurement of certain chemicals in her godfather Drosselmeier's workship and laboratory, Ree had emerged with a very noticeable slash of pure white. Melisande and

Louise were always searching for new ways and new hats to cover the offending stripe.

Tonight it was a charming green top hat, miniature in size, pinned sidewise over the streak, with a bit of black lace that flopped becomingly, and part of a broken clock face perched just so. The hands of the clock were striking midnight, and the pins that Melisande used were shaped like tiny keys. Most of the stubborn white stripe was covered well enough, though if you weren't distracted fully by the odd hat, you would catch glimpses of the silvery strands peeking through. Most of the time, Ree slapped a bowler hat over her head and their strange follicles, but no such disregard for fashion would be allowed tonight. Louise, especially, would never have stood for it.

Tonight was the Stahlbaum's annual Christmas party, and everyone who was anyone would be there. Ree was equal parts thrilled and dismayed. There were sure to be lavish gifts – and though she might be less greedy or vain than most girls her age, Ree was no saint, and she enjoyed a good present as much as anyone – but there was also sure to be boredom. Boredom didn't sit well with Ree, and she was already itching in her scratchy, new crinoline. *Easy on the starch Melisande, you're going to give me a rash.* She longed to pull the key shaped pins from her hair. She had a decent book on organic grease powered inventions she was anxious to see the end of, and a tin of cheddar and apple biscuits secreted away under her bed. The two combined made the prospect of making small talk with the rich families and dancing with their grabby sons seem like torture. Normally, she could count on Louise taking all the dances and all the boys flocking to her, but lately – and no one was more irritated by this than Ree – a small percentage of the young men had been flocking to her. Enjoying the chase and the challenge, Ree could only assume, but she would do everything she could to see Louise properly married off and out of Ree's own hair. White streak and all.

But on the other hand, she thought, determined to find a silver lining in the prospect of dancing and making small talk all evening, *Dross will show up like always, and no matter how many ways I've failed the family by then, he will do something splendidly inappropriate and outshine me.*

The thought boosted Ree's spirits and she was nearly as enthusiastic as the rest of her family when at last they all stood in their proper spots in the grand room. Every year for as long as Ree could remember, they had stood thusly: Mother and Ree arm in arm (probably to keep Ree from darting off at an inopportune time), Dr. Stahlbaum at Mother's left, Louise opposite, and then Fritz, though Fritz usually got to stand wherever he liked, being a boy and all. This year Fritz was in his dress uniform, and Louise naturally, looked stunning in her gown of pink and gold. Her hair was curled and swirled and looked a bit like a plop of meringue, Ree privately thought. But on Louise it worked. All the young debutantes would be imitating it by tomorrow. She had a golden and sparkling set of goggles perched atop her meringue, and Ree mentally rolled her eyes. They weren't even functional; whatever was the point? It was humiliating to anyone with even a scant knowledge of technological education. Ree straightened the oversized bow in the back of her gown that Fritz had obnoxiously yanked on moments earlier, and glared at her brother, sticking her tongue out for good measure. Mostly grown he may be, but he was still a disobedient boy in his sister's hazel eyes. He widened his own brown eyes and adopted an air of innocence as he shrugged at their mother, who was watching them both like a hawk.

"That's quite enough, Marie," Mrs. Stahlbaum murmured firmly under her breath. She pinched her daughter on the underside of her arm. "You're too old to be egging on your brother."

Ree rubbed her arm and thought if she had an everlasting mark from each pinch her mother had ever given her, she'd be spotted like a Dalmatian.

And then the party guests began to arrive. Of course, each and every one were fashionably late; since they all had the same thought, it meant they arrived together, piling in through the doorway like giddy children. No sooner had the butler robot, Hoffman, taken their overcoats and capes, then the next batch would come in out of the snow.

And what a snow it was. Ree didn't remember such a storm as this; not ever, and certainly not on the eve of their annual party. She was surprised it dared to snow so heavily on her mother's celebration night, though the guests seemed captivated and charmed by it. The young ladies had flakes in their hair that set off the sparkle in their eyes, and gave them reasons to shake their heads prettily in the direction of the young men. Hoffman had his metal hands full, moving from room to room with the cloaks, and after four families arrived at once, two with impossibly difficult Russian names, he gave up announcing everyone. Robotics were not supposed to sulk, not having emotions, but if ever one did, it was Hoffman. It seemed to be a glitch of sorts, probably deep in his cerebellum compartment. Ree patted him in sympathy and untangled a reticule from the wires protruding from his head.

"I said we needed more help tonight, m'lady," he puffed his words. Small clouds of steam came from his metal ears, and he was hot to Ree's touch. "I simply cannot be expected to take the place of an entire staff! Half a staff, yes, but not footman and valet and gatekeeper, too!"

"I know, I know," Ree soothed. "But you're doing marvelously, you really are. No one in all of Bavaria has a Hoffman Model I, and we appreciate you so."

The robot seemed mollified and the steam went down to a slighter puffing. The wires atop his head stopped quivering, and Hoffman nodded towards Ree before moving along to serve the punch with Melisande, who was juggling far too many wine goblets and appeared terrified. Melisande was a living, breathing maid, not a robotic, though with her humdrum personality she could easily be mistaken for one. Secretly, Ree agreed with Hoffman – they should have hired more help for the party, especially if some of the longer traveling guests stayed overnight due to the storm. Ree bit her lip in anticipation of Hoffman and Melisande's woes if that were to come to fruition.

"Ree!" someone called gaily, from across the room. It was Jessamyn Pratt, youngest daughter of one of the oldest and most respected families in Germany. The Pratts were also close friends with the Stahlbaum family; a lucky twist of fate that enabled Ree and Jessamyn to see one another often. Jessa's shiny, straight hair had been curled within an inch of its life, and she was wearing the brocade gown she had gone on and on about over the last week with Ree. The corset had been pulled so tightly that her waist-line was positively miniscule, and Ree knew she'd be fanning herself most of the night in order to avoid the vapors. In spite of drastic leanings towards a preoccupation with fashion – something Ree put up with, but didn't encourage – Jessa was a level headed girl, with a witty sense of humor and a love of adventure. At least, she was pretty certain she would love adventure. As rich as the Stahlbaums and enclosed in a country mansion nearly year round due to Lady Pratt's delicate and high strung character, Jessa had never been given opportunity to test her theory. Anytime Adventure came calling, it was turned out on its ear by Petipa, their version of Hoffman. Lady Pratt was American though, so at least Jessa had that scandalous part of her upbringing to boast about when life got too dull to bear.

"Did you see how desperately it's snowing?" Jessa widened her blue eyes and gave her head a merry shake. The tiny, frosted snowflakes that were caught in her brown hair scattered like diamonds and they began to melt and disappear right before Ree's eyes. They both laughed, and Jessa tucked the other girl's arm underneath her own possessively. "Come now, there will be nothing for it but for some of your out-of-town guests to sleep here. You'll have such fun! Why do I have to live so very close to you and have the best horseless carriage? I'll never be allowed to stay over." She pouted prettily.

Ree elbowed her in response. "You're always welcome here, you know that, silly," she replied. "And with my luck, it will be only the very uninteresting, the most gloomy, and the frightfully proper. I shall be a withered old crone when next you see me, having been talked to death by Mama and Papa's ancient associates. Such a way to go."

"Better not let them hear you say that – the ancient associates, I mean," broke in a male voice from behind Ree.

She turned around to find Fritz with a mischievous look on his face. "Oh go away, do." Ree wrinkled her nose. "It's bad enough I have to share a home and parents with you; I draw the line at sharing my time and my friends, too."

"Ah, but Jessa here is my friend, too, I'll remind you. Isn't that right, darling?" Fritz bowed to Jessa in a grand fashion and took her hand. "And in fact, she promised me a dance tonight, so be a good girl, little sis, and go fetch us some punch, would you?"

"No, I will not, and bring her back immediately." Ree glared at her brother, and also at Jessa, who appeared to be much less upset about the whole dancing debacle than Ree thought she had any right to be. "And don't call her darling!"

The evening progressed much like it had at many Christmas Eve parties past. Old Mrs. Spratz had entirely too much spiced wine, belted out Auld Lang Syne at a frightening decibel, and many a tot fell asleep underneath and around the furniture. Melisande had her hands full filling glasses and goblets and passing around trays of cookies and cakes. Poor Hoffman began to quiver and overheat again and Ree had to take a moment to escort him into the kitchen where she patted his gears down with a cooling oil dabbed onto her handkerchief, and talked him out of quitting as soon as the pudding was served.

"And Herr Drosselmeier hasn't even arrived yet, m'lady!" Hoffman clapped his metal hands over his face – or what had been designed to look like a face. It was really more of a smooth dome, round as an egg, with two swirls of copper that resembled eyes. He spoke through a tiny speaker mechanism where his lips should rightly be, and though he had no nose, there were faint markings where Ree had tried to draw one on for him last week. Hoffman was rather vain for a robot, and the Hoffman IVs had recently been released for purchase. With noses. He had been appalled and embarrassed at his lack of a proboscis. He had retired to his bed in the broom closet and refused to come out until Ree arrived with her paint set. When the drawing hadn't looked quite right (and utterly profile-less), Ree had promised to shape him one out of metal as soon as possible, and weld it on.

"And whatever does Herr Drosselmeier have to do with anyone?" Ree cocked her head, inquisitively. The old butler really was getting odd. He was certainly past his prime, and the warranty had expired years ago.

"For one thing, he makes a terrible mess, each and every time he visits. And who do you think has to pick up after him?"

Melisande, most likely, Ree thought, but didn't reply.

"And he brings the most peculiar things, m'lady. You know that! Why, they're – they're-" Hoffman trailed off, evidently at a loss for words.

"Progressive? Futuristic? Mind bending? Fantastic? Incredible?" Ree suggested, helpfully.

Hoffman only glared at her, if it were possible for a robot with no facial features to glare. "Unnatural, m'lady." He drawled it out in a splendidly stuck-up tone, and to top it off, he sniffed.

Goodness, even the mechanical devices in my life are snobs, Ree thought. Really, it was too much. "Now that's quite enough personal opinion on my godfather," she answered, sternly. "Herr Drosselmeier is a genius, if a bit...eccentric. All the best artists and inventors are unconventional, and it's always the high point of the season to see what he's brought me. I mean, us. What he's brought us." She coughed. It was no secret Ree was her godfather's favorite.

Hoffman sniffed again and snatched a beautifully shaped bottle of Pear Schnapps – a favored indulgence of Dr. Stahlbaum's – from the pantry. "I'm sure you're right, m'lady." His voice implied otherwise. "I'll just be on my way then, if you'll be so kind as to spruce up my hair."

Ree obligingly fluffed up the seven wires that poked in random directions off of Hoffman's head. There used to be at least two dozen wires, but they had been put there strictly for decoration and were cheaply made of thin copper. Most had broken off over the years and caused a bald patch in the center. The Hoffman IVs had custom made pompadours in special order colors, like chartreuse, magenta, and lavender, but Ree hoped he didn't know that.

"There, handsome as ever, though I think you need a trim," she said with a smile. "Now, go buttle something."

The butler moved out of the kitchen, whirring gently. Ree stayed behind, thinking of her peculiar godfather. He was odd, she wasn't going to argue that point too vehemently, but that was one reason why she was so fond of him. Christian Drosselmeier was the Justice of the Peace and also a clockmaker and inventor. Ree was more interested in the latter profession. Gears and gadgets and mechanics had always fascinated Ree, and the older man had humored her, first by gifting her with strange and wonderful inventions during Christmas, and then later when she was older, allowing her the use of his laboratory. He wasn't home much, and if his absences coincided with a certain spotting and adventuring of a well-known pirate airship, well, he was too well connected and too powerful for people to say so out loud. There were times when decorum and politeness came in handy, truth be told. Ree was simply glad to be his apprentice of sorts, and planned to learn as much as humanly possible from the genius. Why, she wasn't entirely sure, but she had no plans to knit her way to oblivion like a proper lady when there were gadgets to tinker with, gears to grease, and fabulous ideas to take wing. She loved the tiny mechanisms and her quick fingers were small and suited to the task of rewiring and fiddling and experimenting. She could fix the broken Grandfather clock in the hallway by the time she was seven, and she'd always had a gift for the robotic staff. She'd upgraded Hoffman more than once and privately thought he was nearly as good as a Hoffman Model IV, even if they did look smarter and more posh, what with their noses and perfectly manicured coiffures. Ree also had a way of designing her most usual inventions into cleverly disguised hair pieces. The key pins that held her hair in place tonight in fact, were actual keys.

Keys to Drosselmeier's workship. And should the night prove boring or tortuous as she thought it might, she fully planned on using them.

Chapter Two
The Gifts

The party in fact, was not as dull as Ree had feared. Once she had wrangled Jessa away from Fritz, who was clearly enjoying torturing his sister, Drosselmeier arrived with his usual panache and flourish. Hoffman even announced him, though not with any sort of glee.

"Christian Drosselmeier, Justice of the Peace," he droned, and turning swiftly, he glided back into the shadows.

Ree's godfather was very tall and spindly in build. He was of an indeterminate age, perhaps of the same number as Dr. Stahlbaum, perhaps older, or perhaps younger. He was always dressed in black, but in the finest and, most dramatic, and expensive of styles. Beaver skin top hats, impeccably pressed trousers, and a cape that appeared to be woven of night itself. He was always and forever accompanied by a walking stick of an irregular nature. It was very ornate and made of several different materials, including mahogany, silver, gold, marble, beech wood, and various gems. Each knot of wood had been carved, whether in words or forms it was difficult to distinguish unless you were standing quite close, and not many had the gumption or self-confidence to do so. Besides, Herr Drosselmeier had such a commanding way about him that if you were to stand near, you would not be able to pull your gaze away from his face and his one eye, that some swore, saw into your soul. The top of the stick was a heavy gob of silver, molded into the shape of a rat. The nose was long and pointed and fierce, the ears perpetually perked and at attention, and though there were none, you would swear to see whiskers twitching had you pulled your eyes off of the owner. The eyes of the rat were rubies and they glinted when the light of the candles shone upon them. The stick was equal parts intriguing and frightening. As a child, Ree was one of the few who would approach Drosselmeier without trepidation. She had never minded rats.

Now, this Christmas Eve night, as he had so many others, Drosselmeier clapped hands with Dr. Stahlbaum, pecked Mrs. Stahlbaum on the cheek, and made the rounds amongst the guests. Some held back, nervous at the enigmatic party goer and his reputation, but most would not let the opportunity of being in the Justice of the Peace's good favor slip by for another year. Christmas was a time for jolliness, peace, and levity, and while Drosselmeier was intimidating at best and terrifying at his worst, he was jovial this night.

Finally, he embraced Ree fondly. In past years she would have been more elated to see him, but as she had been learning at his side for the better part of six months now, Ree saw her godfather often and did not have to go months and weeks without having him in her sights. Still, she was as giddy inside as she always was on Christmas Eve because she knew he had been working on some amazing gifts for the guests. She knew of the first – she had helped design it – but she had a sneaking suspicion Drosselmeier had been working alone on a project specifically for her.

"I see you've been in my Hydraulic Serum again," Drosselmeier mentioned casually, as he bent down to kiss Ree affectionately.

Ree blushed slightly. "Why, whatever do you mean?" she hedged.

"You smell of it and you also left the workship table in an irritatingly disorganized fashion." He pursed his thin lips and narrowed his eyes, or at least one eye. The other was gone, removed after a mysterious battle and injury he never spoke of to anyone, and was covered by a patch of midnight silk, held in place by a strand of silver chain fastened beneath his hair.

Ree blushed, further embarrassed and irritated with herself. She was extremely disorganized, but it was usually due to losing track of time (in spite of the Clock Bob she had made herself and wore each day on a chain around her waist) and therefore not having the luxury of a period to clean up after herself. She was, more often than not, racing to the workship in a flurry of petticoats and anticipation, and leaving hours later, in a flurry of soot and panic that she was late – again – for supper.

"I'll come by tomorrow and spruce up," Ree promised. "I'll even alphabetize the chemicals."

"Don't bother." Drosselmeier frowned and shook his head. "I expect you will be too busy, as will I."

Ree wanted to press him for details about his odd statement since she had absolutely nothing planned for the morrow other than the usual Latin and art lessons, but the Justice of the Peace had already moved off and dismissed her. The clang of his strange stick was loud on the floor, in spite of Mrs. Stahlbaum's lavish Turkish carpeting. Ree thought he did it on purpose, as he was typically very silent in his movements, like a swift, noiseless bird, even with his limp and reason for needing the heavy stick. He simply liked being the center of attention at the party.

When the children had been properly satiated with puddings and tea, not to mention small presents of dolls and wooden stick horses, Drosselmeier had his largest gift delivered. It was wheeled in on a table that had been fitted with small rolling balls on its feet, and it was covered with a huge sheet. Ree knew what it was. It was the miniature of her own home and she had assisted the inventor with the smallest of the parts. Drosselmeier's expertise with gears and clockworks was unparalleled, but with his one eye, he sometimes found trouble with the tiniest of parts. That was usually where Ree came in; when his eye blurred and tired, she took over, with her magnified goggles and a tiny set of tweezers.

The miniature Stahlbaum home was elaborate. Ree even thought so, and she found herself drawing in her breath along with the guests as Drosselmeier pulled the sheeting away dramatically. It looked even more detailed and impossibly complicated than she had thought earlier, and was the tiny variation of Louise wearing pink? How on earth did he know what she would wear? Of course, he must have asked. Or he simply gambled, since Lou did wear an enormous amount of pink.

The guests leaned forward, each complementing the artist, gently fingering the details, and moving in a clockwork pattern, so that each could view every side. The house itself was made of wood, carved one panel and rooftop at a time, and assembled painstakingly. There were trees made of marzipan, and a fine dusting of sugar to represent snow had been sprinkled atop the silver plate roof shingles. As the party goers watched, the sound of a cuckoo clock chimed merrily, and the tiny versions of the Stahlbaum family began to move. The little Louise moved in circles, gliding around and around; it was obvious she was practicing her dancing. The real Louise smiled and bowed her head as if she were the one receiving the compliments. The little Fritz marched – actually marched, with knees held high – out the small door, to a wooden horse. The tiny Fritz bent low as if bowing to his mount, then swung his leg up and sat atop grandly. Ree glanced at her brother. He looked suitably impressed, and stroked his red beard thoughtfully as he watched. Of course, Fritz had no use for horses – no one did these days, animals being dumb creatures and entirely unnecessary, unless they were being consumed for dinner – but still, it had been a nice touch.

Next, the miniatures of Dr. and Mrs. Stahlbaum sat at the table in the representation of the dining hall. The tiny Doctor pulled out the chair for his wife first, then sat opposite her, while the miniature of Hoffman buzzed in with a tea tray. The real Dr. Stahlbaum laughed heartily, and patted Drosselmeier on the back. He did not reciprocate the friendly gesture. Ree couldn't be sure, and she certainly didn't know the reason, but she was rather certain her godfather wasn't overly fond of her father.

The miniature of Ree herself was dressed in a tiny replica of Ree's own ball gown, with the bright blue and green. Of course, Ree had known what her dress would look like so that was hardly as surprising to her as Louise's gown had been. Ree had helped sew the little costumes and though she had never really been a girl to play much with dolls, preferring mechanics, she had had fun dressing them, and painting on their smiling expressions.

Just then, the diminutive version of Drosselmeier himself exited the tiny Stahlbaum mansion. It was with a flourish and he moved with incredible speed. His cloak of the darkest black billowed behind him as he exited through the front doors, which had moved of their own accord. The small clockmaker whirled to face the mansion, and the inhabitants, and he bowed grandly.

That was it. It was all that Drosselmeier had programmed the model home to do, and his audience clapped cheerfully.

"I say, old chap," commented Lord Soothsayer, "that was quite remarkable!"

"Yes, do it again!" chimed in one of the children. Ree removed the child's sticky hand from where it had been reaching for the door to the toy mansion. "Make the horse whinny!"

"Make the robot fall down!" shouted another child. Ree thought she saw Hoffman, the real Hoffman, slide backward towards the shadows and a puff of steam escaped his ears.

"No, no! Make him climb the tree!"

There were several suggestions as to how to better the display, and Drosselmeier listened to them all in silence for a moment. Finally, he waved his hand in impatience.

"They cannot do anything else, children." His voice, a rich baritone, was smooth as honey. "They are clockwork. They do only what I have programmed them to do."

"But can't you make them do anything more?" clamored the sticky one. She frowned prettily. It was obvious she was used to getting her own way. "We've already seen them do that once already!"

"I told you," Drosselmeier was firm. "It doesn't work that way at all. They perform for you, but only those movements."

The little girl crossed her arms and glared. "It's boring," she proclaimed, haughtily. "You should have had them do much more."

"Shall I play it again?" Drosselmeier asked, though he seemed to be offering through clenched teeth.

"No," said the little girl, and the others seemed to agree. Even half the adults had wandered off by now, less enamored by the gift and more intrigued by the spiced wine that Melisande was passing out from a gilded and mirrored tray. "Did you bring anything else?"

"I did. But I do not think you are ready for it."

"I am!" The little girl uncrossed her arms.

Drosselmeier pretended to think about the matter. "I do not think you are."

"I am!"

"Goodness, Christian! Don't tease the child," Mrs. Stahlbaum admonished. She leaned in to her old friend. "It's a lovely gift and a stunning invention."

The toymaker seemed placated. He whirled, his black cape billowing just like the miniature version had done a moment before, and he snapped his long, thin fingers loudly. The door to the parlor swung wider and the same servants who had brought in the model home of the Stahlbaum mansion before, now entered again. This time they were pushing an enormous box.

The box was tall, taller than any person in the room, even Drosselmeier himself, and Fritz, too. It was wide as well, and it could easily have accommodated anything from a Bengal tiger to a...Ree's imagination failed her. For all she knew, it was a Bengal tiger. She supposed they still existed somewhere, where animals hadn't become quite so extinct. She moved closer, as did all of the party guests. This must be his special surprise, and she had no clue as to what the box might contain. It was decorated with lavish paintings that included constellations, galaxies, stars, and moons. The paint fairly danced off the box, shining and shimmering and full of light and the whole effect was nearly three dimensional and very beautiful. Ree had never seen anything like it, yet she knew what was inside would likely put the amazing box to shame.

Drosselmeier was content to let the guests stew a bit in their own anticipation and eagerness. He waited, watching their faces in a manner that was almost sly. He motioned to one of the servants, and the man grasped a handle on the box that Ree hadn't noticed before.

"Step back," her godfather instructed the group. They all fell back as one, but unable to restrain herself, Ree stepped towards the box instead of sliding back with the others.

The servant turned the handle and swung the door to the box outward.

Inside the shadows of the box were two figures. Human shaped figures. As Ree watched, her bottom lip between her teeth, one of the figures moved. Not only moved, but stepped lithely out of the box.

It was a clockwork doll. Seeing such a thing moving about, seemingly with a life of its own, was as shocking as coming across a ghost. One of the party goers shrieked, though Ree thought that reaction was a bit much.

The doll paused, and seemed to survey her surroundings. She took another tentative step, and was fully out of her box now. She was marvelously painted and sculpted and Ree knew Drosselmeier must have spent hours and hours building her. Her hair was blue, an electric shade, the exact color of Dross' Hydraulic Serum actually, but done up with much fussing. Her skin was very pale, the epitome of porcelain. There were cracks in her skin, in her face and on her arms, where pieces of clockwork and gears peeked through. She was dressed in a ballerina costume, with frayed ribbons and lace, and a choker of black velvet ribbon was tied around her slender neck. Her lips were painted red and were more of a heart shape than a rosebud. Two smudges of pink were her cheeks, though one was obstructed by the clockwork crack. Her legs were long and covered by striped stockings. She stood stock still now, after exiting her box, and the audience barely breathed.

Drosselmeier stepped forward and removed something from beneath his cape. It was an overly large, gold key. As long as Ree's forearm, with pearls inlaid inside, it was one of the strangest keys she'd ever seen. Ree absentmindedly fingered the key pins in her hair as she watched. Her godfather inserted the key into the back of the doll – which was disconcerting in itself, really – and then twisted it hard. The doll was so very lifelike that it was almost as though he had stabbed and twisted a knife, and Ree couldn't stop the tiniest cry of alarm from escaping her mouth.

The doll's face, though, didn't as much as quiver. She began to move, one arm at first, jerking a bit as she raised it above her head. Her head and eyes – rather lifeless eyes, actually, and jet black - followed her own arm. Then her feet moved. It had taken a moment for Ree to realize, but when Drosselmeier had turned the key, a tinkling sound of music had begun. The doll was dancing to the music. Her fingers flexed to the sound of the piano coming from deep inside her chest cavity, and when the melody changed tempo, so did she. Her movements were not beautiful, nor were they difficult, but no one could take their eyes off of her performance. One thing it seemed the doll could not do was to jump, but she could turn and twirl. One such round of twirling brought her very close to Ree, and when she stopped, they were nearly eye to eye. One set of hazel eyes, amazed and intrigued, and one set of black eyes, dead and unseeing. *I wonder why he didn't work harder and longer on the eyes*, Ree thought. *They're simply black pools of paint.*

The doll seemed frozen again, this time so close to Ree that had she any breath, Ree would have felt it blow across her skin. She didn't feel anything, though, besides a fascination and fondness for the strange plaything. She reached out and touched the arm of the doll. It was cold and hard, like fine china. She turned in expectation to her godfather to ask if she might try the key, but when she did Ree was confronted by a terrifying sight.

The second figure had emerged from the box.

Chapter Three
Unexpected Developments

He moved more gracefully than the clockwork doll. He was tall, though somewhat slight in build, and dressed in shades of cobalt blue and silver. One arm was completely fashioned from mechanical devices and gadgets, giving him an ungainly posture as it was obviously heavy and unwieldy to use. There were leather bits that looked to be supple enough, but the metal joints created a look that was altogether awkward and uncomfortable. The hand of the mechanical arm was made from polished copper that gleamed in the candlelight, and the brass knuckles clenched and unclenched with a slight squeaking sound. Part of his face was created from metal scraps, and nearly one whole side of his jaw up into his sideburns was a mixture of silver and brass. His hair was dark and slightly long, flaring up a bit where it brushed the top of his coat. His legs however had no metal parts visible, though perhaps they were only hidden beneath his clothing.

But it was not all of these observations that had caused Ree to nearly scream. She was used to devices and robotics and the like, and she had been crept up upon by Hoffman many times in the dark when she had oiled his parts too well and he moved silent as an apparition. She had been left behind alone in Drosselmeier's workship before, with only the gas lighting of his peculiar, hand shaped wall sconces to light her way as she bobbed gently in the dirigible. No, it wasn't the silent movement of the new doll – for that must be what he was – or even that such a thing existed, but it was his eyes.

They were nothing like the black pits the clockwork doll had painted on. They were alive and questioning and searching and seemed to be the window into his very heart and soul. Flecks of gold glinted in a way that pierced, and the surrounding iris was a cognac color, swirling with bronze and caramel. They seemed wise beyond his years.

And yet. Nonsense. This was a doll. A created thing. A robotic, though a very, very good one. One that would likely make Drosselmeier richer than ever. Mechanicals this handsome and realistic would sell, and quickly too.

He had no wisdom, no soul, no beating heart, no real kind of knowledge, at least not of the emotions, and he had no years either. He was probably only hours old.

Ree pulled her own eyes away from the odd mechanical eyes that held her momentarily captive, and brought herself back to reality with a start. The figure too, unlocked his own gaze from hers, and turning slowly, he bowed to the clockwork doll. Ree felt embarrassed for them somehow, as they began a slow and stroppy waltz to the tune that emitted from the clockwork doll's body. The audience was delighted, and Dr. Stahlbaum pulled his wife into the center of the room where they too, began to waltz. Soon dozens of other bodies joined them, and the children lost interest in the whole proceedings, and scampered off to bother Melisande over the promise of gingerbread cake and sugared milk.

Ree was left in the center of the room, with dancers milling around her, and she felt out of place and discombobulated. Someone brushed her sleeve and she was vaguely aware of a boy bowing near her and asking her to dance, but she instead instructed her feet to move away, and move away she did, leaving the boy to flush angrily and spend the rest of the evening spreading rumors about her flirtatious and teasing behavior. Ree had lost sight of the two dolls in the swirl and confusion of rippling petticoats and bodies, and she wanted rather desperately to see those eyes again. There was something about them. They must have taken hours to design and create. She was pulled from her goal by Drosselmeier.

"And what do you think of my invention?" He appeared pleased with himself, and he puffed expertly on a steam and flavor infused pipe. Steam rings formed perfectly in front of his face.

Ree waved the spearmint scented rings away impatiently. "They are quite wonderful, godfather," she admitted. She could hear the begrudging tone in her voice, in fact she almost sounded petulant, and she gave herself another mental shake. She knew the reason for her discontent. She was hurt that he'd considered and created these robotics without her by his side. She was itching to know the secrets behind their intricate and elaborate design. For example, why did the clockwork doll jerk so, but the male doll move with grace? Why did the gears show through the skin fabric of the dancing doll as if coming from the inside out, but the young man figure had such unwieldy outer mechanics? Were they powered by steam or by gas, or did they have special batteries inside their chest cavities? Were they only programmed to dance and bow and play music, or could they speak, like Hoffman? Why did the windup girl have a key, but the other did not? And more importantly, how did he make them so lifelike – the man's eyes especially? Ree had so many questions and demands she wasn't sure where to start. Drosselmeier wasn't one for questions and small talk. The constant pepper of children's ramblings and cross-examinations he had no patience for. She opened her mouth, then shut it again with a clacking of her teeth that made her head rattle.

Her godfather laughed heartily. "You sound like my nutcracker man." He puffed again on his pipe when he finished his laughter. "Clack, clack!"

Ree frowned. "Nutcracker man?"

"Oh yes. My automaton. His jaw was busted and broken, so it's hinged now with silver and gold. He makes a dreadful clacking and banging sound when he speaks. A lot of power in those jaws. I had him cracking walnuts for me at a splendid rate earlier. He's worth his weight just for that alone, I rather think. You know how fond I am of nuts."

Well, that answered one question. The toy could speak if he wanted to. Or if he was programmed to anyway. "I rather think he can do more than crack nuts for you, godfather," she replied, drily. "How on earth did you build him?" There, an open ended question that would inevitably lead to plenty of answers, or at least Ree hoped so.

"Ah." The man waggled his long finger at Ree playfully. "You don't know all my secrets just yet, apprentice though you may be. I have a lot you don't know about me, I do."

"Obviously." Ree was annoyed to hear the petulant quality in her voice again, and she cleared her throat and began again. "I mean, of course you have hidden depths and you are a genius first rate." She smiled. Dross loved compliments.

He laughed again, wholeheartedly. "Butter me up, will you? It won't work. These dolls are full of parts it'd boggle your pretty brain to see. Far too advanced. I'm taking them to Sea Level tomorrow to sell."

"Sea Level?" Ree was astonished. Very few ventured that low, at least not those in Ree's circle of acquaintances, though now she was recognizing that perhaps Drosselmeier wasn't quite one of them as she had always supposed. Ree herself had never been off the Bavarian Alps, and though Fritz had, he was a soldier so that was to be expected. He had had maddeningly little to say on the matter when Ree had pressed him for details of what Sea Level and the people there were like. Poor, he had drawled. That she already knew. Only the poor would live at Sea Level, and the wealthy and important drifted high in the sky and nestled in the Alps where they could properly keep an eye on things below. At least, that was what Ree and her friends had always been taught. Then the second part of Drosselmeier's words hit her brain. "Sell them?" Now Ree wasn't sounding petulant, she was sounding upset. "But you can't sell them!"

"Why ever not, child?" Drosselmeier's one good eye gazed at Ree, unwavering. "That is what I do. I am a clock maker. A businessman. I spend money, I make money. I will use the earnings to make something even better. I was envisioning perhaps a singing monkey? A traveling robotic circus? A self-propelled zeppelin with an integrated mapping robotic within the walls?"

"Don't tease." Ree was not amused. "And your plan doesn't make sense."

"Which one? The singing monkey? It does when you realize it can out sing the finest operatic trained voices of our time and is available for parties and bar mitzvahs." He raised his eyebrow slyly. "I'll make a fortune."

"No, not the monkey! Selling the dolls at Sea Level." Ree frowned. One of her key pins slid down and she caught it before it hit the floor. She shoved it back in carefully; it wouldn't do to lose her only way into Drosselmeier's workship. Now that she knew exactly what kinds of things he was keeping – and building – without her, she was determined to preserve her way inside. "No one there can even afford such luxuries."

"Ah, Ree." Drosselmeier looked disappointed, even crestfallen. "Have you been buying what the elite socialites have been pandering to you?"

"What do you mean?"

"You have, haven't you? I had such high hopes for you, girl. And now I see they've gotten you tight in their calfskin and patent leather clutches." He shook his head. He made as if to walk away.

Ree grabbed his cloak. "What are you going on about? No one has me in their clutches!"

"No one there can afford such luxuries ..." Drosselmeier whirled and faced her, his voice becoming girlish and affected as he mocked Ree's earlier outburst. "What a bunch of poppycock!"

"But-" Ree's frown deepened. "If I'm wrong, godfather, then tell me the truth." She was utterly confused, and being confused motivated Ree Stahlbaum. It was the reason behind most of her thinking, her inventions, her late nights, and her intelligence. Being confused about something annoyed her deeply, and gave her the impetus to do something about it. She hated not knowing something.

Dross puffed again on his pipe and the steam rose. It curled his graying hair on his temple. He studied his goddaughter, and thought long and hard before speaking.

"I'm not sure what I'm disappointed in more. Your complete lack of a brain at the moment, or that you didn't even notice the miniature of you is the only one who had no function. Disappointing. You have brought me low. However, I'm not your nursemaid, child. I must attend to my dolls," he replied, and turning into the crowd, he disappeared.

Ree wanted to scream, but instead she took a deep breath and straightened her skirts, flicking them back into shape. What she really wanted to do (after screaming adequately) was follow Drosselmeier and his automatons – examine them, get closer to them, get a peek into their gears and mechanics – but she wouldn't give him the satisfaction. She felt insulted by his words, by his insinuations that she had been bought and brainwashed by her family and friends, and also that the miniature doll of herself had no purpose, no movement, no point. Did they all see her as a prop then? If all she knew was the upper world of the Alps, that was hardly her fault, was it? It wasn't as though she owned her own personal dirigible or had a way off this mountain. No one vacationed or holidayed at Sea Level. It hadn't really crossed her mind very often that things below might be different or interesting enough to seek out. Still, Ree felt oddly chastened and that was as bad a feeling as being confused.

Her resolve to ignore the clock maker and his inventions held out for approximately five minutes. She could see from across the crowded parlor that the automatons were standing beside the Stahlbaum Christmas tree and the party guests were examining them and complimenting Drosselmeier. The inventor puffed on his pipe and smiled amiably. Ree swallowed her pride and made her way over to the enormous tree.

The tree was artificial, made of metal and immense in stature. Sharp as a tack, the pointed silver needles had been hand designed and made by a tribe of West Indian metal workers, and the decorations had been collected and purchased – or commissioned – by Mrs. Stahlbaum. It was a feat of engineering and art, made no less impressive by the pure gold angel at the top. The tree was mechanical and adjustable, so that once the ornaments and decorations had been removed, one could press the mechanisms in the bottom of the tree hidden beneath the lowest branch, and the whole thing could fold in on itself like a giant parasol. It stored nicely beneath the stairs when not in the Christmas season. Being adjustable, Mrs. Stahlbaum could lower and raise it depending on her whim, though she had not yet raised it as far as it could reach. No one could admire the angel properly if it were too high, was her thinking, and she also preferred a fatter, more rounded tree. Mrs. Stahlbaum had experimented with the height this year and knew if it were any higher it would have that lanky, sparse look she didn't care for.

It was certainly stunning. The more protective mothers thought it was also ridiculously dangerous. The needles could easily kill someone if they were unlucky enough to fall into it. And if the whole thing were to topple over? It didn't bear thinking about it. Those particular mothers had long, stern conversations with their little ones before attending the Stahlbaum party. *A mechanical death trap*, they whispered behind their fans at Mrs. Stahlbaum's back.

Still, though, it twinkled and it shone and the dozens of tiny candles that Melisande had painstakingly lit hours before made it shine in a magical way. Even the dubious mothers had to admit it looked gorgeous, though they still instructed their offspring to keep a wide berth. Now not only were the silver needles sharp as knives, but they were hot, too.

"She's elaborate, old man," Dr. Stahlbaum was saying to Drosselmeier as Ree approached. They appeared to be conversing over the clockwork doll. The doll herself was crumpled in the corner. The girl with the sticky hands was poking her in the bodice. Ree wanted to smack her, though she didn't quite know why. She was only a doll. Ree herself had been known to remove her own doll's body parts, cut off all their hair, and draw all over them, at the same age. Still. It seemed wrong to do such things to a life size and realistic looking plaything.

"Elaborate, eh?" Drosselmeier didn't seem to be listening fully, a common occurrence when speaking with Ree's father. "Indeed."

"Used clockwork inside, did you? All the same parts? Gears and whatnot? Will they strike the hour? Ho ho!" He laughed at his own joke.

Ree felt mildly embarrassed at her father's questions. Of course the doll wasn't as simple as that. Gears and whatnot. She felt she must rescue the doctor from further humiliation. If Dross were to respond with sarcasm, the whole party would begin to go downhill. Dr. Stahlbaum might finally have enough of the inventor's eccentricities and forbid Ree to work with him any longer.

"Papa? Mama craves a dance with you." Ree gestured across the room. It was a lie, but a romantic one, so she figured it was acceptable.

Her father clapped her godfather on the back once more – making the one eyed man wince – and left. Ree saw the sticky little girl lean forward to the clockwork and lick her on the cheek.

"Shoo, you little cretin!" Ree hissed, and swatted her away. "Mind your manners!"

The girl scampered off, but not without making a spoiled and saucy face at Ree. Ree sighed and turned to look at the nutcracker man. He had been placed at the doll's side, but instead of lying in a heap on the floor like a ragdoll, as she was, he was standing straight at attention, his hands clasped behind him. He was wearing a hat now, kind of tri-corner soldier's hat that had been placed at an angle that should have seemed jaunty, but instead seemed sorrowful. His unusual eyes were staring straight ahead at nothing – they looked unfocused and blank now – and Ree wanted to look and look at them, waiting for them to blink, but she squashed the impulse. It wouldn't do to have a staring contest with an automaton. She reached out and touched him, stroked his gold jawline, as so many other guests had done. The action made her feel nearly ashamed, as though she were party to some indecent lechery. Not just party to it, but accessory to it. She removed her hand quickly.

She turned to leave the nutcracker man and his sad companion, but as she did so, her bright green skirts close enough to brush against his clothes, she felt her hand caught fast in what was literally an iron grip. It was the automaton.

Chapter Four
What Happens at Midnight

The hand in Ree's was firm and smooth, warm to the touch the way Hoffman's metal parts felt when overheated, and it was heavy and large. It was also crushing her.

"Let go!" Ree whispered. She tried to pull away but it was as impossible as escaping an iron chain wrapped around her body. The automaton still stared blankly into space, but he did not relax his grip on Ree. It was as though the party was frozen around her; she was moving, pulling away, speaking, but it felt as though she were the only one. No, not the only one; Drosselmeier was once again at her side.

"Unhand her, Nikolai," he murmured to his invention. He turned to his goddaughter. "Excuse him. He hasn't had etiquette lessons. Then again, he won't need them where he's going, of course." He chuckled.

The automaton – Nikolai – did as he was told by his creator. Instantly, and with a creaking sound, he relaxed his hold on Ree. She rubbed her hand. She did not chuckle along with Drosselmeier. Even if he had hurt her, and scared her a bit too, she didn't think it in good taste to joke about being sold, like a common tea kettle or a silver tray. She looked up at Nikolai and was startled to find his golden flecked eyes looking back at her. She flinched as though she had been struck.

"Come along," Drosselmeier snapped his fingers at him, "Back in the box with you." Nikolai turned his gaze once more on Ree, left it there for a moment, and then turning on his heel, he marched to the box and disappeared into the blackness.

Ree watched in silence as Drosselmeier bent low to pick up the clockwork doll. She did not move positions as he picked her up in his arms, grunting as he did so. The doll was put away and the door to the wonderful black box was swung shut with a bang. The key to the clockwork doll was hung upon the door.

The rest of the party was uneventful. The snow flurried and blew to such an extent that Jessa Pratt's premonition was proven correct. Several families decided to stay overnight at the Stahlbaum mansion, while Hoffman was in a panic, and Melisande was nowhere to be found now that she was desperately needed. Mrs. Stahlbaum was busy for at least an hour showing guests to their rooms and seeing them settled.

* * *

Ree tossed in her bed that night. She hadn't fallen asleep and was beginning to think she never would again. Every time she closed her eyes she would see Nikolai's face, and that of the clockwork doll, with her blank, black pools of paint. Mechanicals with such realistic features (the female doll's eyes notwithstanding) would fetch a high price for Drosselmeier, and it wasn't as though Ree were unused to robotics and such. Still...it seemed unnatural to sell them. Cruel somehow.

She tossed again, and finally, with a loud groan of frustration, smacked her feather pillow, threw off her blanket, and lowered her bare feet to the floor. They were cold, her feet, so she knew she had been tossing and turning in her bed for the better part of three hours. The Pleasant Foot Warmer had been programmed to stay on for a good two hours, and it was definitely not giving off its soft, warm puffs of steam beneath her covers now. She hung low over her bedframe and fumbled in the dark beneath her bed for her furry slippers. She came across them and slipped them over her cold toes.

Ree pulled her blanket with her, wrapped it around her shoulders, and padded across her room. She would just check in on the automatons. See that they were...what? Comfortable in their box? See if they needed anything? A cup of tea? A tightening of their nuts and bolts? Ree mentally slapped some sense into herself. Fine, then; she wouldn't so much as check in on them like they were important guests, but examine them.

Like she would any other invention. Just, in the dark, under cover of night, where no one would see. Nothing unusual about that.

She lit herself a fat candle from her bedside, and cupped her hand around the flickering flame as she moved down the hallway. The flame danced wildly and she could only guess that the storm had still not abated; it was causing breezeways throughout the house. She felt chilled and wished she had taken the time to put on her ermine cloak instead of her lightest coverlet from atop her bed. She could hear the distant sound of someone snoring mightily; it must be old Lord Croftenspot. His snoring was the stuff of legends. The great grandfather clock – one of Drosselmeier's oldest and grandest creations – struck the hour as she passed it, nearly giving her a heart attack.

"Oh, shut it," she hissed at it, once her heart had quit its palpitations. The huge wooden carving of an owl, with its massive wings spread around the top of the clock, stared down at her, as if in judgment. She'd never really liked that owl. Its hooked beak of a nose was thin and cruel looking, and its eyes had always seemed to follow her about the room. It reminded Ree of a lonesome, but mischievous gargoyle, perched above her head, ready to pounce. It didn't help that once, as a little girl, she swore she saw the wooden feathers ruffle, as though it had just lit upon the clock after flying about the room when no one was looking. She used to stare at it after that for long periods, until her eyes crossed and her head ached, trying to catch the owl in the act of coming alive and moving. Of course, she had been too old for that kind of nonsense for many years now. Well, at least a few anyway. Two at the lowest estimation.

The house seemed frozen, and Ree knew if she were to gaze upon it from the outside, it would appear that way, too, with this winter storm freezing everyone in their tracks. Like an enormous snow globe, with Ree trapped inside. Shake it and she had an irrational fear that she would tumble out, a bit like Drosselmeier's miniature of their home, petticoats swirling and ribbons floating around her head.

Ree felt a huge, comforting feeling of relief when she entered the Grand Parlor and saw the massive box next to the steel Christmas tree where it had been left. Drosselmeier himself had left for his home – a blizzard was no match for the eccentric Justice of the Peace – but he had left behind his toys, claiming he would fetch them in the morrow. Still, she had worried in her bed that she had dreamed the whole thing up. Would they appear as magnificent when she opened the door as they did coming to her in her memories of this night?

Only one way to find out, and Ree opened the door to the box. The large, ornate key that wound up the clockwork doll, swung and clanked loudly against the box as she did so. She gulped, and looked about guiltily, but there was no one around to hear.

The inside of the box was dark as midnight. Lifting her candle only seemed a joke; as she peered inside she might as well have tried to light a long buried and long forgotten tomb with a flame no bigger than a pinprick. She could vaguely make out shapes in the back of the box. How could it seem even larger on the inside? Some trick of the dark, she supposed. She swung her candle in further but it flickered dramatically with a draft from the box, and she didn't want it to go out. Instead of reaching in any further – she had no further to go anyway, her arms could only extend so far – Ree grasped the doorway, and stepped inside, taking her meager light with her.

Now, she could see a bit better. The mechanicals were huddled together on the floor of the box, as if for warmth. Ree found that strange. She herself had seen the boy automaton, Nikolai, march inside and remain standing as the door had shut him up in his prison. She brushed aside any fretting about it, however, as it had already proved obvious that Nikolai was a bit more advanced and of a higher quality in technology than the clockwork doll had shown herself to be. Ree lowered herself down to the ground of the box with the dolls, wishing she had better lighting, not to mention more elbow room. If she wound up the doll with the key, could she exit the box, she wondered? Or if she simply commanded Nikolai, would he leave with her? Or would he only respond to the timbre and tone of his master's voice? It would be next to impossible to examine them thoroughly in the dark like this, squished up against the side of the box with no room to maneuver, and she so longed to do so without the prying eye and sarcastic comments of her godfather. Ree lifted the candle and came face to face with Nikolai.

His eyes were open. She wondered frantically if he even had eyelids. His face looked...angrier than it had before. She shrunk a bit, remembering the ironclad grasp of his mechanical hand and how trapped it had made her feel, even in a room full of people and gaiety. There had been scores of people to help should he attempt to harm her; here she was alone with only a windup doll to save her. She felt very foolish, though she wasn't sure if it was that thought that caused the feeling, or the fact that she was frightened by a plaything.

"What are you doing here?" Nikolai's voice was hoarse and labored, as if unaccustomed to being used. It sounded too like he had a thick accent – though perhaps it was his metal jaw line that was obscuring his speech. If his face looked angry, it was nothing compared to his voice.

Ree swallowed back a scream, and steeled herself to show little emotion or surprise. So he spoke; godfather Drosselmeier had intimated as much. Nothing to be alarmed about, though it was unsettling, especially as he was demanding something from her. Most mechanicals only responded – not initiated conversation.

Ree found herself at a complete loss for words. Shut up inside this musty box with a nutcracker man and a life size doll. She would have laughed had she not felt so uncomfortable and confused. She couldn't very well tell him she wished to examine him like a dissected frog on an anatomy table, could she? Then again.

"I wish to examine my good godfather's creations."

Nikolai stared at her. She felt his scrutiny, even more than she watched it. He could blink. She watched his eyelids lower and open again. He looked less angry now. More...annoyed.

There was a sound then from outside the box, coming from the parlor. A sort of scratching, scrabbling sound, like fingernails on a chalkboard. It was merely instinct that caused Ree to blow out the candle, and almost instantly, she wished she'd thought longer and harder about the consequence of such a rash decision. The box was blacker now than anything she'd ever experienced. It was like a living, breathing thing. It was suffocating and dank...and it was closing in on her.

I'm claustrophobic, Ree suddenly realized. *Isn't that lovely to know?*

She swallowed down her fear as if it were the last bitter dregs of a cup of cold, black tea, and strained her ears to listen for the sound. It came again, louder this time, and confusion as to what it could be gripped Ree with enough firmness so as to lessen the claustrophobia. It sounded like metal scratchings. Was it coming from outside? On the windows, perhaps? There were more scratching sounds, and then the sudden and bizarre noise of something or someone squealing. She could hear her own breath, coming in shallow, paper thin noises that sounded more like autumn leaves blowing across cobblestones than it did a healthy girl with strong lungs. She could even hear what sounded like Nikolai's breath, very near her right ear, warm and somehow comforting. It was likely steam escaping from his mechanisms, but it still made Ree feel as though she were not so alone in the dreaded box with the mysterious noises coming closer. The scratching was odd, but the squealing was worse.

It sounded like a piglet – or dozens of them – were taking up residence in the Grand Parlor. Whatever it was, it was going to wake the whole house at this rate. Ree moved, determined now to not only exit her prison, but to find what was making such a racket. She was held in place by the lightning fast reflexes and grip of the nutcracker man.

"Stay here," he instructed, though with his accent or impediment, Ree had to strain to understand him.

"I will not," Ree hissed back. Being told what to do by a robot? Now she'd seen everything. As if there weren't enough people in the world telling her what to do, where to go, what to read, how to sit, when to speak. Her irritation overcame her claustrophobia and her fear of the noise both, and she shook him off like a fly. She exited the box by flinging herself through where she knew the door to be...and came face to face with a nightmare.

34

ACT II
The Battle

Chapter Five
Enemies of Steel

The parlor was lit by a faint red glow. The glow was coming from something on the floor – some things, in fact – and they were crawling at such a speed that the whole Turkish carpeting seemed alive and pulsing. They were mice. And not just mice, but rats. And not just rats, but mechanical, steel rats. Moving at an incredible speed on their gangly, silver legs, they moved as one living, breathing organism; turned as one, sped up as one, and slowed down as one. There were so many that Ree's horrified brain estimated as many as one hundred, and there were more arriving through the fireplace. The red glow was emitting from their tiny, bejeweled eyes, which seemed to be some sort of ruby, used in an unbeautiful and obscene way.

Ree felt her gorge rising and her feet had hardly touched the floor – brushing against the cold, cold steel of a rat – when she immediately double backed into the box. It was high enough off the floor that some inner voice in Ree's imagination hoped desperately the mice couldn't jump or climb. When she realized she had basically leaped into Nikolai's arms, she flushed and disentangled herself. His metal arm was heavy against her, but not in the same sort of prison-like way it had felt before, when he grasped at her hand so insistently. This time it felt safe, and Ree missed it instantly when it was gone.

Nikolai looked at her in something like amazement – there was enough of a glow to light his features now – and Ree stammered an explanation. She intended to sound brave and in control of the strange situation they found themselves in, but she sounded wheezing and terrified out of her wits, even to her own ears.

"Rat mechanicals! Everywhere!" seemed to be all she could stammer.

"Rats?" Nikolai's scratchy voice was even angrier than usual. How odd that she knew already the timbre of his tone after only a few sentences. "Here?"

"Coming in through the fireplace," Ree gasped, and then screamed a breathless sort of scream.

The rats could climb, it seemed. One was making its way towards them, its evil looking eyes trained straight upon the prisoners in the box.

It may be remembered that Ree never minded rats. This logic didn't sway her nerves. There was something about the small, robotic things that was perverse. They scuttled about the floor like crabs, and at an astonishing rate. They moved with insidious purpose and drive and Ree knew whatever they had been programmed to do, it was not to tuck little children in at night, or deliver biscuits. They weren't here to brush ladies hair, or to tie the men's cravats. They had been created for a purpose, and whatever that purpose was, Ree didn't trust it in the slightest.

Nikolai moved with a speed that would have given Ree pause had she time to admire it. He struck at the rat with a ferocity that left Ree no question as to whether or not he agreed with her assessment of the rat's goal. His metal arm lowered onto the rat with such force that it was surprising it didn't crash them all through the bottom of the box. The rat was disabled certainly; it lay in a heap of silver and copper parts, gears and gadgets, and it leaked blue liquid that pooled around it and shimmered. The eyes blinked quickly, as though malfunctioning, and then went out altogether. It was only a pile of harmless parts now. Nothing more terrifying than the contents of a lady's sewing bag, or what you might find in Ree's Hair Ribbon and Toiletry Robotic. Nikolai and Ree stared at one another.

"We have to contain them!" Ree suddenly gasped. "We can't let them leave the parlor. The guests, my family!"

Without another word, she attempted to push past Nikolai. Her fear had wings now, but so did her anger at this intrusion into her home. She would have leaped outside straight into the mess of rats if he hadn't shot his arm – his flesh arm – out to stop her.

Nikolai held her fast. He nodded toward the clockwork doll, still crumpled in the far corner of the box. "Wind her up," he instructed, "or she won't stand a chance. I'll close the parlor doors."

He was gone before Ree could respond. She could hear the crunching, the terrible sound of metal shrieking and screeching against metal. She felt frozen on her feet for a moment, and then she remembered the doll. She wouldn't stand a chance, Nikolai had said. If what? If the rats attacked her? Would they devour a doll? And should they care? It was only a doll. But so was Nikolai, and she would never just leave him to be eaten, or dismantled, or nibbled upon, or whatever it was these nasty things were apt to do.

Ree exhaled in a deliberate and slow rush of breath, blowing her white streak of hair out of her eyes the way she always did when concentrating. It was shaky, but it gave her a firm sort of resolve and calmness. She moved to the very edge of the box. Concentrating on removing the key from where it swung gently on the other side of the door, she purposely ignored what was happening in the parlor. Multi-tasking had never been her strong suit, and Drosselmeier always teased her about her one track mind. Getting distracted from her goal would never do. The sounds around her, surrounding her, suffocating her, though...it took all her concentration to keep her eyes trained on the door.

Ree swung her body through, her feet still in the box, her hands grasping as high up on the doorframe as she could reach. If she had to completely exit the box in order to get the key, she didn't like her chances. She didn't have to look down to know the rats were right beneath her, the floor swarming with them. If she fell...it didn't bear thinking about. Death by mechanical rats was not a fear she ever knew she had, but she knew it now, and doubted that fear would ever leave her side from this point.

Sufficiently distracted by the vision of such a death, the key was in her hand and she had ducked back inside the box before she knew it. She wished she could close the door, close herself and the doll inside where she could have a moment to think and come up with a plan, but the inside of the box door was smooth as glass. There was no handle to grip, nothing with which to pull it closed and give them refuge. Besides, she couldn't just abandon Nikolai out there with the monsters. The sounds of shrieking and screeching and scraping and smashing had not abated. How had the guests not awoken? Ree found herself wondering. Of course, they were all in the other side of the mansion – an entirely different wing. Still. It was odd. But not the oddest part of Ree's night.

The key was heavy and awkward, and the doll was not placed at a good angle to use it. Her back was propped up against the wall of the box, covering the lock that the key fit into. Ree grasped the doll's porcelain hands and yanked, hard. The doll crumpled to the floor, face down. She hoped she hadn't added more cracks to the poor thing's face, but there was no hope for it. She didn't know what Nikolai expected once the doll was functional and moving (did he expect it to arabesque to safety? Pirouette for help?) but Ree trusted him.

"Hold still now," Ree murmured, and bit down on her bottom lip as she fit the giant key into the doll. It slid in easily enough, but it still felt weirdly like inserting a scalpel or knife deep into a human body, and Ree felt queasy as she began to turn it. Why did Dross have to make the thing so lifelike? It wasn't at all like his other mechanical inventions. It wasn't natural. She licked her lips and tasted blood.

The key was hard to turn. It grated and objected and Ree broke out into a sweat. "Lefty loosey, righty tighty," she whispered, double checking her rotation. "Come along now, blast it!" She heard a tinkle of music from inside the doll's cavity, and the doll began to twitch her fingers. Ree breathed a sigh of relief. She gave it one last crank, and then pulled the key out. She didn't toss it aside though; a heavy metal object was a decent enough weapon and she couldn't cower in the box all night. Might as well keep it with her. It wasn't a proper deterrent, but it was better than the nothing she had to compare it to. What else would she fight with? Her furry bedroom slippers? Now there was a ludicrous thought.

The doll was moving now, in her jerky way, and had come to a standing position. The music was a merry and incongruous background noise to the sound of the battle only a few feet away. "If you can do more than spin and twirl, dolly, come along. If not, maybe you should stay here." Ree felt ridiculous talking to her, but for all she knew the doll had some responding capabilities or could obey simple commandments like Hoffman.

Ree moved to the doorway of the box again and braced herself. She could see Nikolai in the dim gloom of the thousand glowing red eyes, and he was fighting like a warrior. The door to the parlor had been shut; Ree breathed a thankful sigh of relief. He had succeeded in that at least. And now he was leaving dead rats in his path. They littered the floor, and the living (Were they living? Well, the mobile ones then) scattered and climbed over and around the bodies with no regard for their fallen comrades. Shimmering pools of blue blood seeped through the Turkish carpet. *Mama will be furious.*

Brandishing the huge metal key, Ree jumped out of the box. A rat turned instantly towards her as if gone rogue, for the others were all after Nikolai, and Ree swung the key down and smashed it. She heard a satisfying crunching and breaking sound, but took another swing and yet another before she was convinced it wouldn't rise up again and attack her. The eyes flickered, fast at first, then slower, and then went out. She had no time to congratulate herself; another rat turned from the pack and began to crab walk rapidly towards her. The speed at which they moved was incredible. They were more like spiders than rats, clicking and scraping along, and able to move from side to side, as well as forward and back.

This one seemed to anticipate her move with the key and it had disappeared from her line of fire before Ree could even bring the weapon down upon its metal back. With a squeal of alarm and also of pure terror, she realized it had scuttled beneath her nightdress and she could feel it scratching at her ankles. With a speed she didn't even know she possessed, Ree kicked hard and simultaneously brought the key down on her own shin. The spider and rat hybrid flew through air and crashed against the floor, knocking several of its own kind as it landed. Ree shivered in revulsion.

Unexpectedly, all the mechanicals ceased their assault. They simply froze in place, their spike-like legs still as statues. They were all facing Nikolai, except for the dead ones, which were facing every which way, some with heads detached from their awful bodies. Ree looked up and met Nikolai's eyes over the fray. He looked as confused as she felt.

"Behind you!" Ree shouted. Something had moved inside the fireplace. Something much, much larger than a small mechanical rodent.

Something human.

Chapter Six
Choosing Sides

The figure in the fireplace straightened to its full height. Though slender, very slender, in build, it was nevertheless very tall. Taller than Nikolai, and certainly much, much taller than Ree. It stepped out into the light of the glowing red eyes; eyes of whose bodies still had not moved since the man appeared.

Ree and Nikolai, too, were as still as the rats. Only the clockwork doll moved, and she from inside the box, her music still playing cheerfully. It was undeniably out of place in this room of horror, but no one paid her any heed.

The figure in the fireplace had long legs and arms, like those of its minions, which the rats must be. They quieted when he arrived, and as both were unwanted and uninvited in this parlor, so Ree made the leap that here must be the inventor. He was dressed very simply in trousers, boots, and a dirty brown coat. They all fit loosely and limply, as though over a man who had been dead a long time and only his skeleton remained. He wore a plague mask, with the pointed beak of a bird. The mask covered his entire face, and the eyes were goggles, framed in brass. On his head he wore a top hat, but it was a battered old thing, torn and frayed and with a dent in one side. Only his gloves were white, and they fit more closely to his fingers than his clothes did his body. Fisted in one glove was a large bag, seemingly empty.

"Cullen Souris." Nikolai's voice was flat. Unemotional. Ree looked at him in surprise. "I should have known it was you."

"Hello, brother," the man replied. From behind his mask, his voice was muffled.

"I'm no brother."

Ree looked from one to the other in confusion. "Could someone let me in on what is happening, or should I simply go for my father?"

Nikolai and the man called Cullen ignored her, which only served to boil Ree's blood. "Fine then," she snapped, and began to step over the motionless rats. There were so many that in order to get to the parlor doors she would need to use them as stepping stones and the thought gave her pause. What if her weight awoke them again? She bent to wipe her shin where some blood was dripping. She wasn't sure if she'd been bitten by the dreadful thing or if she'd injured herself with the key while trying to get the rat off of her, and then she saw that the liquid was blue, not red. It wasn't her blood then. And where was the key? She had dropped it. The music box inside the clockwork doll had finally stopped playing, ground to a total halt. Ree looked at the box and saw the doll with one delicate leg posed halfway outside the box, as if about to step down, but her mechanism had paused in mid-stride. If she hadn't been leaning the slightest bit backwards, she would have toppled out; instead she was frozen in place and the sight would have been comical if it hadn't been so pathetic and strange.

Before Ree could take another step, the parlor doors swung open from the other side. It was Fritz. And he wasn't alone.

"Steady!" Fritz's voice was commanding and booming. "Halt!" Ree had never heard him like that; it was a far cry from his usual teasing and boyish manner. He was wearing full uniform, but not the same one as he had at the party. That had been his dress uniform, while this one was for combat. A peculiar looking weapon, a sort of gun with clips of brass and bronze and a cylindrical tube of fluid, was in his hand. It was leveled at Nikolai, and another smaller version of the gun was pointed at the floor, in the vague direction of all the rats. It seemed ridiculous to tell a group of motionless things to halt, but Ree didn't feel – for once – like making fun of her brother. She'd never been so glad to see anyone in her life.

The group of soldiers behind Fritz were an astonishing crew. A well-groomed militia, all with the same atypical weaponry, they appeared fierce and ready to fight. That wasn't what made them astonishing. What made them astonishing was that they were women, some in fact, no older than herself.

Ree would have gaped, if she'd had the time, or the lack of manners. She knew of course that her brother was in charge of a specially trained group, a well-organized and secretive select batch, but she'd had no clue that he was the only male among them. He used to brag often at the supper table about his elite assembly of super soldiers, but Ree had mostly ignored him; or if she had allowed herself to be taken in by his boasting and asked for more details, Fritz would get obnoxiously mum and waggle his finger at her and tell her she wasn't capable of understanding. She was just a girl. It made her crazy. Now, seeing his girl army, she saw the irony of his humor. She wasn't particularly amused.

The man in the fireplace, Cullen, made a sudden move. He pulled from his bag a type of filigreed pocket watch. He flipped it open and it glowed a strange green. He pressed some sort of button in the device and a sound like a musical note emitted from the watch that likely wasn't a watch at all. Ree recognized the sound as the same she had heard from inside the box, before she had caught sight of the rats. It seemed to be a sort of signal, a remote controlled trigger effect, and the rats once again began their frenetic activity. This time, they all about faced, so they were no longer facing Nikolai. Now they were scurrying with fantastic speed towards the open parlor door. And towards Fritz and his girl army.

"Shut the door!" Ree shouted. She was impressed when they followed her orders, and even more impressed that they did so with all of their selves on the inside of the parlor doors and not on the opposite side. It seemed reflex and human instinct would have forced them to save themselves, but not so with soldiers, it seemed. They were all ensconced in the parlor now – this parlor that would never be the same, Ree realized vaguely, what with all the blue fluid everywhere, the shattered remains and shards of metal animals, and the furniture that she had no doubt would be destroyed in a matter of minutes. But at least, the rest of the house wasn't infested yet, and for that Ree was grateful. *Small mercies*, she thought to herself.

The rats were swarming the soldiers. The peculiar guns were leveled at them, and Ree panicked when she saw that they must be broken. Leave it to Fritz to bring useless guns to a battle. But no, the mice were crumpling around her. Smoking and writhing their silver bodies. The guns were working after all; they were simply quite silent when fired. One soldier seemed younger, or at least smaller, than the rest, and Ree watched in horror as a dozen mechanical rats scurried up her body as though she were a set of stairs. She toppled to the floor, grasping at the metal legs and heads, and shoving and throwing them off her. Another soldier leaned down to help her, and shouted instructions, all while firing at the rats on the floor. The small soldier made it back to her feet, but she was battered and bloodied. The soldiers didn't bleed blue.

Nikolai and Cullen were engaged in some sort of circling, hunched over, wrestling match. They ignored the battle around them, but focused in on one another, swinging with their fists, and kicking each other's legs out from under their opponent. Cullen was slight of build and seemed no match for the nutcracker man, especially with his arm of steel, but he was also quicker and lighter on his feet. Nikolai's heavy arm of metal was no good if he couldn't make contact with the faster man.

The rats were entirely focused on the women soldiers and Fritz, and Cullen and Nikolai were entirely focused on killing one another, so Ree used the moment to collect herself. The doll was about to topple right out of the box onto her porcelain face, so she was no help, the rest of the house's inhabitants were sleeping too far away to hear, or under some sort of spell (or dead), and Ree had absolutely no idea what to do besides jump in somehow and do her part. She spied the giant key on the floor, lying in a shiny pool of blue rat blood, and grabbed it. It was slick with the fluid, so she sniffed it curiously. It appeared to be oil of vitriol combined with sulfuric acid. The stuff could burn mightily on contact, and could also cause blindness. It was probably only colored blue like that to alert the inventor when he spilled on himself. Dross and she used the same trick when using deadly liquids. She wiped her hand hastily on her nightdress, and wiped the key too. It left a huge smear of electric blue on her gown. This nightdress had been specially ordered from the sister nuns at the Our Lady of the Snows in Nova Scotia. It had cost a fortune. *Mama really is going to kill me if the rats don't do the job first.*

* * *

When Ree had retrieved the key from the floor, two rats had come up along with it. Now these two robotic monstrosities seized their opportunity and used the key as a bridge to scurry across and leap onto Ree's arm. She shook violently, trying to upend them, but their small, silver feet were steady and sure and dug into her arm like an unhinged parrot with a fear of flying. A silent bullet must have hit one, for it fell suddenly to the ground. Ree looked up just in time to see the small soldier, the bloody one, lower her weapon. Ree nodded her wordless thanks and the soldier smiled grimly.

The second rat Ree dispatched with a satisfying fling of her arm; it went flying through the air and crashed against the Christmas tree. Had it been a real rat, made of fur and bone and muscle, it would have been impaled. As it was made of steel and brass and gadgetry, the vile thing made a clanging sound and fell to the floor on its back, where it lay, wiggling its legs impotently in the air. They seemed to be like turtles in that way, as they were both feeble and confused when laid upon their backs. If only it were a simple thing to flip them like a gorgonzola and walnut omelet, Ree thought. But reaching down to pick them up seemed a dangerous thing and one she wasn't quite brave enough to try. Yet.

She realized she'd been bitten by the stupid device, with its razor sharp, silver pronged fangs. She looked down at her arm, where blood was seeping through the fine satin of her nightdress. It didn't hurt – not yet – but she felt woozy at the amount as it spread. The rats at her feet seemed to lose interest in her. They scurried away from her, and away from the line of fire coming from the soldiers too, and headed as one towards the fireplace.

Cullen seemed to know instinctively they were coming, or maybe he had called them with his magically evil pocket watch device. Ree didn't know. If he had pressed the button that caused the glowing green color and played the musical notes, she hadn't noticed them, what with concentrating on not fainting. Cullen dropped his bag to the floor and opened it wide. The rats raced inside, over and around one another, in a hurry. It was such an odd sight that even Nikolai stood still and watched, though he had been about to swing an impressive punch with his mechanical arm just a moment before. When the last rat had entered the bag, Cullen straightened. The bag was large and pulsing with life and had to be quite heavy. He swung it over his bony back as if it weighed nothing. Ree was reminded of an evil version of Santa Claus, who was some sort of gift wielding and chimney traveling elf, which Jessa had told her the Americans celebrated during Christmas.

"Where do you think you're going?" Fritz challenged. "This battle is not yet done!" His voice was dreadful. Ree was impressed, through her haze of pain.

"Another time, brother," Cullen bowed. He stepped backward, and before Ree could even blink, he had disappeared. There was nothing left but soot.

* * *

Soot, and the dozens and dozens of dead rat robots. And puddles of blue liquid that would be dangerous to wipe up, and a clockwork doll that chose at that exact moment to fall right out of her box with a crash. And an enormous metal Christmas tree that looked very much the worse for wear, and several fierce looking soldier girls, packing weapons. And an automaton with seemingly a mind of his own. And here Ree had thought she'd be bored this eve. She wanted to collapse on the floor, but didn't dare get anywhere near the oil of vitriol.

"Your arm," Nikolai moved towards her, concerned.

"You went and got yourself bit?" Fritz was incredulous. "Marie, for goodness sake!"

"Well, I'm sorry." Ree glared at him. "It was hardly intentional! I didn't ask to be bitten by bloody vermin from hell!" The occasion seemed to call for a small amount of cursing, even if she were a lady of quality. And her arm burned. It made her irritable. "Hellfire and damnation it all to...to hell and back! Hell's bells!"

The soldiers seemed to be holding in laughter, but covered it politely by rearranging their guns and holsters and tending to their own injuries, which miraculously were minimal, other than the small one, who had been scratched rather savagely.

"Only you," Fritz was disgusted. "Everyone else managed not to get bitten. Here, sit down."

Nikolai had reached her already though and Ree was surprised to find he was the only thing standing between herself and an appalling increase in gravity. She would have sunk to the floor right then if Nikolai weren't holding her up. "I'm rather in pain," she said crossly, as her legs gave out altogether. She felt a fraction of time where she was floating when she began to topple, and then she was scooped up, as easily if she were a kitten and Nikolai a child.

Chapter Seven
Recovery and a Visit from Drosselmeier

The next several days were a flurry of activity and panic for Hoffman, who had been employed with the task of cleaning and putting to rights the Grand Parlor. At first, Ree felt terrible for him and promised to help as soon as Mama would allow her out of bed, but then she realized the spilt oil of vitriol that the rats had bled would be safer with the robot than cleaned by human hands. The Christmas tree was busted and dented in a few places, and would need some tender care before the next holiday season, and the chaise lounge and the Turkish rug had been removed from the house and destroyed. Mama was livid. She had adored that rug.

That wasn't even the worst of it. Old Sir Croftenspot had expired during the night of the rats, evidently of a heart attack. There was blue blood in the parlor and a dead body in the guest bedroom.

Ree relayed the strange happenings of the strange man, Cullen, and his army of rodents as many times as she was told, until her good temper finally snapped and she faked twelve hours of sleep just to get out of reliving the tale again. Fritz and his army of women soldiers had disappeared as mysteriously as they had arrived, once Ree had been carefully put to bed and their father woken to tend to her wounds. They hadn't been back since, and now Ree was the one who was livid. She was itching to know precisely what and who Cullen Souris was, and how he had come to know Nikolai and have such a vicious military of rats. She couldn't ask Nikolai, because he was back inside his dratted box with the clockwork doll, and she was stuck in bed, halfway across the mansion, like an invalid schoolgirl.

The effects of the bite had left her blurry and confused at first. She was embarrassed to remember babbling something about her nutcracker prince and his rescue of her, and she desperately hoped those ramblings had bubbled out of her delirious mouth after Nikolai had returned to the parlor, and not as he was carrying her, as she rather thought. Automaton or not, Ree was pink with the memory of her wayward gushing over him.

Why he had chosen to return to his box, Ree was at a loss to explain to herself – unless it was out of acute mortification at her words about him - but she had been assured by Hoffman that indeed, the toys were there. It was possible they had run out of whatever had been used to power them, and needed to recharge themselves. Or mayhap Nikolai didn't want to leave the doll alone in case the intruders returned?

The only other person Ree believed could explain the adventure was Herr Drosselmeier, and he was annoyingly absent from her sickbed. She told Melisande to pay him a call, and when that didn't work, Ree sent a mechanical pigeon with a politely worded request to see her favorite godfather. When that didn't work, she sent another; this one not so polite.

Must see you immediately. Matter of life and death. Quit floating around in pirate territory and get here NOW!

The pigeon was equipped with a homing device that could only go from Drosselmeier's workship to Ree's home, and vice-versa, but she received no reply. She wondered if it had wandered off, or if its mechanics had failed, mid-flight. Or if Dross wasn't at home, he wouldn't know of her plight, and the pigeon was probably pecking around his workship, turning about in circles, and bonking into walls, the way it did when it was activated but had nothing to deliver. Ree sighed from her bed and tossed a silk pillow at the wall in frustration. She'd never been a very good patient. One summer, as an eight-year-old, she'd broken her leg climbing a tree, and three nannies had quit before autumn had arrived. And one of the nannies had been a robotic, with no emotions and a fully built brain that was wired to be more patient and long suffering than most. That had been embarrassing.

'Wound fever' was the official diagnosis now, and Ree was insulted by the vague label, wondering if it was just a made-up conclusion to explain away her fanciful story. It didn't seem like an actual malady. Her tale of the mechanical rats and their evil ruler who came in and out of the fireplace was received by her parents and the doctor with polite smiles and pats on the head. Only Mama seemed somewhat inclined to believe her, and that was likely due to the state of her Turkish carpet and its mysterious stains that could hardly be chalked up to a party goer's spilt punch. No, the blue goo had to have come from somewhere and while she wasn't apt to stomach Ree's whimsical ramblings, she had no other explanation. However, she was busy with Sir Croftenspot's family and mourning, and couldn't dedicate her full attention to Ree anyway.

Christmas in general had been awful. Ree's family tromped through her bedroom to bring her her gifts, but since she was getting too old for such things (it was only Drosselmeier's presents that had piqued her curiosity lately), they sat in a dejected heap by her bed. Mama had gotten her practical things, like crinolines and corsets, and Lou had given her a copy of a book entitled, *Anyone Can Be a Lady: How to Turn a Sow's Ear Into a Silk Purse, Volumes I-IV*. Ree planned to use the pages for fire starters, and she figured the tomes would come in handy for stacking as a footstool. Especially when her boots were muddy.

The door to Ree's bedroom opened while she was intent upon her musings, and when she saw who was behind it, Ree clapped her hands like a little girl. Immediately, she sat upon them and turned her grin into a frown. It wouldn't do to indulge Herr Drosselmeier's behavior. He had some smoothing of her ruffled feathers to do first. He had been so rude at the party. And then? Taking his sweet time to visit his ailing goddaughter.

"Well, it's certainly kind of you to come," Ree muttered. She plumped up one of her satin pillows behind her back and glared at him. "I nearly died, you know."

"Poppycock," Drosselmeier waved his hand in the air, as if he were waving away her ridiculous notion. "The chances of that were very slim indeed. Well, if not slim, then middling anyway. Why ever are you lying there? It's mid-day. Get up, for goodness sake, child." He walked over to the window and flung it open. "It's like a sick bay in here. Ugh."

Ree gaped. "I nearly died," she repeated, enunciating better this time. "Wound fever? Oil of vitriol poisoning? Ever hear of it?"

"Piffle. That stuff was likely diluted with something harmless, like vegetable oil, or lard, or lady's hand cream, or some such thing. The worst it could do is give you a headache, a few hallucinations, and possibly some light scarring."

Ree glanced down at her arm, ensconced in her covers and bedsheets. She had an ugly bite mark in the shape of a half moon. She'd bet dollars to donuts there had been no lady's hand cream mixed in with that electric blue fluid. "Yes, I do have a lovely scar, thanks very much. It will serve nicely to remember this rotten Christmas for all of eternity, if the memories etched into my very brain don't do the trick."

"Don't be sarcastic; it annoys me. I came to keep you company even after you berated and abused my poor pigeon."

"I did no such thing."

"You nearly twisted off his cute little feet attaching the message."

"Well, you designed it poorly. The clasping is difficult. And I was sick. I had wound fever, remember?" She scratched her itchy scar, irritated. Her leg hurt too, where the pink, zigzag lines went up and down; a little something to remember those hellish rats by.

"There's nothing difficult about the clasping mechanisms, you simply have the grace of a troll when you're upset. Now, enough with this wound fever nonsense. Are you getting out of bed and coming downstairs, or do I leave without you? The air in here is making me ill."

"I'm so sorry you're not comfortable, Godfather, dear." Ree seethed. She flung her covers aside. "Of course, let me see to your every whim. I only hope my leg is able to support my weight." She tested it gingerly, wincing as she did so.

"Probably should have passed by the creampuffs at the party, my dear," was his only response. He left her bedroom, assuming she would follow.

"What?" Ree limped, following.

"You must maintain that girlish figure if you want to marry well," Drosselmeier responded, and began to mimic the mincing steps of a schoolgirl down the hallway. He pranced and whirled, and ended in a bow.

Ree raised her red eyebrow at him, refusing to play his silly game. Her leg still hurt and burned a bit, and she was frustrated with the whole situation. "And just where are we headed anyway? I'm supposed to stay in bed another day." *So the doctor can pat my head and ignore everything I say.*

"We're checking on the state of the dolls. I'm off to Sea Level, and I want them in the best possible condition so I can get the best possible price. And also, you need exercise."

"Creampuffs?" Ree answered, sarcastically.

"Indeed. Come along."

"Must you sell them? I thought they were a gift."

"The creampuffs?"

"No, you irksome man. The dolls." She hobbled along behind the clock maker with all the grace of a hippopotamus. Perhaps she did need exercise after all. Just this little walk was causing her to break out in a fine sheen of sweat. If Lou came upon her now, she'd get an earful. *Young ladies of good breeding do not perspire, Marie! Stop shining immediately! Ugh.* "And may I come if you're set upon this journey?"

"To Sea Level?" Dross put on his best mock horrified face as he whirled around to face Ree once more. His thin lips formed a perfect O, and his one good eye widened in pretended shock. He left it that way, looking like an old, mysterious owl, so long that Ree's own eyes began to water.

"Oh, must you tease?" she finally grumbled, as it seemed he could stare that way for all of eternity until she caved. "I want to go, too. I'm going to die here, you know, if you don't save me."

"Rubbish, child. What is this preoccupation with dying? So morbid. If you want to come along, I certainly can't stop you. You'd only hide away in my ship anyway. Can you move faster, please? I want to get to the parlor before Easter." He scampered faster and faster and reached the stairwell, not even pausing to help her down. He disappeared from sight, and Ree picked up the pace, shining all the way.

* * *

"This is dreadful. Much worse than I thought," Drosselmeier said as he rocked back on his heels and smoothed the ends of his mustache. It was a bit disheartening to see, because Ree knew he only did when he was particularly distracted, or out of ideas.

Nikolai and the doll were in bad shape. The doll had cracked her skull in several new places and most of one ear was sitting next to her foot. Her cheerful, striped stockings were torn and ripped, and half of her fluffy crinoline had been gnawed and chewed on. *Why ever would mechanical animals do such a thing*, Ree wondered. *Unless it was simply for spite.*

Nikolai looked even worse. His jaunty tri-cornered hat had been smashed to smithereens, he was covered in soot and blue fluid, his smart blue uniform was ruined, and quite a few of the brass fittings in his mechanical arm were hanging loosely or missing altogether. He also had not said a word or acknowledged Ree and Drosselmeier's appearance since they had swung open the box door. Ree assumed he had run out of whatever power he ran on, but she still felt a sharp jab of disappointment. Nikolai then, wouldn't answer any of her questions. She'd have to rely on her godfather and his ever changing and maddening moods, though he might not even know a thing about Cullen and his army of rats.

Well, there was simply no other way. She'd have to help Drosselmeier with the restoration of the dolls, even if the price was allowing them to be sold. It may feel wrong, but after all, they were only robotics. It might pain Ree to think of selling Hoffman, but it would hardly be morally unacceptable. Why then, did she feel such disenchantment in herself? She shook off her jumbled and pointless thoughts and set herself to planning.

"I can fix the doll if you have the original paint you used for her hair. And I should be able to reattach the ear, poor thing. You know I'm no wizard with a needle, but I'm sure I can patch up the skirt. The stockings though." Ree pursed her lips in thought. "Louise has a pair she used for a school play years ago. I think I could find them."

"Do it then." Dross was preoccupied with working the robotic arm of Nikolai up and down. He wrenched it with such force that Ree winced in sympathy, though Nikolai's facial features didn't budge in the slightest.

Ree unfolded her body gingerly from where she had perched it several moments before, and stood. "All right then. I'll go and procure those stockings. Though Lou hates it when I enter her space uninvited. If you hear screaming, it's me."

"Mm. Yes. That's fine." Dross wriggled the fastenings on Nikolai's arm and a shower of bolts fell to the ground with a tinkling sound.

"She may in fact, murder me for trespassing and stealing."

"Hmph." Dross pocketed the bolts with a sigh.

"And then you'll have no one to help you."

"Make haste, child! Stop dawdling. My buyer is an anxious fellow and won't wait."

Ree felt queasy in her stomach at his words. Help her eccentric godfather she would – help him get his inventions back in working order. But after that...she would give him no guarantee of her loyalty in his schemes.

Chapter Eight
Thievery and a Funeral

Getting in and out of places she wasn't allowed to be in in the first place was a bit of a specialty for Ree. However, she'd rather sneak into Dross' workship or in Jessa's window on a midnight escapade, than enter her older sister's lair. A grown adult and a lady to boot, but at heart Louise was still a vindictive and easily angered sibling. Plus, her giant bedroom reeked of rose petal perfume and was a complete and utter mess.

Lady she might be all right, but Lou was a total slob.

Ree gingerly picked her way through a pile of petticoats, lying in a heap like a pile of dead seagulls, and tripped promptly on a pair of dainty heeled boots. No, just one boot. Ree rubbed her shin and sat where she had fallen, surveying the scene. Oh, there was the other boot perched atop a tray of half-eaten roast duck. They hadn't had roast duck for at least a week. *She's going to attract rodents*, Ree thought to herself. Then she shuddered. Rodents. Blech.

Ree picked herself up, her ears pricked for any noise that might signify the appearance of her sister, and bit her bottom lip. The stockings should be...well, never mind where they should be. The roast duck should be in the kitchen and the boots should be in their proper place and they weren't, so obviously logic wouldn't be of any help.

At least Lou couldn't possibly notice a little ransacking, not with the state of this room. Ree abandoned all pretense of sneaking around or being careful, and simply began to go through the room; searching through piles of clothing with a wrinkled nose. The rose petal scent was overwhelming, and the faint odor of molding duck also wafted by every few moments. Had Louise any fondness or trust in the servants – robotic or otherwise – this room would be clean and spotlessly organized. However, she had a deep mistrust of the hired help, and Ree also thought she rather liked the mess. "Though I don't know why," she muttered, pinching a crumbling sugar plum between her fingers in disgust. She flung it over her head, where it bounced off a rag doll's face and landed in a heap of underpinnings.

Ree moved onto the wardrobe in the corner. There were the stockings, wadded up in a ball and sitting dejectedly with the rest of costume. During Lou's coming out year, she had participated in everything she possibly could. This had included a performing arts and dramatics phase that Ree would rather forget. While Lou was beautiful to look at, it was best that she didn't sing or have any lines to perform. Her portrayal of Titania would be remembered for years in the Stahlbaum family, but for all the wrong reasons. Ree secretly thought the play acting might be the main reason why Lou was an old spinster now—still on the shelf at the ripe old age of eighteen. With a shrug, she pocketed the ball of stockings. They were diamond patterned, not striped, but she didn't think Drosselmeier would care. He was a man, after all.

* * *

The action and the plan to action was all Ree needed to invigorate her. She forgot about the dull ache in her leg and the burning sensation in her arm as she and Drosselmeier secreted away the automatons.

Well, it wasn't so much secreted away as it was loudly making a fuss. The box was as heavy as it looked the night of the fateful party, and the wheels were sticky with the remains of blue fluid that Hoffman had missed. It caused the wheel mechanisms to squeak and stick.

Once outside the mansion however, things moved more speedily. Herr Drosselmeier had one of the finest and most lavish horseless phaetons ever made and the open ended, four sided design was the perfect fit for the box, though there was an alarming banging sound as they lowered it to its side. Ree flinched in sympathy, knowing it was the dolls inside, falling.

"Meet me at the workship," Dross instructed, as he fit his lithe frame inside the phaeton. "And be quick about it. No time for dilly-dallying or primping. Just get dressed and bring your toolbox." He looked down at his goddaughter and raised a brow.

Ree had forgotten she was in her dressing gown. Hurriedly, she clasped the fine lace around herself and rushed back into the house. "Don't start without me!" she shouted, before slamming the door closed behind her.

* * *

Outfitted with her favorite bowler hat and her oldest gown (it was already stained with goodness knows what and torn in several places, so it was the perfect dress for the workship), Ree packed her toolbox. It had been a gift from Dross a year earlier and when folded properly it was an unassuming little thing, almost like a reticule. Opened, it revealed a dozen cleverly designed compartments and tiny drawers; ideal for concealing vials of chemicals, assortments of gears and gadgets, and Ree's beloved tools.

She nearly tripped over someone in the hallway as she raced around the corner. Old Lady Croftenspot. She was dressed all in black, complete with an over the top dramatic veil with a papier-mâché crow over one ear, gloves, and pointy toed, heeled boots. Ree stifled a groan, and righted the woman, who glared at her through her black lace.

"You've already killed my husband, Stahlbaum chit, don't finish the job with me now!" Lady Croftenspot snapped.

"I'm so dreadfully sorry, ma'am. Please accept my condolences. I wasn't trying to finish the job, I assure you." Ree bit her lip, feeling contrite and sorry for the old widow. She'd had a Christmas to remember as well, and not fondly.

"Well." Lady Croftenspot seemed mollified. "I suppose you're here to pay your respects? Right this way, and stand up straight, child. I can't abide poor posture."

"Oh, I –" Ree wasn't certain how to get out of paying her respects to the old man she'd hardly known without offending his surviving wife even further. "I mean, yes. Yes, of course. I would like to say goodbye."

The old lady shuffled off, looking like some sort of rare, black bird (though perhaps that was the effect of the crow), and Ree followed dejectedly. She wanted nothing more than to get to the workship, but fifteen years of Victorian upbringing and training from English nannies and tutors prevailed. There was only so much one could do to undo all that, she thought.

Old Sir Croftenspot had been laid out in the drawing room. The shades and curtains had been drawn and a sense of doom and gloom invaded the gray spaces, like a heavy shadow. Ree stifled another sigh and wondered how long she'd be required to stay here. There were no other visitors, other than Melisande, who was standing stiffly with a tray of refreshments and looking terrified to be in the same room as a corpse. Ree was beginning to wonder if they paid their staff enough. Really, it was too much what they had been through lately. Hoffman would be in a stink for weeks.

Ree approached the body and steeled herself to bend down and kiss his cheek, hoping the gesture would seem sincere and appropriate. His face was waxen and cool to the touch, a bit like the clockwork doll actually, and the scent of dried herbs and flowers clung to him. Her mother and Lady Croftenspot must have dressed him; he'd hardly have died in his fancy Christmas clothes when he was in bed, asleep. He'd probably been in some sort of dressing gown. And the odor...it was coming from the pressed flower in his breast coat pocket. He really looked ancient and rather like he'd been dead awhile, instead of only a couple of days. But then again, he'd looked a bit like a walking cadaver before succumbing to his age.

"Well," Ree said brightly, straightening, "I feel much better seeing how peaceful he looks. As he, er, goes to his eternal reward and whatnot. I do hope we will see you again next Christmas, Lady Croftenspot."

"Sit down, little girl. I need the company." The elderly woman lowered herself into the nearest settee and patted the cushion beside her. "My own kin haven't arrived yet, you know."

"No?" Ree replied, weakly. She longed for the workship.

"I'm sure they're coming. Yes. They wouldn't desert their father and grandfather." Lady Croftenspot began to cry, which alarmed Ree greatly. She never knew what to do when people cried; it was such an odd activity and one Ree didn't indulge in herself unless in great pain. Lady Croftenspot dabbed at her ancient blue eyes. This was more difficult than it looked, seeing as how her massive veil was blocking her attempts. She fluttered about like a bird caught in a chimney flue.

"Now, now. There, there," Ree murmured, and helped disentangle the woman from her black lace. "Come, come." Were comforting words always said in pairs? "Here, uh, here."

"Oh, you're a nice child." She sniffled and hiccupped. The sniffles and hiccups multiplied into weeping and nose blowing. Ree, not surprisingly, had no handkerchief, and offered the use of her middle petticoat. "He was just so young! So much youth in that man! Why, he had the heart of a thirty-year-old, my Reggie did! So young to die! Too, too young!"

Ree held her tongue. Dear Reggie had to have been ninety-five if he was a day, but she supposed it was true what they said about age being a state of mind. Or at least she *thought* that's what they said. It was a grownup idiom, and Ree tried not listen overly much to grownups even though she was nearly one herself. She realized she should likely start. The thought was unbearably depressing.

"There, there," Ree said once more, and snuck a glance at her Clock Bob, which had barely escaped being rained upon by Lady Croftenspot's dripping eyes and nose. Dross would be very unforgiving of her lack of punctuality. What if he left for Sea Level without her? He wouldn't care a fig for Ree's show of sympathy for the old widow. Dross didn't have a sympathetic or polite bone in his body.

"Why doesn't Melisande fetch you a fresh pot of tea and you can spend some time with dear Reggie, just the two of you?" Ree snapped her fingers at the maid, who looked extremely grateful and nearly flew out of the room.

"Yes, yes, dear, of course." She blew her nose one last time on Ree's petticoat. "You're a good girl."

Ree couldn't help but be pleased at the praise. Being a good girl wasn't a compliment she received often. A tiresome girl, a smart girl, an energetic girl, a rich girl, a clever girl, yes. But she'd never been accused of being good. It felt nice, even if her petticoat felt soggy to the touch.

The good feeling didn't last. As Ree rose from the settee at last and made to leave the drawing room, she watched the widow raise her dead husband's hand to her quivering lips. The hand had a faint smear of blue goo under his fingernails.

It was no heart attack that killed Sir Croftenspot. Or if it was, it had been brought on by fear. Ree's skin turned icy cold. At least one rat had to have made it out of the parlor that night in spite of Fritz and his army's attempts to keep them contained.

Ree raced back to the widow and threw her arms around her. "I'm so very, very sorry for your loss," she whispered in her ear. But this time, she meant every word.

Chapter Nine
The Workship

By the time Ree made it out of her home and to her godfather's workship – hanging in the sky like a giant eagle – she was beginning to feel feverish and exhausted. Maybe wound fever was a thing after all, and if so, she seemed to have it in spades. She tucked a lock of hair beneath her hat, feeling her clammy jawbone as she did so.

Drosselmeier's workship was a thing of marvel. It was not beautiful; in fact, it was an eyesore; something his unlucky neighbors pointed out frequently over pints of ale or cups of tea. It was a monstrous thing, huge and looming; or at least it seemed monstrous. It actually wasn't as large as it appeared; it was its haphazard style and architecture that tricked the eye. There were two floors to the floating laboratory. The bottom was open in design and was really just a huge room for his creations and half-finished inventions. No parlors or drawing rooms or any such nonsense for Drosselmeier. He had those things in his own house to be sure, but they were covered in dust and rarely used for their purposes. The second floor of the workship was a maze of rooms that supposedly were used strictly for storage, though Ree suspected differently now. He must have used one of them to invent and make the dolls since she knew full well they hadn't been below at any point. Above the second floor was a ramshackle roof made of all sorts of things, including a regular crazy quilt as a lid for Dross' ship. Part of it was tile from America, some of it was peat and moss from Scotland, and here and there were patches of hay and even grass growing. Honestly, it looked as though a smattering of sheep wouldn't be amiss, and Ree would hardly have blinked should any be seen lazily grazing on the roof. Above the odd looking top was the balloon that held the whole thing aloft. It was large enough to cast a shadow on the entire neighborhood, and the balloon was held to the ship with long ropes. Another rope tethered the monstrosity to the ground below by means of an iron anchor that Dross had assured Ree had come from a drowned pirate ship in the Caribbean. The anchor was fixed to the wrought iron fence belonging to a certain Lord Anklesby, who Ree was quite sure would be peeved as a wet hen when he returned from his holiday to such impertinence.

"Hi ho!" Ree shouted, and waited expectantly for a reply. Again, but this time cupping her hand around her mouth and turning up the volume a notch. "Hullo! Godfather! Hi ho!"

"Come up, come up, child, and stop screeching throughout the neighborhood!" Drosselmeier appeared at the first floor window, several stories high above Ree's head, and scowled. He waved her upwards impatiently and slammed shut the window.

"No, thanks, I'll manage on my own," Ree muttered, thinking crankily of wound fever. She hiked up her skirts and began the long and tedious process of climbing a swaying rope ladder near the anchor. It was made of sturdy enough rope and planks of wood, but it might have been made of dreams and wishes the way it felt beneath Ree's feet. It swayed alarmingly in the wind and her petticoats and skirts whipped around her legs, making life in general more problematic than it had any right to be. Ree wished desperately for one of the uniforms that Fritz's girls wore. She could shimmy up this rope like a monkey in a banana tree. Or at least, she was pretty certain she could.

Finally, secure in the workship (or as secure as being so far off in the air and tethered to the ground by a stolen pirate anchor could possibly be), Ree could breathe a bit more easily. Drosselmeier was hunched over the body of Nikolai in one corner of the ship. He had not said a word to Ree since hollering at her out the window minutes before, and he paid her no mind. He seemed to be immersed in whatever it was he was doing, and Ree decided wisely not to interrupt him. Instead she wiped her shining palms on her skirts and set her toolbox down next to the clockwork doll.

She was even in worse shape than she had been only hours before. Likely from being tossed around inside the box as the phaeton traveled through town, or from pulling herself up the rope ladder. Ree couldn't imagine how Dross had managed that feat but assumed he had to have hired help. Or perhaps lowered the workship closer to the ground while he loaded his cargo? She made a mental note to ask sometime, when he was in a better mood. He was positively glowering at Nikolai and the poor nutcracker man's injuries. As if they were his fault!

Ree sighed and examined the clockwork doll critically. Most of her blue china ringlets had broken off, leaving sharp shards hanging by her ear. The other ear was safely tucked inside Ree's toolbox. She may as well start there. She wasn't sure whether or not the ears served any real function for the automaton, but it seemed cruel to not put them both back in their proper place. Machinery she may be, but every girl had some vanity, even if she had no flesh to be vain about.

Ree mixed up a batch of glue and then tinted half of it blue to match the doll's hair. She wrestled the doll atop a table and then felt like the strangest doctor in the world as she bent over the body.

"Turn her on then," Drosselmeier snapped, as he raised his head to look at Ree. "She can't tell you what ails her if she's asleep, can she?"

"Oh." Ree hid her surprise at the suggestion. "The key?"

"The key is just for show. There's a button beneath her shoulder blades." Dross had already dismissed her and was back to screwing in small silver screws into Nikolai's elbow.

Ree frowned. "But I used the key before and she came to life."

Dross growled audibly. "Came to life?" he mimicked. "Is that what you call it when you wind your Clock Bob? It comes to life, does it? You must have knocked the button when you used the key is all."

Ree didn't think so, but she knew better than to argue. She rolled the body of the doll over a bit to expose her china back. She pulled down the tattered part of the crinoline skirt that covered the hidden button. There it was. A switch more than a button, but still. Ree held her breath as she flipped the little mechanism and gently laid the doll back down.

The pools of black ink that served as the doll's eyes didn't change, but they did seem to twitch. Almost like a puddle that you toss a stone into, they rippled and seemed to change shape. Her fingers twitched too, and her tiny, ballerina feet. Ree heard the doll take a breath, and it felt if she laid her hand upon the chest of the doll, she would somehow feel the air going in and out of her lungs.

Except of course, dolls didn't have lungs. Or any breath in those nonexistent lungs. Ree told herself to stop her romantic imaginings; it really wasn't like her at all.

The doll made a mewing sort of sound, a bit like a kitten, and it was simultaneously cheering and pathetic to Ree's ears. "Well, hullo, there!" Ree said, brightly. "I'm here to fix things right up for you. Is there a particular place you'd like me to start or examine?" She felt a little awkward talking to a doll but was bound and determined to sound professional.

The doll cocked her head in a curious fashion and seemed to regard Ree through her black eyes. Or at least pointed them in the direction of Ree anyway. From deep inside her chest cavity, Ree could hear the distant piano keys of the automaton's music box. "I can't hear you very well," the doll said. Her voice was tinny and tinkling, much like the music that accompanied her.

"Yes, that's no surprise. You've lost an ear in the fray, I'm afraid. But I've got it right here in my bag and I'll fix that up first thing." Ree smiled optimistically, though she wasn't sure the doll could see her anyway through those strange puddles of black paint that served as her eyes.

The doll smiled back, much to Ree's delight. The heart shaped bow of her pink lips lifted at the corners, and a tiny dimple appeared in the smooth china of her cheek, right beneath the crack where the clockwork gears showed through. "Thank you kindly, miss," said the doll.

"Not at all. Now hold still if you can. I'm just going to make sure of the placement before I add the paste. It wouldn't do to have it glued on backwards now, would it?" Ree stifled a chuckle, though it felt as awkward as speaking, and twice as bizarre.

"Yes, miss, thank you, miss. I can hold quite still."

And she did, for quite some time, until Ree instructed her that she could move once again. The ear was reattached and held in place by a clamp until the glue was completely dry. Next they moved onto the next project, which was to repair a deep gash across the doll's shoulder. Ree felt less like a surgeon than she did a clockmaker or some such tinkerer, and it was odd to be fishing around inside someone's body and coming up with silver and gold wires and gears. The doll seemed to be sectioned off in neat compartments. Her body was a map of hinges and square shaped boxes, with tiny, hairline seams. She was like a woman made entirely of jewelry boxes that fit together like a jigsaw puzzle. Each shoulder was a box, each elbow was a box, there was a rectangular shaped compartment beneath her neck, and one where her heart would be. Ree was curious to open the heart box, but contained herself. Curiosity was no good reason to go snooping. She did wonder which one held the music box.

There was a complicated and detailed pulley system in the shoulder compartment, and once Ree figured out the basic mechanisms, she could fit the wires back in their proper places and like magic, the shoulder and arm were as good as new.

"You are the most perfect patient ever," Ree declared, as she carefully closed the shoulder box. "Now, besides your outfit, which needs mending and replacing, is there anywhere else that hurts?"

The doll seemed to think for a moment, then she shrugged a delicate shrug. "I always hurt a bit, miss," she said. "I'm not sure what it's like to not."

"Oh, dear." Ree frowned in sympathy. "I'm sure that's not how things should be."

"It's always been this way, miss. I don't mean to complain."

"Of course you're not complaining. I will speak to my godfather about it. In the meantime," Ree suddenly felt shy, "do you have a name? And you needn't call me miss. Ree will do just fine."

"We call her China." It was Nikolai's voice, coming from the other end of the room. He sounded tired.

"China. That's lovely. Now, about these stockings? I'm afraid the rats made a meal of yours, but I have these to replace. Will they do?" Ree held up Louise's diamond patterned stockings.

"They're lovely! I only wish they were pink." China confided. She lowered her voice to a whisper, as if nervous the two gentlemen would overhear. "I've always longed for a pair of pink stockings."

So she could see through her strange eyes then. Ree smiled. "Well, I know what to get you for your birthday then."

A gentle rippling sound came from China's mouth. It sounded like water trickling down a stream. It was her laughter, and the doll covered her lips with one delicate hand as it bubbled out of her. "That won't be until the autumn. I'll be sixteen, but thank you. These will do nicely."

"Are you two ninnies done chatting?" Drosselmeier's impatient voice cut through their exchange. "We've much more important things to do than giggle like schoolgirl chits. Ree, I need your help over here. Hold down Nikolai. I need to wrench this leg back into place and it keeps slipping gears."

"Ree, wait," China covered Ree's hand with her own, "About the other night? I was so scared, but you had pressed my Demonstrate Button which meant I could only dance. I couldn't help. I just wanted to apologize. I know I was useless to everyone. I'm so embarrassed. It's like I'm trapped inside my own silly body sometimes. I want to be more alive, but I'm a slave to my programming."

Ree was appalled. "Don't apologize, please! It was a horrible night and I'm so sorry it happened at my house. You were very brave."

"Ree!" Dross was seething. She could tell by the way the vein on his forehead was popping out. She could see it from the distance, pulsing and throbbing angrily like a purple worm. He really had a temper problem. No small wonder he had been a bachelor for...forever.

"I'm coming already! China, try to lay still while this glue finishes drying. I'll be right back."

China smiled brightly. She really was excellent at holding still.

Nikolai's face was turned away from Ree when she reached his side. He had parts and gizmos and gadgets strewn about on the table. It made Ree's stomach turned when the thought occurred to her that they were in fact, strange bits and pieces of body parts. Her stomach clenched further when she noticed bits of rust colored staining on some parts.

"Is that oil or blood?" Ree picked up a gear and frowned at it. The rust colored substance was sticky. She put it down hastily.

Dross looked over, impatiently. "Don't worry about it. Hand me that wrench, would you? And be quick about it."

Ree did so, but her gaze went back to the gear on the table. The liquid seemed to shine and shimmer at her, as if begging for her attention. It really did not have the consistency of oil. "But...," she began, but her godfather let out a furious roar.

"Stop pestering me, child! I need you to either help me or go home and do some needlepoint!"

Ree clamped her mouth shut and bit her tongue. "I'll help you, but stop yelling at me. What do you need me to do?"

"Hold down his leg like so. No, not there, put your hands above the kneecap, like this. Yes. Good. Now put your weight on it. More."

Ree had nearly climbed atop the automaton and straddled the poor thing's leg before Dross gave a grunt of satisfaction. She made a point of not meeting Nikolai's eyes. This was unbearably awkward. She would be vastly embarrassed and mortified later, she was sure. For now, she needed all her concentration on what she was doing.

"Ready?" Drosselmeier asked.

"Ready."

He gave a mighty shove and Ree heard the sickening sound of bones popping into place. Nikolai groaned and she felt his leg quiver beneath her. She felt as though she needed a minute to compose herself, not only from the exertion and the bizarreness of the procedure, but because of what the whole ordeal had shown her.

Blood and bones.

Nikolai was no doll. At least not entirely.

Chapter Ten
Uncomfortable Realizations

Ree felt sick. She felt like retching over the side of the workship. She said not a word to Drosselmeier and on wobbly, weak knees she made her way back to China.

China. Good Lord, did the clockwork doll have human parts as well?

What kind of monster scientist was her beloved godfather?

Ree sank down into a hardback chair that was near China. She wanted to cry, or at the very least, cover her shocked face with her hands and whimper a little, but she didn't give in to the feeling. She needed to pull herself together first. She could fall apart later, at her own house, after she had figured out what to do.

This kind of work, this kind of perversion – it wouldn't be tolerated if people knew. Robots made to look human were one thing; but human parts used to make robots? Not even the most progressive among Father's social circles would put up with this monstrosity. Dross would be run out of town on a rail, or tarred and feathered. At the very least, he'd be tried and sent to court and likely, prison.

The irony didn't escape Ree. The Justice of the Peace sent to court? Who would wear the white curled wig then?

"May I move just a bit now?" China's polite voice cut through Ree's imaginings. "It's just that I think I may be lying upon a screw."

"Oh, goodness!" Ree jumped up and carefully helped China rock slightly from her back to her side. "China, I'm dreadfully sorry. How careless and clumsy of me. Yes, here it is." She pulled out a dull screw. It had left a mark in the doll's smooth porcelain skin. A scratch. A pink scratch. The sick feeling returned. Scratching porcelain shouldn't have a pink tint. Unless she had pink paint beneath the ivory hue. Or unless there was human blood beneath the surface somewhere.

"Oh, that's much better, thank you ever so much! I'm sorry to be such a bother. I'll continue lying still now." China crossed her arms over her chest. The shimmering pool of her eyes seemed to wane a little, and Ree somehow knew that she had closed them.

"I think you're safe to move around actually. Why don't you get up and see if there are other areas that need addressing?" Ree offered her arm and China took it. She helped the doll (girl?) off the table.
China's legs seemed a bit shaky, though to be sure, they always seemed that way.

"Right as rain!" The doll gave one of her bright smiles that Ree was beginning to recognize. She was a very optimistic and obedient thing. Of course, she had been programmed that way, but even so. Hoffman certainly had his grouchy moods, and Ree was forever tinkering with his Emoticon Panel to little or no avail.

"Shall I try on those stockings then?" China bit her heart shaped lip. She had tiny, white teeth. Ree remembered Nikolai's human bits and winced. Surely the teeth weren't real? The sick feeling in the pit of her stomach returned, and with enough force to make her visibly shudder.

"Yes, yes, of course. Here you are." Louise's stockings passed from flesh hand to china hand. "There's a partition there you can change behind." In case the robot had modesty? Ree believed she did.

China walked on her thin, jerky legs to the screen, and Ree watched her go. She stole a look back at her godfather and at Nikolai. She could tell that Nikolai had either been turned off, or had lost consciousness. He was laying on the table completely limp, not stiff as a board like he had been before. Dross was hammering at the automaton with a hammer and a long, wicked looking nail, right into his metal arm apparatus.

"Good as new!" Dross proclaimed, straightening his lanky body and removing the protective eyewear he had been sporting. "In fact, even better than new. The Sea Level women – they like a man with a few scars. Character! It's the vintage vibe. Gives him a story, eh?" He brushed his hands on his trousers. "We call it the distressed look. I'd wager I can sell him for even more now."

Oh godfather, what have you done? Ree wanted urgently to ask, but she knew it was a bad idea. A very bad one. One worse than putting frogs in Louise's bed that one time when she was seven, and she had regretted that one right quick when Fritz tattled on her. If Drosselmeier knew she had suspicions, and that she wasn't pleased about what she knew, then there was every chance that he'd write her out of his life, take the automatons, and just disappear. She was under no illusions about his temper.

No, she needed to think. She needed to get the dolls away, but where in the world to? Could they survive on their own? Selling them now was no longer an option; not now that she had inklings of how they were alive in their own human right. But she could hardly steal them and keep them in her own house either. There had to be something she could do to get them away, and to a place where they wouldn't be bargained for like an antique side table.

Fritz. Fritz and his army of specially trained soldiers would know what to do. They had to. Ree didn't like to be dramatic or theatrical – that was Louise's department of expertise – but this time the situation called for it. Fritz was her only hope.

* * *

Her only hope was uncooperative, cranky, and didn't believe his sister for a minute.

"You're being ridiculous, Marie."

"Call me ridiculous one more time!" Ree was seething. Lord, brothers were maddening! Couldn't he see she meant every word? "I swear, I will stab you with my hat pin!"

"Don't talk about stabbings." Fritz stroked his red beard. He looked tired. Ree had thought at first she was the one making him tired; now she wasn't so sure. This was more than just sibling rivalry. Work must be getting to him.

"Why not?" She crossed her arms in front of her chest and glared at him, stifling any sympathy that was welling up in her.

"Because Lily didn't make it, that's why." He sighed. He rubbed his eyes with his fists; something he'd done ever since he was a baby when fatigue set in.

"Who? What? Whatever are you talking about?" Ree was completely lost.

"One of the soldiers with me that night. She was stabbed by Mother's tree."

The great, metal Christmas tree. Ree gasped in horror. "But – how – no one even saw?" She was flabbergasted.

"Adrenaline does strange things, Ree. It can protect you in times of stress, but it can also mask your symptoms. Lily didn't know how bad it was until after we left the house. She lost too much blood. We couldn't save her."

Ree didn't know what to say. First old Sir Croftenspot, now the soldier named Lily. Two deaths in one night, and in the wealthy, comfortable mansion she called home.

Her godfather was piecing together human body parts with robotics for his material gain, and her home was a house of death. This was not shaping up to be the best Christmas season of her life.

Even more reason to make Fritz see the seriousness of the situation then. Resolved, Ree straightened her shoulders, and tried again.

"I need your help to get the automatons away from Herr Drosselmeier. Please, Fritz."

"I can't, Ree. I'm being serious. I have too much to deal with right now. There are more important things-"

His sister narrowed her eyes cynically at that excuse.

"Namely," Fritz continued, "This character named Cullen. He's a bad egg, and I want him out of our city. Rats included."

Ree stopped narrowing her eyes and tried raising them instead. "Ah, big brother, I see you haven't thought this through then. Don't you remember who knew Cullen?"

Fritz frowned. "The nutcracker man?"

"Don't call him that; he has a name. But yes, they seemed to know one another. Don't you think you should question him? He may have knowledge that will help you." Ree waited, biting her lower lip.
He seemed to take forever and a day to answer.

"I suppose so," he acquiesced at last. "But questioning him doesn't mean I'm conspiring to get him away from Drosselmeier, or whatever hare brained scheme you're hatching. He's a grown...whatever he is. I'm not in the mood to rescue him."

"I'm not hatching anything. I wish I was, actually." Ree meant it. She really didn't have a plan; hare brained or otherwise. She'd just have to take it one step at a time.

And step one was in motion.

*   *   *

"Hell's bells!" Ree kicked Lord Anklesby's fence with all her might. All she got for her trouble was a sore toe and an even bigger surge of temper. "I never should have left! Drat that man! Drat him, drat him, drat him! And his stupid flying laboratory!" She glared up at the blue sky. There was nary a cloud in sight, but that wasn't what was infuriating her. What infuriated her was that there was also a grievous lack of a workship hovering above.

Fritz watched his sister, bemused. He allowed her to continue her tantrum and her assault on the fence, then pointedly coughed. "Well, we tried. Another time. I've got to return to work."

Ree grasped his coattails. "Not so fast! Think this through with me. Nikolai has got information you want – critical, political, top secret information." Did he? She had no idea, but it didn't seem too farfetched. "Plus, the trouble with Cullen started when Nikolai and China showed up at our home. It stands to reason if we find the dolls, we should find Cullen."

"Who in the blazes is China?" Fritz made as if to leave.

"The clockwork doll! Please pay attention, toad face. This is important!"

As a retort, Fritz knocked her hat askew. "Insulting me won't soften my heart."

"You started it." She reached up and yanked on his beard. "So there."

"Ouch!" Fritz jumped as if he had been bitten, and glanced down in alarm.

"I didn't pull it that hard," Ree said. "Baby."

"Not you. I stepped on something and nearly broke my foot. Good grief, what is this?" He bent down and retrieved something from where it had been nestling near the iron fence post.

"It's the pigeon!" Ree exclaimed in delight. "Give it here. Hello, darling," she cooed. The mechanical pigeon stayed silent. It seemed a bit tarnished and dented. She turned it over to inspect it. "Poor thing must have fallen out the window. Dross always did fly recklessly, and his takeoffs are dismal. Well, we've a stroke of luck after all, haven't we?"

"If you're expecting me to ask why, you'll be disappointed. I've played nursemaid long enough for today, thank you. I'm going back to work before I lose my position."

"Hang on! The pigeon will take us to the airship, don't you see? It's programmed to return to it. All we have to do is follow it."

"And why would I do that?" Fritz was walking, and at a brisk pace, too. Ree hurried to catch up.

"Because your very small, inexperienced, little, baby sister is going to do just that, and you wouldn't want her to show you up, that's why."

Fritz snorted. "Try again."

"And also because I'm going to follow it all the way to Sea Level. And if Father finds out you knew and didn't protect me, he'll be furious. And also because if you don't come with me I'll tell everyone you kissed Inga Silberhaus Christmas night."

"Little sneak! Go ahead and tell then."

"Her father will make you marry her."

Fritz stopped in his tracks. "You're a right proper little blackmailer, aren't you?" He couldn't keep the respect out of his voice, though Ree could tell he was still annoyed.

"Yes, I am." Ree nestled the dented pigeon inside her cloak. "I'll need to make sure he's in working order and pack some supplies. You'll be ready to go in one hour, won't you?"

"I suppose I will," Fritz sighed.

Act III
The Land of Snow

Chapter Eleven
A Sleigh Ride, and an Enchantment or Two

Ree had the pigeon inspected and repaired, a basket of food spirited away right under Hoffman's nose (or lack thereof), and the Stahlbaum's massive steam powered sleigh packed high with blankets and her toolbox, in a little less than one hour. That was quite a feat considering she also had to sidestep her mother's questions. It was yet again another example of how difficult it was to be any kind of heroine at all. No wonder orphans had all the adventures. No one was forcing them to eat their stewed peas, get their rest, or turn in early.

She tapped her booted foot impatiently in the stable where the sleigh hummed quietly, and waited for her brother. She resented needing him this way, but she had no desire to wander down a frozen mountainside alone until she happened upon an airship driven by a madman, scurry her way inside undetected, and then shimmy back down a rope with two life size dolls. She bit her lip. Even with her large, red headed soldier brother, this was going to be rather difficult. Normally, wearing trousers made her feel as though she could take on the world, but even her favorite brown tweed pair wasn't enough to calm her stomach. She couldn't imagine how jittery she'd be in a skirt.

"All right, little brat. I've arrived." Fritz looked decidedly unhappy to be so. He flopped in the sleigh with all the grace of an albatross. "What's the plan then? We follow the brass chicken?"

"It's a pigeon," Ree retorted, haughtily. "But yes. I've slowed down his mechanisms so he won't fly too fast, but as an alternative, we could tether him to the sleigh?"

"I'd rather not. This whole thing is embarrassing enough without sliding through town with my little sister and her pet fowl. Which is why I'm wearing my hood." He pulled up the folds of his black cloak until his face was completely hidden.

"Oh, wonderful," Ree answered, sarcastically. "Now I look like I'm being kidnapped by some stranger, instead of off on an innocent lark with my caring older brother. We're not supposed to be drawing attention to ourselves." She sighed. "Not that it really matters. We aren't going through town."

"We're not?" Fritz lowered his hood, and looked at her suspiciously. "Which direction are we going exactly?"

"Down," Ree replied, sweetly.

* * *

She knew the Bavarian Alps were high, of course she did. Nevertheless, Ree had never gone plummeting down the side of them, through the snow, in a sleigh that seemed to have a mind of its own, with a panicking brother (some hero he was turning out to be), and a seemingly hell-bent robotic flying pigeon tethered with a hair ribbon. She didn't mean to scream – she'd never fully screamed in her life – but the sound came out of her mouth, unbidden. She also didn't mean to close her eyes since that seemed an impudent thing to do when you're supposed to be steering any type of vehicle, but the snow and the wind did it for her.

"This is the worst idea you've ever had, Marie!" Fritz bellowed, as they raced down the mountain. His grip on the side of the sleigh had turned his knuckles white.

She was inclined to agree with him, but the rushing snow and her fear made it impossible to form a reply. The snow stung with the force of a thousand icy needles, and even in the midst of Ree's fear of possible death, she had the presence of mind to be thankful she had stowed her favorite bowler hat in her bag. It would have blown away forever, and that would have been a disaster.

There was a point during their descent that the mountain leveled out just enough to slow them down, and Fritz began to get the hang of steering the sleigh, at least a bit. With the combination of the two siblings leaning and shifting their weight, and with Fritz discovering the ornate wheel that they had at first assumed was merely decorative had a very important function – that of a ship's steering wheel - they continued down the mountain. Their stomachs settled a bit, and Ree began to feel as though they might possibly, maybe, if they were lucky, survive. Perhaps.

They were still going at such a reckless speed in spite of themselves that the first time they caught sight of the human reindeer, both Stahlbaums blinked and shook their heads to remove the fanciful image. It had looked as though a girl...with antlers...but no. That would be impossibly strange. Perhaps a deer, though Ree wasn't sure she'd know what one looked like if she saw one. Or maybe a girl...in an odd headpiece?

There it was again; another one this time. This reindeer girl's dress was blue, with a white apron. She glanced at the sleigh as it slid by, and she seemed as frightened to see the humans as the humans did to see her.

"Did you see-" Fritz began, his jaw slack. "I thought I-"

Ree craned her head around behind the sleigh. "I know, I thought I saw it too. Go back, stop!"

"I can't!" Fritz snapped. "If there are brakes, I have yet to discover them."

"Well, I'm sure there are, for goodness sake! Push that pedal thingy there. No, not that one, the other one!"

"Why don't you just jump out and I'll slow the contraption down when I run over you?" Her brother suggested, teeth grinding.

Ree ignored him and began pushing pedals and levers. The stupid invention seemed to have dozens of completely useless features, but there had to be one or two that would actually come in handy for drivers on the brink of wrecking. Or those who needed to stop to gaze at bizarre and incredible creatures.

Something worked; the sleigh began to glide to an elegant stop. Ree scrambled out, snagging her cloak on the way. Impatient, she yanked on it, and heard a tear as it came free. *Mama is going to be livid.* Wool from the vicuna llamas in the Andes was extremely expensive. Some beasts were still held in high esteem.

"There! I see it! Her!" Ree pointed towards the tree line. It was a miracle they hadn't collided with any trees during their madcap descent down the peak. She would have to give Fritz some credit then. Later maybe. "Look!" She put her index fingertip to her lip, motioning her brother to be silent.

The little reindeer girl peered back at them, from her shelter behind the tree. She was a slender girl, even in her flowy blue dress, but the tree she had chosen was not large, and Ree could see the antlers coming out from either side. Her hair was golden, flaxen colored, and wound in braids that went around her head. The antlers seemed to sprout right out from them. She had a curious, childlike beauty about her, and the strange thing was, the antlers didn't seem amiss at all. In fact, they were rather pretty. Ree was certain the ladies of her city would wear them upon their hats should they get a look at this girl. Ree cringed just thinking about it. On those women, they would look ridiculous. An owl suddenly hooted and swooped low. Ree jumped, and the reindeer girl cried out and cowered behind her tree even further.

"Come out," Ree called. "We won't hurt you."

The reindeer girl hesitated. She looked behind her at the thick tree line, as though pondering running.

"Please?" Ree persuaded, taking a step towards the reindeer. "We only want to speak to you. And see you closer. We've never seen anything like you."

"You have no weapons?" The reindeer girl spoke in a breathy voice. She was obviously still frightened. Ree had to strain her ears to hear her. She took a few more steps closer.

"No, of course not."

"It isn't hunting season. You'll receive a ticket and a fine if you shoot me."

Ree stopped in her snowy tracks. "My goodness, we would never! Have you been hunted?"

The reindeer girl nodded. "We're only out today in the open for the flowers that bloom in the meadow here, through the snow. We're running out of food in the forest. And it isn't hunting season. Hunters are shrewd and wicked and hard to catch. You don't look like hunters." She narrowed her wide, doe eyes, "Though many of our bodies could fit on your sleigh. Even more heads if you leave our bodies behind."

Ree grimaced. "I don't want any heads or bodies, I promise you. What a horrible idea." She hoped secretly that the hunters weren't friends or associates of her father's. As far as she knew, they simply hunted hares and deer and foxes, and those were robotic replicas. "Can we help?"

"I don't think so, unless you're a hunter of hunters." The reindeer girl finally stepped out from behind her tree. She looked curiously around Ree at Fritz, who was still sitting in the sleigh, looking flabbergasted and like he wanted to be elsewhere. Anywhere else. "Who is that? He is very handsome." She unwound a bit of her wispy braid and chewed on it, contemplatively.

Ree wrinkled her nose. "That's my brother, Fritz. I'm Marie. And you are?"

"Hope." She continued to stare at Fritz and nibble her hair. Her large brown eyes were deep and wide and the color of molasses. They had long lashes – improbably long - the color of her flaxen hair. Her antlers were huge and winding and had been polished to a sheen. Ree wondered if carrying the weight of them ever gave Hope a headache. "He's lovely." Hope sighed, pensively.

Ree began to wish she'd never left the sleigh. What an awkward and odd conversation she was having with the reindeer girl. She'd never had much patience with moony eyed, love struck teenagers, and she'd been known to smack Jessa over the head when she got that way. *Someday*, Jessa had said once, *you'll meet someone who makes you loopy, too.* Ree had rolled her eyes, but with a stab of embarrassment, she now recalled her gushing over Nikolai the night of the rat invasion. Of course, she'd just been through a rather trying evening, and she had had wound poisoning. It hardly counted.

"Is he married?" Hope asked. She straightened her apron. "I'm not. It's very hard to find boys here."

"Aren't there any males of your...species?" Ree couldn't help but notice Hope had human fingers, but the toes peeking out from beneath her skirts were hooves. The oddity made her swallow any other words she had been forming.

"No, only girls." Hope looked even sadder now. "The boys were all killed. There are only a few of us sisters left. We're quite rare, my sisters and I. That's why we're hunted. Oh, speak of the devil." Hope scowled as she looked over to her left. "There's Faith. You can't have him!" she called to her sister.

Faith – the reindeer girl Ree had thought she had seen first, while careening down the mountain – meandered nonchalantly into the clearing. She looked like Hope, but her dress was green and she wore no apron. Her hair was darker, and cut short, like a pixie. It made her shiny antlers look even more impressive and grand. Faith ignored both her sister and Ree, and instead wandered shyly but purposefully towards Fritz and the sleigh. Ree wasn't sure whether to be alarmed or amused. She chose the latter. Fritz looked like he might have a coronary. He gripped the wheel of the sleigh and his eyes were wide as the reindeer girl strode towards him. Ree stifled a laugh and turned her attention back to Hope.

"Who protects you?"

"Winter and her tribe mostly, but they can't be around always. They're often at the Waltz, of course, and then it's open season on poor us."

"The Waltz?"

Hope looked impatient. She glared at her sister, who was attempting to climb inside the sleigh. Fritz was backing away from the antlers, and looking equal parts irritated, flattered, and confused. "Yes, the Waltz. It's all the rage at Sea Level. They used to hold it yearly, but it's such a popular affair that now they have it weekly." Hope sighed again.

"How close are we to Sea Level?" Ree asked, forgetting the Waltz.

"I don't know," Hope pouted. "It isn't as though I'm wanted there. Nor up there." She gestured with her head up the mountain. "Up Top they'd likely eat me, and down there they'd probably mount my head and stuff my body for their museum. Or is it the other way around?"

To her shock, Ree wasn't sure either. Surely no one atop the mountain – her home – would do either to an innocent and love starved animal girl. Surely they wouldn't? But she had just left her beloved godfather who had been sewing and welding human parts onto robotic ones, and one of the more popular and decadent meals served in the Stahlbaum house was stuffed baby swan. Her world was upside down already without this new moral dilemma.

"Is there anyone I can ask at Sea Level to help?" Ree asked, politely, but the girl only shook her head, and Ree was glad to put an end to the strange conversation. She had spent enough time with Hope, and she was beginning to worry for Fritz's state of mind. Besides, the daylight wouldn't last forever. She certainly didn't want to be in this strange forest after dusk without shelter of some sort.

Hunters and human animals. Needlepoint, piano forte, and Latin lessons had hardly prepared her for this.

Chapter Twelve
At the Bottom

Ree had never seen Fritz so very happy to see his sister. He nearly embraced her, and the look on his red whiskered face would have been comical if it hadn't look pained and vulnerable.

The reindeer girl named Faith watched with a mournful expression on her pretty face as the siblings readied the sleigh to move once again down the steep and treacherous slope that was the Bavarian Alps. The pigeon was flapping sluggishly, still tethered to the sleigh but going nowhere.

Faith and Hope waved sadly as the strange vehicle left them behind, then picked up their skirts and galloped away. Fritz and Ree stayed silent for long moments afterwards. Ree kept wanting to speak, to ask if what they had just encountered really happened or whether it was, perhaps, a side effect of wound fever, but all she had to do was turn to Fritz's baffled countenance and she had her answer.

"That was the oddest thing," she finally ventured to say. Now that they had gotten the hang of the sleigh, they were no longer moving at such a frantic, breakneck speed. In fact, if they hadn't been chasing a madman in a flying house, and hadn't just left impossible animal women hybrids, Ree would have relaxed and enjoyed the ride. It was quite picturesque really, once you got over the shock.

Fritz snorted at his sister's understatement. "Odd doesn't begin to cover it."

"Do you think they're real? I mean...could they have been made? Or enchanted?" Ree bit her lower lip thoughtfully.

"Meaning they can't possibly exist like that in nature? I'm inclined to agree with you." Fritz used his free hand – the one not gripping the steering wheel – to rub his chin. "We would have seen them by now."

"But she said the hunters know of them."

"Well, it must be some sort of underground hunting club then. No one I know is mounting anything other than the occasional falcon or wild turkey or boar." Fritz snorted. "The lower we go, the more backwards everything will get. They still use magic down there, and they even keep pets. They're totally uncivilized. Father will have my head when he finds out I've let you down there."

Ree sighed. "Well, this whole thing is getting out of hand. How long till we reach Sea Level?"

Her brother rolled his eyes. "How should I know? This isn't exactly the main thoroughfare. I wanted to take the highway." He pondered their options for a moment. "There should be a cable carriage on this side, but I don't know if it's even manned anymore. We'll have to leave the sleigh behind. You should have planned better, Madame Mastermind. I hope you brought food."

Ree glowered. "I'm sorry I didn't plan better, posterior face. It isn't as though I knew I'd be half eaten by robotic rats, learn my brother has a secret army of girl warriors, discover my godfather might in fact be an evil genius, and plot my way down a mountainside I've never been on, to a town I have never set foot in!" She finished her glowering, but since it was obvious Fritz was blithely ignoring her, she gave up and changed subject.

"She spoke about Winter like it were a person, not a season." Ree rifled through the basket of food, and tossed a meat pie at her brother.

"Yes." Fritz looked uneasy. "I've heard of her. Some Snow Queen or some nonsense." He unwrapped his pie and munched on it with gusto.

"Do you think we'll get to meet her?"

"If you'd have asked me an hour ago about Winter, I would have told you to stop believing in faery tales," Fritz replied, speaking around his food.

"And now?"

"When talking reindeer tell me something, I'm inclined to listen."

Ree grinned. They went over a large snow berm and she bounced uncomfortably in her seat. She rubbed her bottom, muttering.

Fritz abruptly used the braking pedal and the sleigh glided elegantly to a silent stop.

"What?" Ree began, but Fritz hushed her.

"Look there." He gestured with his meat pie towards the horizon.

Herr Drosselmeier's workship was floating amidst the trees just a mile or so ahead of them. Ree held her breath, wondering if they could be seen, bright against the white snow, if one were to glance out the window of the flying laboratory. Just then, the pigeon began to make an alarming beeping sound. It echoed in the stillness of the forest.

"Hush!" Ree frantically began winding up the long ribbon that tethered the mechanical. "It's the homing alert. I told Dross it was an unnecessary and annoying addition. He wanted to make it authentic, I suppose. You know that meowing brass cat he fashioned for the stairwell at home that Mother took a hammer to?" Yanking the pigeon out of the sky, Ree turned it over and pressed a button. "Yes, we know you found it, silly thing. Now be quiet."

"Well," Fritz switched off the steam of the sled as well, "now what? What's your big plan?"

Ree swallowed. "Just give me a minute. I didn't expect to find them so rapidly. I kind of assumed we would catch up with them at Sea Level."

"We may yet. I think it's actually moving."

Sure enough, the workship did seem to be slightly further away than it had a moment ago. Ree felt a bit of relief that she had more time to come up with a plan to rescue the automatons; she didn't like the feeling of being answerless when peppered with questions by her brother, who didn't want to be here in the first place.

"We're on enough of a slant right now, I believe I'm going to keep the steam power off and we'll just coast. Less noise that way. Did you shut off that chicken's squawking?" Fritz demanded.

"Yes, it's running low on power anyway. It needs to recharge. And it isn't a chicken. Chickens are...fatter, I think. Aren't they? I've never seen one unless it's stuffed with apricots."

"Well, with any luck, we won't need it again anyway. Not like we can misplace a floating house now that we've found it."

"You mean, since we've found it after losing it the first time?" Ree responded, dryly.

"Very funny."

"Why, thank you," Ree said, primly. She found her bowler hat where it had been rolling around gently in the bottom of the sleigh, and she placed it back upon her tangled red and white curls. With her hat and her toolbox and the workship in sight, she felt more courageous and up to the task ahead, whatever that might prove to be.

From a tree nearby, the same owl from the reindeer clearing watched them silently. Without a sound, it lifted its huge wings and soared away.

* * *

Fritz and Ree and the silent pigeon soon found themselves nearing a waterfall.

"Why, it's frozen solid!" Ree exclaimed, in wonder. "Have you ever seen anything like it?"

Even Fritz seemed duly impressed, and typically he wasn't one to be taken in by beauty, unless of course it was of the female form variety. "Will you look at that?" he murmured.

They paused the sleigh long enough to admire the sight. The water had frozen in midstream, creating an astonishing effect. The stream of ice made Ree think of powdered sugar being poured from above, and the icicles surrounding the fall were taller than she was. It looked like a giant, beautiful spun sugar creation, and it glistened in what was left of the sunlight. The pool beneath was frozen, too, except for the smallest section where the icy spray entered it.

"It's magical," Ree whispered. "I'd like to sit here and paint it."

Fritz looked at her, appalled. "I've never heard you say anything like that before. Your teachers would be shocked into heart attacks, I'm sure."

"Haha. I enjoy artistic pursuits as much as any lady," she responded, haughtily. Though her brother did have a point. Last time she had a painting lesson she had fallen asleep at her desk. She had sported a blue forehead the rest of the week where the paint had dried, and Fritz had laughed so hard at supper he had nearly choked on his roasted peacock.

"Well, paint a picture in your head, Madame; the dirigible gets away from us while we stand here gawking." Fritz pointed ahead, and sure enough, the floating workship seemed to have picked up speed. The very top of the balloon was all that was visible now as it neared the bottom of the mountain.

Ree put all thoughts of the romantic waterfall aside, and began to worry again about what she might do once they reached Sea Level. She couldn't very well march into the workship and demand the dolls back; Dross wouldn't stand for it. And they did belong to him somehow, in some sort of unnatural fashion. It seemed wrong for a man to own another person, even if that person was mostly made of metal and gears. Shouldn't there be a law in place, banning one from this sort of thing? Ree bit her lip. Drosselmeier was in charge of the law where she was from. He obviously knew his way around any regulations of the sort. She sighed. She could buy the dolls herself; she had brought plenty of money in her toolbox...but would that make her any better? She didn't like the thought of owning Nikolai or China. What exactly would she do with them? Keep them in the kitchen with Hoffman and have them fetch things? Set them free? Where? To roam the snowy mountainside with enchanted reindeer? To wander through Sea Level at their own risk? Or worse, to be on the streets of her city where she could push the Toiletries Robotic nonchalantly by as she shopped for ribbons and crinolines and petticoats and pretend not to know them? It didn't bear thinking about.

"We'll be in the village soon." Fritz looked carefully over at his musing sister. She was chewing on her fingernails now, which meant she was either deep in thought plotting something, or she was nervous. He assumed both. "You'd better think of something. I can't spend too much time down here; I'll lose my position, especially after what happened with Lily."

Ree glared at him. "I'm thinking, I'm thinking! And yes, you said that already." Add to her list of troubles, her brother's gainful employment. She stopped gnawing on her fingernails and donned her warm gloves again. "I'll come up with something. In the meantime, tell me why your soldiers are girls."

"That's classified information." Fritz was annoyingly condescending.

"Classified, my great Aunt Fanny!"

"You know perfectly well our great aunt is named Marigold."

"I dislike you greatly."

Fritz pushed Ree's bowler hat over her eyes. "I love you, too. Now stop your ceaseless conversation. We're approaching the village and the last thing we need is to make a scene."

"Oh, because a floating ship and a steam powered sleigh will blend right in as long as we're quiet?" Ree snickered. "That's perfectly logical. No wonder they put you in charge of armies and saving the world." She tipped her hat back up where she could see properly.

90

What she saw made her sit up taller, and yet simultaneously made her want to sink down lower in her fur covered seat. The village outskirts were unlike anything she'd ever seen in the city where she had grown up. The snow had steadily gotten dirtier as they approached and what she could see of the city gate at this distance was not impressive. They wound their way silently through the last bit of trees and came to a crossroads. On one side was a group of tinkers; their wagon overloaded with goods and things to sell, including tea cups, kettles, pots and pans, and bags of candy. It was manned by three whiskered men who were both big and burly. They wore tall, fur hats and black, muddy boots that reached nearly to their knees. The coats were red, with black braided trim. They all had thick, black and silver beards and mustaches, but one had a mustache that stuck straight out and curled up most impressively at the ends. This man stroked his beard and all three men watched the sleigh warily as it slid past them.

Ree nodded her head politely at the men. "Good afternoon," she said, rather weakly. The men were intimidating. She felt glad she had brought Fritz after all, and part of the reason was his odd looking, silent rifle she knew he had hidden beneath their seats.

To her surprise, the men broke their rough grimaces and grinned at her. "Welcome, lady," the mustached one said in a deep voice. The sleigh continued to glide past them, and Ree craned her head around to hear him. Still, she missed the next part of his greeting.

"What'd he say? I didn't catch that," Ree directed this at Fritz, who hadn't so much as acknowledged the men.

"Something about being careful, I think." Fritz shrugged.

"What? That seems important! Perhaps we should go back," Ree looked behind her. The men were watching them.

"I don't trust Russians, I don't trust tinkers, and I especially don't trust Russian tinkers."

"Oh piffle, you don't trust anyone."

"True."

On the other side of the crossroads as they approached was a sign, and it made Ree forget the Russians altogether. It was made of many planks of wood, some older than others, all with a point at one end, as if pointing them towards a destination. The destinations themselves read:

Divertissements ahead!

Finest tea this side of China at Mr. Ceylon's Leaf Emporium

Miss Ginger's School for Young Criminals – Absolutely no unsolicited drop-offs.

Sea Level's Finest Bakery and Chocolatier

Enchantments and Unenchantments – By appointment only.

Sea Level's Famous Waltz and Ballroom – Subject to availability.

E.J.'s Taxidermy – We specialize in reindeer, faeries, and elves-on-a-stick.

The Scurvy Dogs Pirate Floating Saloon – Cold ale and slightly less cold women.

And finally, written in black paint beneath the last sign were the hand painted words, scrawled in as if in afterthought...

Outsiders, Strangers, and Updwellers enter at your own risk.

Chapter Thirteen
Angels and Updwellers

The floating workshop had docked itself with its pirate anchor dead center in the middle of the village. It drifted above like a monstrous puppet master, the town below its puppets. Knowing Drosselmeier, Ree thought the imagery was rather apt.

Leaving the sleigh behind made Ree nervous, and Fritz even more so, though he slung his rifle over his back. "If it's still here when we return, I will be shocked. And when it isn't here when we return, you will be the one to inform Father." He crammed the last meat pie in his mouth.

Ree ignored his threat and released the pigeon with a message for her mother. It flew off with a creak and a groan, back up the way they had come. She hoped it would make its destination or Mama would be inventing new punishments for Ree's rebelliousness, like assigning extra chapters of her Latin book, or polishing Lou's smelly boot collection. Her feet were more odiferous than Fritz's. She shuddered. "Come along," she said, briskly. She pulled her hat lower over her hair, brushed some wayward snow off her trousers, and tucked her beloved toolbox beneath her elbow.

The gates to the village were even more dilapidated than Ree originally had thought when she had spied them from a distance. They had once been painted a cheery red and white stripe, like giant candy canes, but the red had faded to a pink and the white to a dingy gray. No one manned the lookout tower, which brought to mind more of a play fort to Ree, and that was hardly surprising, since it didn't look as though the town offered much to pillage. Something fuzzy streaked by Ree's legs and she swallowed a gasp.

"Cat," Fritz said. "They run wild here."

Ree nodded, as though she'd known that all along. They didn't have pets Up Top. They were unnecessary and dirty and left hair and other questionable piles behind them. If someone desperately wanted such a thing, there were robotic animals for such eccentricities. They'd had a mechanical cat once; the one that had met its demise under Mrs. Stahlbaum's hammer.

"You look like you could use a guide, you do!" chirped a sudden voice.

Ree whirled, wondering a bit hysterically if it were the cat talking. Instead she came face to face with a remarkable little urchin child. It (he? She?) was grubby beyond all reason – Melisande would have fainted dead away and upon awakening would have got out her harshest lye soap – with a mop of gold curls streaked with dirt, a bag slung over its shoulder that was larger than the carrier, and a huge eyepiece that magnified its wearer's eyeball by a disturbingly large amount. The eye itself was a green color and appeared to be intelligent and full of mischief. All in all, Ree put the child's age at about eight years, although it was the wildest of guesses.

"I am the best guide in the village, let me tell you, lady! Why, I know every nook and cranny this wonderful place has to offer, and I knows all the inwards and outwards of every person, too. Want information? Want lodging? Want grub? I'm your Angel!" The child plopped its hands on its hips in a cocky and confident pose. The pack on the child's back slid to the ground with a thumping sound. It may have been her imagination, but Ree thought she heard a meowing sound.

"An angel are we?" Ree cocked a red eyebrow at this revelation. "Shouldn't there be wings or halos or, at the very least, a harp to strum?"

"Aw!" The Angel waved its hands and chuckled. "Not us Angels, lady. We're more of the earthly type if you will. My name is Georgie and you need my protection if your stay here at Sea Level is to be memorable and luffly!" The Angel pronounced the last word as though it had several syllables and also as though its mouth were full of ambrosia.

"Memorable and luffly, eh?" Ree pretended to think about this. "I suppose there is a charge for each? Is it half price if I just choose the luffly tour?"

Fritz was not so polite in his disinterest of Georgie's protection. "Shoo, kid!" He batted at the Angel, annoyed. "Get lost. Scram."

"Don't shoo me, mister! You don't know who you're dealing with, you don't. You need me." The one eye batted at him like butterfly wings.

"Like heck I do. You'll pick my pocket soon as look at me." Fritz glared at the child. He turned his attention to his sister. "The Angels live at Miss Ginger's School for Young Criminals."

"Gifted Young Criminals," Georgie corrected him. "Miss Ginger's School for Gifted Young Criminals. They just ran outta room on the sign is all. Miss Ginger is very discriminating; only takes the best. We ain't your typical pick pockets, no sir." The Angel (Ree still wasn't entirely sure of its gender) puffed out its chest, proudly. "Why, you won't find no better crooks and petty thieves if you searched the whole planet Earth! I'm your girl, mister. For sure and certain."

Ah, a girl then. Goodness, but she needed a bath even more with that confession. Ree couldn't help being a bit charmed by Georgie, but Fritz didn't look amused in the slightest. In fact, he was walking away.

"I think we'd best find our own way, Georgie." Ree reached out to pet the girl on the head, but getting a closer look at the dingy curls, she retrieved her hand hastily.

A single tear rolled down the eye that looked imploringly out at Ree. "Oh, mistress, must you? Leave me here to fend for myself, you would? On the streets? Oh, you wouldn't! I'm but seven years old!"

"Ree! Come along!" Fritz shouted. He was inside the gate already.

"Goodbye now," Ree told Georgie, and began to catch up with her brother's long legs. The crocodile tear was good, but after all, Ree was the baby of her own family; she recognized the scam.

"Oh all right then! I knows a hard bargainer when I sees one!" Georgie scrambled after them. "Today's your lucky day! Why, it's Thursday and I never charge a fee for my services on Thursdays!" She beamed.

"Then you'll come along with us?" Ree stifled a laugh as the Angel reached her side. "For free, I mean?"

"You bet your boots I will," Georgie promised, fervently. "Now, where is it we're going 'zactly?"

"Well," Ree paused in her walking, "Do you see that ship there? That's where we're headed."

Georgie scowled up at the sky. "Borrrrring. I was hoping there'd be adventure with the likes of you, lady. You didn't seem the quiet, meek type. Don't tell me we're going for a ride? Not when there's perfectly luffly escapades and quests down here where the ground is nice and solid beneath our feet!"

"Scared of heights, are we, Georgie?"

"A bit," she admitted.

"Well, don't fret too hard. I doubt we'll be going for a ride. I'm more interested in acquiring what's inside the ship frankly."

"Oo, it's to be thievery, is it? I'm sooooo your Angel." The green eye widened and the brow above it wiggled. "What's it to be? Treasure? Loot? Food? Gold? Diamonds? Stolen property?"

"Something like that."

They were beginning to encounter people now. Fritz strode purposefully a few feet ahead of the two girls. They passed a group of very small Chinese acrobats who were practicing some sort of performing routine outside of a dilapidated old inn. One twisted herself into a shape that called to Ree's mind a Bavarian pretzel she had eaten once. There was a horse stabled outside a blacksmith shop and Ree skirted around it hastily. She'd never seen a real horse before. They were much larger and much dustier than she had supposed. Fritz had mechanical horses, but those were polished and gleaming and didn't have any teeth. Or any scent.

"Have you been to the market, lady?" Georgie asked.

"What market? And please call me Ree." She imagined her mother would have a small heart attack by that disregard of propriety, but she couldn't picture Georgie calling her Miss Stahlbaum. She'd much rather be Ree.

"Why, Sea Level's famous market, of course! The one and only! It's to die for. Really luffly and scrumptious, too. Of course, it's a little...well, not dangerous exactly, but it's a little unpredictable for Updwellers. You don't mind, do you?" Georgie's green eye looked up at Ree in concern. The other green eye seemed miniature in comparison.

"Look, do you have to wear that? It's very distracting."

"This?" Georgie pulled off the contraption. "Oh, no, it's not for my eyesight; I just like the way it makes me look. And it does come in handy for some jobs. Magnifies, don'tchaknow?"

"Yes, I gathered that from the eyeball the size of your head. That's much better." Ree looked down at her companion. She really was a cute little thing, even if she'd smelled much worse than the horse back there.

"What's so unpredictable about the market, and what makes you think I'm an Updweller, huh?"

"It's kind of obvious, no offense." Georgie sounded apologetic.

"None taken. At least, I don't think there is. Do you get many down here? From Up Top I mean?"

Georgie shook her head fervently. "Oh, no Miss Ree. Not often. They don't mix well with us. Like oil and water, we are. Well, present company excluded! You and I, we're gonna be great friends." She said as she winked up at Ree.

"Where is my brother?" Ree asked as she looked around and settled her free hand on her hip. The other hand was holding her toolbox. They were in more of a crowd now. People were jostling by her while snippets of conversations floated by in the ether. A large man with a leather apron nearly knocked her down as he rushed by, and didn't as much as glance at his victim. Ree scowled at his retreating form and wondered if he were the taxidermist. The apron had had several nasty looking stains on the front.

"Uh oh," Georgie muttered. She pointed to their left. "There he is. One of them faeries has him in her clutches."

"A faery?" Ree frowned. There was no such thing. Of course, she would have made the same claim about talking reindeer a mere day ago, but still. If there were faeries, surely all the Updwellers would know. They'd be booking them for parties and other entertainments.

"Nah, not real ones. We just call 'em that because of their wings. Kind of like how they call us the Angels. 'Cause of our cherubic faces." Georgie fluttered her eyelashes and beamed her dimple towards Ree as an illustration.

"Oh, I see." Ree felt a pang of disappointment. A real faery would have been a treat. Jessa would have been enthralled with that revelation. She took a closer look at the faery with Fritz. No wonder he'd stopped to talk. She was quite lovely, and exactly his type. Perky, pretty, and gazing up at him with big, innocent eyes. She had a sweet, upturned nose, and rosebud lips.

The faery was dressed in a billowing skirt that Ree personally thought was entirely impractical for flight. It had a tight bodice and she wore shoes that curled up at the tips. Her hair was a shiny black that was piled high on her head. The wings that Georgie had mentioned were fashioned from brass and copper and fitted to her back by straps. Little lights blinked on and off, and Ree was fascinated by the device. Could the faeries really use them to fly? How inventive! Deep inside, the inventor side of Ree was slightly irritated she hadn't devised this herself. Still, perhaps she could purchase one from this market. Mama would be...well, Mama wouldn't have to be told.

Georgie pulled on Ree's sleeve to get her attention. "You'd best tell your brother to stay clear of the faeries. They're trouble." She wrinkled her nose.

Ree looked down at the child, and readjusted her toolbox. "Why? Don't tell me they'll put a spell on him, or curse him, or some such thing?" She was only teasing, but Georgie didn't laugh.

"Nah, they won't do that, but they can't be trusted neither. They're thugs for hire is what they are. Mercenaries. Plus, they aren't too smart neither. Flying around in those unpredictable wings. They're always crashing into windows and buildings. Miss Ginger had to scrape two of 'em off our roof just last week. They'd been in the cider." She tipped her head and spoke primly, as if she were much older and confiding something vaguely scandalous – but expected – to Ree.

Ree grimaced. "Well, that's...ghastly. I'll tell Fritz not to go off on any moonlit flights with her."

"Seriously! It took a spatula the size of my leg to scrape what was left of 'em off the side of the house, don'tchaknow?" Georgie shook her head, remembering.

Ree paled.

"And not to mention, they are addicted to glitter," Georgie continued. "They like the way it sparkles in the moonlight so I swear, they pour it on by the bucketfuls. I'm gonna be finding glitter and sequins up and down the shingles for weeks." She paused, then clapped her hands together briskly. "Well, anyway! To the market?"

"To the market," Ree repeated, dimly. This was shaping up to be an even more peculiar day than she had thought. After what she'd already been through today, she didn't think anything in the whole world would surprise her.

She was wrong.

Chapter Fourteen
The Market and its Peculiarities

Fritz seemed to lose interest in the faery girl, and joined both Ree and Georgie as they neared the crowded marketplace. It was taking place in the town square (which really was a square), and the sight was bustling and busy and brought to Ree's mind a memory of owning her own ant farm when she was seven years old. People of all shapes and sizes and colors moved almost as one organism, from booth to booth, and Ree was caught up in it, both literally and figuratively.

"Keep moving, Updweller!" barked a man to her right. It was the butcher/taxidermist again.

"Pardon me," Ree replied, stiffly. "Feel free to go around."

With a martyred humph, the man did so, pushing past rudely.

"What a peculiar place," she whispered to Fritz. "Is it always thus?"

"You haven't seen the half of it," he whispered back. "Caramelized pig ear on a stick? They're delicious. I've had four already."

"No, thank you."

"Everything's better on a stick," he pressured.

"I said, no, thank you." She took a deep breath and tried to take everything in all at once. To her right, where the taxidermist had shoved by her was a cheerful little booth selling everything from *Hair Tonic for Men* to *Deep Tissue Massage in a Bottle* (they appeared to be some sort of eels floating in liquid) to *Broken Hearts Repair* to *Love Sick Charms* to *Weight Loss in a Jar* (again with the floating eels). The woman manning the booth was red-cheeked and cheery looking, with coiled silver hair that stuck out like quivering sea serpents. She shouted out special prices and deals to everyone in earshot.

"Get your Potions here! Sea Level's best white magic! You've tried all the rest, now try the best! No better prices this side of the Alps!" The woman lowered her shouting to a murmur as Ree paused. "Love Potion, dearie?" She waggled her gray eyebrows towards Fritz in a suggestive manner.

Ree wrinkled her nose. "I should think not! How very revolting."

"Weight Loss in a Jar then? This'll give you the results you're looking for, guaranteed, dearie!" She waved a bottle of swimming eels close to Ree's face, who blanched.

"No, thank you. I'm...I'm giving up cream puffs actually." Ree moved along to the old merchant's chagrin.

Ree remembered seeing the advertisement for the next booth on a sign at the outskirts of the village. It said, *Sea Level's Finest Bakery and Chocolatier*. All resolutions for cream puff abstaining forgotten, Ree reached eagerly for what appeared to be a coconut meringue.

"Ah! A lady of quality I see!" the merchant said as he rubbed his hands together eagerly. This one was a small, wizened man who was probably half the age he appeared to be. "No cheap trifles can fool such a lady as you! My lady goes right for the most expensive, the most delectable, and the most exotic of my gastronomic creations!"

Ree paused, with the meringue halfway to her lips. She narrowed her eyes, remembering the reindeer girls and the splattered faeries. "What is it exactly?"

"Why, it's a coconut meringue, of course." The merchant looked crestfallen. "But I use only organic coconut."

Ree was relieved to hear that. She'd been expecting that the coconut flakes might have been pixie flakes or elf skin, but since they weren't, she quickly devoured the cookie in two bites. "Delicious!" She counted out much more than the baker's asking price, as she decided moral living needed to be rewarded in this strange land. She moved on after she paid, but Georgie lingered behind, staring at the goods hungrily, and feeling properly guilty.

Ree pressed a few coins into the Angel's grubby hand. Fritz had moved along once again, but at least the faery was nowhere to be found. What an odd thing faeries and Angels were turning out to be. Ree's personal Angel packed three meringues into her mouth, and then they continued on.

The next booth they came to was so very crowded that Ree at first began to move around it. Then curiosity got the best of her and at the very least she thought she needed to know the reason. Craning her head and standing on tiptoe in her boots, Ree made out the letters on the vendor's awning. It said, *Miss Ginger's School for GIFTED Young Criminals.*

"It's your alma mater," Ree said to Georgie, who smiled in an impish way.

"We're always the most popular booth at market," she replied, humbly.

The crowd was a mixture of both old and young. In fact, it seemed to be a hodgepodge of parents and children now that Ree looked closer at them. Beyond that observation, it appeared to be a hodgepodge of parents attempting to sell off those said children. There were mothers shoving their daughters forward and fathers encouraging their sons to elbow and kick the competition.

Oh, dear.

Georgie stood by her side, watching the fuss as she shoved several more meringues into her mouth. "Miss Ginger won't take any of 'em; she's very particular."

"Then why have a booth at all?"

"Well, it's good publicity, see? And the drama is good for business. Keeps 'em hungry, don'tchaknow? Plus, Miss Ginger can talk to the would-be students and keep 'em motivated, so to speak; so's then they might be up to snuff next year. You have to have very good marks in school, or be exceptional in your community to be considered for enrollment, especially if you aren't a true orphan. We're very particular at Miss Ginger's School for GIFTED Young Criminals." She puffed out her tiny chest. A button that had been hanging on for dear life on her flannel vest gave up the ghost and drifted down to the dirt.

"Yes, you said that before." Exceptional in your community and earning high marks in school to be considered for criminology enrollment? Ree felt as though she had tumbled down a chute into an alternate reality where up was down and right was left.

"My boy is too good for the likes of you, anyway!" A man was shouting at the proprietress; supposedly the alluring Miss Ginger. Ree could see the top of her head. It was a bright, vivid, and completely unnatural cherry red color. "He could steal circles around your sad, sorry excuse for a graduating class, he could! He could beat up your finest henchmen! Why, just last week he lifted the wings off a faery herself, he did! He could steal the beauty marks right off your face, sure as certain! And it might do you some good, you cow faced wench!"

Georgie giggled and munched on the last of her very last meringue. "I love violence in the square."

"Mm, yes. Come along." Ree tugged on the Angel's elbow, getting something dubious and sticky on her fingers as she did so. "We're forgetting what we're here for."

Georgie shaded her eyes and peered up at the workship, which was still floating in midair above the square. They were closer now. Ree followed her gaze and found the rope with the stolen pirate anchor, wrapped around and around a large marble statue of some sort of bearded saint. The rope ladder however, was nowhere to be found. Ree bit her lip in annoyance. Either Dross was down here in the square with the ladder tucked in his cloak, or he had squirreled himself away up inside the workship and hadn't bothered to lower the ladder yet.

Ree looked to her side for Fritz, but as was his habit, he had wandered off again. Ree caught a glimpse of him standing in line at a Lemon Fizz Stand, with the faery again at his side. Ree shrugged; may as well have something to wash down all those meringues. There was nothing she could do to shimmy up to the workship without the ladder anyway; unless of course there was a booth here at the market, selling rope ladders. Of course, if there were, they'd likely be made from troll entrails or something equally nasty.

"Lemon Fizz, Georgie?"

"Don't mind if I do, Miss Ree. Lead on!" In spite of the command, Georgie led the way, pushing past a trio of young men hawking their wares, which included samples of cider, courtesy of The Scurvy Dogs Pirate Floating Saloon. Ree remembered the fate of the splattered faeries that had been scraped off the roof of Georgie's boarding school and shook her head at the boys when they attempted pressing a sample into her hand.

"Don't know what you're missing, lady!" one of them hollered at her back. "Finest cider in the world! Made from apples pressed by local sprites! No added sugar and delivers quite a kick! Blended up or on the rocks, and when I say rocks, I mean ice chiseled from the frozen waterfall of Winter!"

In her hurry to get away from the persistent merchants, Ree tripped headlong into a dark figure that seemed to materialize out of nowhere. "Please pardon me!" Ree gasped, straightening. She untangled herself from her rescuer and tipped her hat back up from where it fallen and covered her eyes.

It was Nikolai.

* * *

Ree desperately wanted to throw herself back into the automaton's arms, but contained herself. She settled for grinning so widely her jaw hurt.

"I've been looking for you!"

Nikolai smiled down at her, and it occurred to Ree that she had never seen him smile before. It seemed a bit of a strain however, and his own metal jaw made a painful popping sound. "Have you now?" His voice sounded tired, but light enough. She hardly had any trouble understanding his accent and his speech impediment any longer. "And why is that?"

Ree tucked her arm under his heavy prosthetic one and turned him away from the crowd. "I'm happy to tell you, but not here. Is there somewhere private we can go? And does my godfather know you're out and about on your own?"

Nikolai's smile faded as abruptly as it had appeared. "Not exactly. Here, let's duck in there." He gestured with a motion of his head towards a building. Sea Level's Aquarium and Botanical Garden.

"What about me, Miss Ree?" Georgie removed Ree's elbow from Nikolai's and wound it through her own instead. She pouted up at them both.

"Can you do something for me, Georgie?" Ree bent down so she was eye level with the Angel.

Georgie pursed her lips and narrowed her eyes. "I guess." Her tone was begrudgingly obedient.

"Can you keep watch? Wear your monocle and look out for a skinny man with an eyepatch and a walking stick with a rat's head. He may or may not be accompanied by a walking and talking human doll."

Georgie stared at Ree for a moment, taking it all in. Then she shrugged and popped her giant eyepiece into place. "Sure thing."

"Come in and warn us if you see him."

"What about him?" Georgie motioned towards Fritz, who was sipping his drink with the faery. She was making coquettish faces up at him. They hadn't seemed to notice the appearance of Nikolai, but instead were gazing at one another and sharing sips of Lemon Fizz.

"He's fine where he is. Oh, and Georgie?"

"Yes, miss?"

"This may be a dangerous job. Are you up for the challenge? After all, it is still Thursday. It's a lot to ask of someone on their day off." Ree kept her tone serious though she was only teasing. Mostly.

"Don't worry about me! I'm ten years old. I can take care of myself. Besides, the Angels look out for one another. I'll get a few more on the case for you, miss." Georgie saluted smartly and turned on her heel. A cloud of dust swirled around her feet.

Weren't you seven just an hour ago? Ree wondered, smiling to herself. "In all seriousness, Georgie," she called after the Angel, "Be careful! He's my godfather and I love him dearly, but he's not to be trusted!"

"The best ones aren't, miss, don'tchaknow?" Georgie winked, her green eye magnified by the monocle and disappeared into the crowd.

Act IV
Divertissements

Chapter Fifteen
Mermaids and Their Appetites

Sea Level's Aquarium and Botanical Gardens cost a dear amount for admission and Ree was grateful she had had the foresight to bring plenty of gold marks. Once in a while it did pay to have wealth, even if it occasionally stood in the path of adventure, purely and morally speaking.

The gold marks were paid through a strange looking box in which sat a Gypsy robot. She was painted in bright and gaudy colors and adorned with cheap looking wrist bangles and earrings. Her hair was made of black yarn and her cheeks were painted red, as were her lips. The lips didn't move as the automaton spoke her thanks and the hours for which the admission were good for, but her hands moved in a choppy way as she swept the marks into a drawer. Privately, Ree thought Drosselmeier was a much better robotics maker – the gypsy model was so badly done it actually pained Ree to look at her - but she kept the thought to herself as it seemed inappropriate to voice it to Nikolai.

It was humid and overly warm in the Botanical Gardens, which was the first area of the building. The walls hung with vines and leaves and strange, exotic flowers. They practically dripped with the moisture that hung in the air, and the perfume was heady. Ree lifted her hair off her already sweaty neck and tucked it up beneath her bowler hat. The lighting was low, and the botanicals made outlandish shadows on the walls that seemed to shift and wiggle and move even though the original plants and flowers were still. The atmosphere was extraordinary, but not in a comfortable way.

The two walked in a silence for a few moments, but whether it was due to the uncanny room or due to the awkward silence that even friends can find themselves in at times, Ree wasn't certain. All in all, it wasn't a bad silence and Ree appreciated the minutes to gather her thoughts.

Does he know what he is? Some sort of hybrid human and robotic? Does he blame Dross? What shall we do? Are there more like him?

A squawking interrupted her musings, and Ree peered upward to the tall cathedral ceilings of the Botanical Garden. "My word! Whatever is that?"

Nikolai looked up, then looked down at Ree. He seemed amused. "It's a parrot. Have you not seen one before?"

Ree shook her head in amazement. "I've seen pictures, of course. But the colors...I had no idea how lovely they would be." She stared at the bird, soaking in the sight. It seemed to blossom under his admirer's scrutiny and it preened itself in a prideful way.

"There are many where I'm from," Nikolai sounded wistful. "And lovelier than that one."

The bird squawked and lifting its wings, it flew over their heads, nearly knocking Nikolai's tri-corner hat off in the process. Ree laughed. "You insulted it. We're frightfully sorry, bird! You're a good enough fellow!" The parrot ignored the apology and nested in the rafters.

They walked a bit further and came to a glass enclosure the size of the Stahlbaum's Grand Parlor. At first glance, Ree didn't see what it was designed for; it looked as though it were full of the same types of flowers and succulents and tropical plants the rest of the building boasted. She moved closer and pressed her hands to the glass, hoping to find it cool. She was shining up a storm in the humid air. Louise would have pretended not to know her if she were here.

The plant on the other side of the glass seemed to shiver and an orange colored python slithered out. Ree swallowed back a shriek and realized what the glass enclosure was. It was a giant snake cage. Several more wriggled their way through the hanging ivy, and the closer Ree looked, the more she discovered. She couldn't help the shivers that went up and down her spine, though she did find the creatures fascinating. At least, as long as they stayed where they were ...

Nikolai took her elbow once more. "Should we move along to the Aquarium section? After all, you did pay full price. We may as well see it."

"Yes, of course." Ree was glad to leave the snakes behind, though she wouldn't have admitted it for the world. She didn't want to seem a frightened school chit, out of her element, and nervous around animals. "How did you get down from the ship?"

"Your godfather is a dreadful flier. He nearly took the chimney off a building in the square trying to park, and I took the opportunity to climb out a window."

"Very ingenious. I approve heartily. And China?"

His expression darkened. "Still there. He must have removed some sort of part from her or something. She isn't acting like herself at all. We'll need to go back for her, of course. That is why you're here?"

"Of course. That's why I'm here." She stood up straighter. A mother with several children moved past them, chattering excitedly, and Ree and Nikolai paused their conversation until they were out of earshot.

"So, am I to understand that you came to rescue me?" Nikolai raised an eyebrow. He had fine, smooth eyebrows that must have taken Dross several hours to apply. Unless of course, they were as real and human as Ree's.

"Hm?" Ree shook off romanticizing Nikolai's eyebrows. How silly.

"It's just a bit unorthodox. I've never been rescued before." His voice was wry, as well as its usual gritty and metallic tone. Still, though, it was lighter than it had been back in Ree's grand parlor. As if he were more free to be himself now that he wasn't being forced into some sort of dancing doll role.

Ree laughed. The sound echoed in the empty room and bounced back to her. "Look, fish!" They stopped at the next glass enclosure. This one was filled to the brim with water, as were all the cages in this area. They must be in the Aquarium section then. Ree put her hand up to the glass and marveled at the fish. There were all sorts, and she was frustrated at her lack of knowledge of their proper names. There was a whole school of brightly colored ones, and some bottom dwellers that floated along lazily. There was a huge tortoise, and an amazing looking gray thing.

"Is that a killer whale?" Ree gasped at the sight of the gray one.

Nikolai stifled a chuckle, turning it into a cough. "No, I believe that's a porpoise."

"Look at this one!" Ree cried out in delight. "Look at all its funny legs!"

"An octopus. Oh, and see the jellyfish?" Nikolai pointed.

They made the rounds of the room in a circle. Ree was enamored by all the sea creatures and completely forgot for a while why they had ducked in here in the first place. Then they came to a small sign at the front of a seemingly empty glass box, separated from the other wall.

Please do not feed the Mermaids. They have a special diet that is monitored by the staff. Also, they've been known to become distraught and violent.

* Sea Level Aquarium not responsible for gnawed limbs or emotional trauma.

Ree held her breath and peered more closely into the enclosure. Mermaids? Surely not. Dangerous mermaids? Even more absurd.

But there was something. Something that shimmered through the decorative sea plants. Something that moved with silent grace. A fish. A woman. Both.

A mermaid.

*   *   *

"Miss Ree! Miss Ree!" Georgie's call was breathless as she raced down the corridor of the Aquarium. "He's here, he's here! The man with the rat walking cane!"

Ree had the ridiculous urge to shove Nikolai into the nearest cage to hide him. Since that nearest cage belonged to a mermaid however, she curbed the impulse and instead merely stood in front of her nutcracker man. Which was equally ridiculous since she was half his size. And also because he pushed her aside anyway.

Georgie came to a sudden stop and caught her breath. "Not here here, but outside in the market here. That's what I meant." She inhaled deeply. "Sorry to alarm you."

"That's perfectly all right." Ree was relieved. She glanced behind her at the mermaid cage. She still hadn't gotten a good look at what was inside. All she'd seen was a shimmering tale of blue, and some floating brown hair. Really, it could just be something manmade, she reasoned. A toy. An automaton that floated. Some sort of wind-up doll with a fish tail even. It wouldn't be that hard to do; though making it waterproof would be problematic. Her mind whirled with the possibilities and idea of such a thing.

"Anyway, I have Pork Chop distracting him for now."

"A pork chop? My godfather is eating pork chops?" Ree was confused.

"No, no." Georgie shook her blond curls energetically. "Pork Chop is my friend. Well, he's sort of my friend. Though I'd prefer you wouldn't tell him I said so, miss. His head'll get awfully swelled."

"Swollen," Ree corrected, absent-mindedly.

"Yes, that's what I said. Oo, looky! A mermaid." Georgie's voice was interested enough, but her feet betrayed her. She took a hasty step backward from the enclosure.

"Is it really?" Ree narrowed her eyes, which gave her an idea. "Let me see your magnifying monocle, if you please, Georgie."

"I call it a Magnocle," Georgie confided to Nikolai as she gave it over willingly enough. She even spit on it and buffed it with her sleeve first.

The mermaid moved at an astonishing speed. It also seemed like it didn't want to be peered at, and kept hiding amongst the kelp. "Hold still, you magical little thing, you," Ree murmured. She attached the Magnocle to her right eye and pressed both hands against the glass.

"I wouldn't get so close, if I's you, miss," Georgie said, her small voice nervous. "Them's not tame. Don't you have 'em Up Top?"

"Of course not," Ree replied, briskly. She caught a glimpse of human hands as they yanked shut a curtain of sea coral. "We don't have the Sea, remember? I've rarely seen a fish. My aquatic education has been sorely lacking, I'm afraid."

"Well, all's you needs to know is that they don't like humans, especially human girls. They're vicious killers, don'tchaknow." The Angel spoke the word 'vicious' with savoring bite.

Ree rolled her eyes, which looked comical wearing the Magnocle. "Don't be a Nervous Nelly, Georgie. You think faeries are hired thugs and mermaids are vicious killers. I don't know what that Miss Ginger is teaching you, but she shouldn't let you get away with such fanciful imaginings. You should be spending less time with the dramatics, and more time doing sums and tidying yourself." *Oh lordy, I sound like Louise!* "I mean, just...never mind. Look, she's coming out!" Ree nudged Nikolai. Georgie took yet another step away from the mermaid in fear.

"I'm going to check on Pork Chop, Miss Ree," she said, and was gone in a flash.

The mermaid swam up to the edge of her glass cage. Her tail was monstrously large and powerful, and it swished with force. Ree gulped. Her tail was long enough and Georgie's tales were scary enough that she worried for a moment that the mermaid could break through the glass and eat off all their fingers. The mermaid swam upward a bit and when Ree's eyes followed she saw that there was a foot or two of air where the water stopped before the ceiling. There was a hole with bars across it in that space.

"Come closer," the mermaid said through the opening. She stuck her long, tapered fingers through and beckoned Nikolai.

"Probably best if you don't." Ree put her hand on his sleeve. She didn't believe the mermaid was dangerous – not exactly – in fact, she didn't even fully believe it was real, though there were no visible technologies or gadgetry. Still, it didn't pay to take chances.

Nikolai seemed to be in agreement. "I wasn't planning on it."

"Look, another one." She pointed behind the first creature.

This one was red headed, like Ree. Her tail was green and it sparkled like diamonds. "This tank is absolutely enormous. I wonder how many they have captured?"

"I wonder how often they clean it," Nikolai replied. He gestured towards some algae that was growing up along the viewing area. There were also a pile of bones in one corner. A few of the skulls definitely looked human.

"I'm sure those are merely decorative," Ree said, confidently.

"Are you? They were delicious. Sorry about the housekeeping. We keep eating the algae eaters they put in to clean us," the first mermaid answered through the hole.

"Oh," was all Ree could think to say. "How unfortunate for the fish."

The mermaid shrugged. "If they'd give us some decent boys to eat, we'd leave the algae eaters alone."

Nikolai stepped back in haste. "What do they feed you then? I mean, on purpose?"

"Porpoise? Mm, I love a good porpoise. Filleted and rolled with seaweed." The red haired mermaid behind her giggled. Ree could tell because the water bubbled out of her mouth.

"Well, that seems a little cannibalistic, since you're half fish yourself, don't you think?" Ree asked, skeptically.

The mermaid shrugged again. "To each their own."

"That's kind of the problem. Oh, never mind. Nikolai, we should go."

"I think that's easier said than done, unfortunately." His voice was low. He gestured towards the way they had come. Ree whirled to see what had made him go so pale.

The entire Aquarium and the hallway as well was filled with the menacing red eyes of the mechanical rat army.

Chapter Sixteen
Trapped!

"Toss them in here. We'll take care of them for you," the first mermaid cooed. "They don't look like they'd swim well. Their feet would be perfect for picking my teeth. I have a piece of boy stuck in my bicuspids."

"I'm not tossing them anywhere," Ree answered, remembering the wound she had gotten from being scratched by a rat before.

"Then what are we going to do?" Nikolai whispered. So far, the rats were silent and still, but they both recalled how fast they could move when they got their signal from their master.

Cullen. Just where was he? She hardly thought the rats were here for the sightseeing. She pulled off the Angel's Magnocle and tried to look past the rats. Unfortunately, that meant taking her vision off them and she couldn't seem to make herself do that. She felt locked in a sick sort of staring contest with the robotic army and their blinking red eyes. She wished desperately for Fritz's quiet and deadly rifle. She wished desperately for Fritz.

"Up here!" Nikolai hissed. He pulled on Ree's arm but she couldn't tear her gaze off the spider rats. They still didn't move, though their ruby red eyes glowed brighter than ever before. Reluctantly, she gave herself a mental shake and looked up where Nikolai was staring. The top of the mermaid cage.

"I'm not going in there," she hissed. She still had a hard time believing the beautiful, mythical sea creatures were violent, but she didn't feel up to testing that theory. "I don't swim. And I don't want to lose any extremities either."

"Not in," he continued, "Up. It's covered. Probably so they don't jump out."

"Or so you don't jump in," the mermaid whispered. She still had her fingers through the little hole in the aquarium wall. "Though the water's fine ..."

Nikolai boosted Ree up the trunk of a tropical tree that was deader than a doornail and used mainly as decoration. In fact, as Ree shimmied up the thing she realized it was manmade, and not a real tree at all. *They can get a real mermaid*, she thought to herself, catching her sleeve on a fake branch, *but went to all this work fashioning a make-believe hibiscus. The world has gone absolutely bonkers.*

"My toolbox!" Ree realized suddenly that it was gone. Where had she dropped it? Put it down somewhere? Perhaps when she was so enamored with the fish? No, it was when she had put on the Magnocle. She looked down as she hoisted herself up on top of the mermaid enclosure. Sure enough, she could see it – hopelessly close to the rats. She had sinking suspicion she'd never see it again. Stupid, stupid, hateful rats.

Which were beginning to come to life.

"Nikolai! Hurry!" Thoughts of the toolbox were gone in a flash.

He needed no encouragement. He was off the Aquarium floor quickly, but his metal arm was heavy and awkward for climbing. The hibiscus tree swayed alarmingly and Ree held her breath. She laid down prostrate on the ceiling – trying her best to ignore the two mermaids swimming only a couple feet below her – and dangled her arms over the side towards Nikolai. A branch snapped. Senseless, shoddy, cheap papier-mâché, she thought to herself. She felt her heart in her very throat as Nikolai flailed wildly, then regained his balance.

The rats were scampering now. Willy-nilly, some turning in circles, some making mad dashes across the floor and running into the walls with loud thumps. They didn't seem nearly as organized as they had in Ree's parlor that night. Instead, they appeared out of control, sped up, and completely crazy. But they didn't seem inclined or capable of climbing up either the hibiscus tree or the mermaid cage either, which was something of a relief. Ree helped Nikolai swing his leg over onto the ledge where she lay, and he lay there for a moment, breathing heavily. The brunette mermaid swam beneath them in lazy figure eights, swirling her tail. Ree looked down through the glass and caught her eye. The creature smiled and broke the surface of the water, just inches below Ree's face.

"Are you sure you won't come in for a swim?"

Ree could barely hear her through the glass, and she pretended not to hear her at all. She turned her head to look at Nikolai. "Now what?" she mouthed, more than spoke. The ceiling – the real one – was only a couple of feet above their heads. Much too close to stand, or even sit. They were stuck lying down, above slyly smiling mermaids and an army of poisoned rats. Would anyone in the Aquarium interfere? And where was Georgie? Ree hoped she hadn't gotten mixed up in the fray. Had she met the rats coming in as she was on her way out to check on Pork Chop? What if she had been bitten? It would be all Ree's fault. She closed her eyes and desperately willed her thoughts to stop their jumbling blame-shifting. She needed a plan, now more than ever. She didn't have the luxury of coddling her self-deprecating thinking. Action. They needed action.

Nikolai seemed to have reached the conclusion even faster. He was already inching along the glass floor, the mermaid with brown hair floating on her back beneath him. She crossed her arms lazily behind her head and winked at him.

"Where are you going?" Ree hissed, inching along after him. She tried not to wonder what would happen should the glass give way. "First enchanted reindeer, then self-destructive faeries, and now obsessive mermaids. The females here at Sea Level are completely mad."

"Are not." The red haired one pouted, and she frowned at Ree as she swam by.

"Are too. And you're all man-crazy, to boot!" Ree huffed and puffed as she slithered along the glass. This was harder than it had looked. "Have some self-respect, ladies. Really!"

"We're not man-crazy." This time it was the other one speaking. She flipped over and turned a slow motion somersault in the water. "We're just hungry. Look at me; I'm wasting away." She stretched lazily, showing off her small waist.

"Can't fault us for being hungry," said the other, twirling her long hair. She blew a kiss at Nikolai, who was actively ignoring them both as he reached the other side of the aquarium.

Ree took a moment to pause and glance down at the rats. They were still running amuck, and Cullen was nowhere to be seen. Thank goodness for small mercies. She wasn't sure she could handle the plague masked villain just now. One arch enemy at a time would be more prudent. And Ree was ever prudent. Mostly.

Nikolai turned over on his back and reached up. There was a door in the ceiling above and now Ree understood what he was thinking and planning. It was a small door, however; likely put there for access to the attic, or perhaps simply as storage for the Aquarium's supplies. Pushing against it and knocking on it and jiggling it had no effect whatsoever. It was much better built than the fake tree had been.

"Kick it," Ree suggested. She had finally reached his side and was out of breath.

"I can't." He sounded frustrated. "My knees won't bend that much with all these pins in them. And even if they did I'm too tall."

"Out of the way then," Ree forced cheerfulness and lightheartedness into her voice. She rolled over, and giving a silent benediction to her trousers as this would have been so difficult in petticoats, she kicked upwards with all her might. She yelped as the wood made contact with her boots (that was going to leave a mark), but the door gave way. She wanted to hoot and holler but checked the impulse. She was taken aback at the sight the doorway had unmasked.

Blue sky. Well, not blue exactly – evening had set in while they had been inside the Aquarium and Botanical Gardens – but it was the sky. The roof.

It couldn't have been more perfect. This was far better than inch worming their way through some sort of ceiling cavity anyway.

Ree went through first, scrambling up and out. Next came Nikolai, and getting his larger body through the small hole gave Ree a moment of panic and finally an attack of the giggles.

"It's not funny," Nikolai panted, half in and half out of the hole.

"I'm sorry!" Ree clapped her hands over her mouth. "It's a reaction to stress! I can't stop!" She wiped away tears of mirth.

Nikolai glared at her. The effect knocked some sense into Ree, and she swallowed the last of her laughter and grasped him by the metal elbow. Below, she could hear sounds from the marketplace; chatter and conversation and the like. She pulled with all her might and with a splintering sound (the roof) and a metal scraping against metal sound (Nikolai's leg), he finally made it through. Ree looked down, feeling a bit dizzy with the effort.

The two mermaids floated on their backs, looking up at their visitors. The rats were still racing around the floor, a long way beneath. Some had flipped themselves over and were wildly waving their spindly silver legs in the air. The red haired mermaid waved sadly at Ree, and the brown haired one stuck her tongue out petulantly. Then they both flipped with a splash, and swam back down into the coral. Ree grabbed the wooden door and dropped it firmly back into place. Let Cullen assume they'd been eaten by mermaids, or poisoned by the rats.

"Going up, brother?" said a voice. Oddly enough, it was coming from above.

Ree raised her head in surprise, tendrils of her hair escaping her pins and blowing in the breeze. Her hat had fallen off at some point. Gone with her beloved toolbox, she supposed. She felt, rather than saw, Nikolai's hand grasp hers with some urgency. Together, they stood on the roof of Sea Level's Botanical Garden and Aquarium and looked up.

It was the workship, hovering silently.

And the man speaking to them – peering through the window in a casual way – was not Drosselmeier. It was Cullen Souris.

120

Chapter Seventeen
In the Sky with a Villain

Expect the unexpected. That had always been one of Fritz's favorite idioms, and while Ree used to think it was an entirely useless and senseless one, she suddenly thought she should have taken it to heart before now. Perhaps she would have learned something from it. For example, expecting to see your mortal enemy flying above your head, and thus having a plan in motion. *Then mayhap you wouldn't be standing on a rooftop with your mouth hanging open like a pelican.* She wasn't sure if it was her own voice in her head, or that of Fritz or Louise. Either way, it snapped her back to attention. She turned to look at Nikolai.

He was glaring upwards at the workship and he hadn't yet let go of her hand. That might have made her blush only a week ago; now she was only grateful for the support, both physically as the roof was rather high, and emotionally as the shock made her a bit shaky.

"Miss Ree!" Georgie's voice was unmistakable. She was on the ground, with her hands on her hips, standing next to several other urchins. The other Angels, Ree could only assume. Georgie looked annoyed, even at such a distance. "Miss Ree! For golly's sake, what are you doing up on the roof?"

"Escaping?" Ree replied in the form of a question.

"Marie Stahlbaum, get down from there this instance!"

Fritz. Perfect. Now everyone could berate her all at once and get it over with. Ree groaned. The workship still floated gently in the air near them. Cullen still leaned out the window, with his disturbing plague mask pointed right at Ree. As she watched him, he reached his bony hand out and crooked one long, skinny finger. Did he expect her – they – to simply come aboard?

To her shock, Nikolai moved forward and reached out his hand towards Cullen. Ree yanked him back with all the force she could muster.

"I think not! Whatever are you thinking, going off with a madman?"

Nikolai turned his glare to Ree instead of directing it at Cullen any longer, and Ree paled at the intensity in his face. "China," he growled.

"Oh." Ree swallowed. He was right of course. How could they just let Cullen float off with the clockwork doll? For all Ree knew, she was at least as human as Nikolai was. Which reminded her; they never had time for the conversation they had begun back at the beginning of their Aquarium adventure. She didn't really know any more now than she did an hour ago. The realization irritated her greatly. She had so many questions. Among them, how did Nikolai know Cullen? Why did Cullen call him Brother? Was China made of human parts? Where was Dross? *Drat that man.* Chief among her concerns was what was the plan would be once they went aboard the workship?

Ree felt trapped in a terrible story; a heroine caught up in a dreadful plot with no end in sight. She'd never had any patience for storybook girls who couldn't figure out a simple plot twist, or just ask the correct questions. How many times had she shouted at a book with a bland and insipid hero who could have wrapped up his own ending if he'd just stopped being ridiculously stupid and took matters into his own hands?

But there was no time to sit down and have a civilized conversation over tea just now. Swallowing her fear and trepidation, she followed Nikolai to the edge of the roof and watched as their enemy uncoiled the rope ladder out of the hatch built into the foundation of the workship and swung it towards the couple.

* * *

Ree had been to many strange parties Up Top. She'd sat through endless teas as a chaperon for Lou and her latest beau (they were torturous), she'd practiced Proper Napkin Dabbing and Sugar Lump Dissolving with Melisande until she wanted to scream, she'd served brunch to her father and his business associates while wanting to poke herself in the eye with the shrimp forks, and she'd even dressed up Hoffman in her mother's hand-me-down Sunday best gown and taught him how to dance a quadrille. But being aboard a dirigible with a foe who gave her the creepy crawlies up and down her spine, and a nutcracker boy whom she was apt to believe was more human than robot, really took the cake, so to speak.

Add to that, the shouts of Fritz and the Angels coming to her in snatches from below, and a large, seemingly discombobulated owl that kept flying against the window, and Ree felt quite uneasy; as if she were having the strangest dream and couldn't jog herself awake.

She kept a discontented position at the front door – which was silly seeing as how opening it and stepping out would likely kill her at this height – and Nikolai was the first to break the silence since they had entered the workship. Until now, the two old acquaintances had simply stared at one another. Ree wasn't sure if it was some sort of male stand-off to see who would begin a conversation or what.

"Where is the doll?"

Cullen watched them. Or at least Ree assumed he did. It was difficult to tell anything with that blasted mask on. She wished he'd take it off...although she had a sinking feeling that his real face might be even more terrifying. That was when her imagination took over. What if he had no face? What if it was just a blank wall of skin, or maybe made of gears and gadgets, like what showed through China's skin? Or perhaps he was some sort of creature – not human at all? Had an animal head instead of a man one? She was so taken in by her own dramatic conceptions, she missed Cullen's response. And then Nikolai was speaking again.

"What brings you here?"

"Making amends."

"That seems highly unlikely." Nikolai was obviously unconvinced.

Cullen shrugged. His shoulders encased in his brown coat were so thin that they looked more like they were hanging on a wire hanger than on a proper human form. He looked as though he'd blow away in the wind if he weren't careful, but Ree wasn't fooled.

"You've left behind your rats," Ree spoke up.

"They were stolen. Well, the device that controls them was stolen." The plague mask turned towards her.

"By whom?"

"That's not important."

"Where is my godfather?" Ree demanded, changing tactics. Was he with China? Was he the one who had stolen the rats? If so, why would he have unleashed them in the Aquarium? Nothing was making any sense.

Cullen shrugged again.

"Where are we going?"

"Up, up, and away." There was a smile in his voice.

Ree noticed that the shouts of her brother and of the Angels had faded away to the faintest of whispers now. She felt a pit in her stomach as she realized she was floating away from the people who made her feel safe. She could drop the anchor and hope it hooked onto a tree or something, she supposed. If she could get to it undetected anyway. And she'd had some experience in steering this workship; usually not for very long and only when Drosselmeier was completely immersed in work. She'd never really flown it before. She frowned. No one was really flying it now either.

"We're going to crash into the Bavarian Alps if you don't know what you're doing," she pointed out. "Or at the very least, take out several eagles."

Cullen waved his hand in the air, indifferent. "We're merely drifting at the moment."

Ree was skeptical. The thought of crashing this monstrosity against the mountainside sounded less than ideal. And Dross would be furious, if she survived to be yelled at.

"I wish to know where you're taking us!" All polite pretense that this was simply a social call left Ree with a whoosh of pent up emotion. "Immediately! If not sooner! And where is China?"

"Hiding somewhere, I believe. I have no interest in the doll, only in your godfather's illegal dealings. I only invited you as a courtesy, and for your own good. And because Nikolai and I are old friends." He sounded very defensive.

"Yes, someone explain that part to me. I'm afraid I missed it," Ree said as she edged closer to the stairway. The first floor of the airship house was really one large room, so if China wasn't here, and she didn't seem to be, then she must be upstairs in the storage area. The very place Dross invented, sewed, and operated on her in. She must be terrified, Ree worried. Maybe if she could get Cullen talking like villains were wont to do, then Nikolai could handle him, and she could scurry off.

The plan seemed to work. In fact, she felt a little insulted that no one stopped her as she streaked across the room and tackled the stairs. Obviously, Cullen had underestimated her, or at least she told herself that as she took the stairs two at a time. Then again, it wasn't as though she could escape anywhere anyway. They were prisoners in this place. Why would he care if she wandered around? There wasn't anywhere she could go. Just then, the airship took a sickening lurch and Ree nearly tumbled. She steadied herself on the wall, breathing heavily, and a loud thumping noise and then that of breaking glass distracted her from climbing any further. She looked down at the landing.

The great gray owl had burst through a window. Dazed and hurt, it flopped around like a fish out of water. Both Cullen and Nikolai stared at it, though neither made a move towards the injured bird. Ree's heartstrings were effectively plucked as she looked at the bloodied owl. She turned and looked back up the stairs, where she thought a frightened China might be hiding. Then back down at the owl.

Sighing, she trudged back downstairs. "No, no, I've got it." She couldn't help the long suffering and sarcastic tone. "You two boys just stand there and look pretty. Come here, birdy. I won't hurt you." Ree lowered herself to the floor by the owl, and tentatively reached for its wing, which was bent at a painful angle. The owl flopped pathetically and looked at Ree with its large yellow eyes. The airship took another dip that made Ree's stomach lurch and flip.

"Do something about flying this thing, would you?" She snapped at Cullen. "I, for one, don't feel like wrecking today."

To her surprise, the man obeyed. The control room was a tiny space, built into what originally had been designed as a butler's pantry. Ree thought her mother would be quite pleased and proud of her at this moment. She'd always said being a lady and being a force to be reckoned with were one and the same if you did them right, and Ree finally understood what she meant. Before she felt any giddier with power, she turned to Nikolai. "Hand me something to wrap it up in," she directed.

Nikolai, too, snapped to attention, and handed her a scarf that had been draped across a chair. All of the furniture in the airship was bolted down to the floor, which was not only a precaution for flight, but also a testament to Dross' dreadful piloting skills. Ree imagined Dross had used the scarf just that morning perhaps, and left it on the chair assuming he'd be back soon. She felt a pang of loss for her godfather, though her emotions on the subject of the clock maker were strained and confused, to say the least.

Ree was concerned that the owl might try to peck her once she touched it (her knowledge of birds was every bit as lacking as her education of fish), but it lay there calmly enough and allowed Ree to wrap it in the scarf. Its feathers were pillow soft – except for the ones that were crunchy and sticky with blood - and Ree stroked it gently once she had the bird swaddled like a babe. "There, you silly thing. Whatever were you thinking, crashing through glass like that? Have you been in the Scurvy Dog's cider?"

Of course it didn't answer her; just stared up at her with those perfectly round eyes. She patted it fondly on the head and then laid it down in the nearest and best spot she could, which turned out to be a soup pot. "Don't fret. It just makes a good sick bed," she assured the owl. "All right. I'm going upstairs to look for China. You," she directed this at Nikolai, "Find a weapon or something."

"We need more than weapons to fight Cullen," he answered. He was pre-occupied with screwing back in a gadget in his elbow that had been wriggling its way out. He winced as it popped back into place.

"Don't be defeatist. He's a man, like any other man."

"I'm just being realistic, that's all."

Ree snorted. Realistic in this crazy place seemed farfetched. The word had lost its meaning altogether, if you asked her. "You and Cullen have had dealings before, I gather?"

"I guess you could say we've got a history together. Are you going to keep him in that pot?" Nikolai said as he peered into it cautiously.

"Why not?"

"I don't think he approves...never mind. Go find China and we'll figure out what to do next."

"At least you aren't being sold to the highest bidder at market," Ree reminded him, climbing the stairs once more. "So...that's something."

"Yes, this is much better," he replied. "Stranded several hundred feet above ground in a floating laboratory with a lunatic in charge."

"It's nice to know your Hilarity and Humor Fluid isn't running low. And Cullen's hardly in charge. I know this place like the back of my hand and he doesn't. In fact, I'd say, he's our prisoner. Not the other way 'round." She smiled brightly and disappeared into the second floor.

Chapter Eighteen
A Faery's Tale

In truth, that last statement uttered by Ree was a bit of an exaggeration. The first floor of the workship, yes. She knew every nook and cranny. But upstairs – in the section she had always been under the impression was only used for storage – was new to her. She walked cautiously, realizing that China could be hidden anywhere, even as large as she was. Had she been told by her godfather never to enter here? Or had she simply never seen the need? Suddenly, she was unsure. Her footsteps faltered.

On the walls were metal hands holding candles; Dross' eccentric versions of sconces. The candles weren't made of wax but were gas powered. The combination of the airship and too much excess gas, though, made Ree rather hesitant and she wouldn't have chosen to light them. She would have preferred to feel her way and rely on what little light came in through the windows. Unluckily for her sensibilities, someone had already lit them. The light flickered and danced and reflected eerily on the walls. It brought her to mind of the one time she'd been allowed backstage at a dramatic opera. It had been strange and dark and full of shadows, and the singers and ballerinas kept creeping up on her on silent feet. She had been only seven years old at the time, and Louise and Fritz made fun of her for years after for being terrified of ballerinas.

There was furniture up here. Great wardrobes, as well as oversized tables and chairs, were all covered in white sheets. So it was mainly storage then. Ree felt relief. Deep down inside, she had been nervously expecting some sort of evil laboratory. Boxes of limbs. Jars with brains floating inside. Cadavers with missing body parts. Ree shuddered at the thought, even though no such evidence existed. Even so, she wished for Fritz's rifle, or even the comfort that the contents of her toolbox had always given her. The toolbox was likely gone forever now.

She moved through the rooms. "China?" she called, softly. "It's all right to come out now. It's Ree. And Nikolai is here, too. China?"

"Is he gone?" came a small, scared voice. It was coming from deep inside somewhere. It was muffled.

Ree moved towards the doll's voice. "Who?"

"The bird man."

Bird man? Oh, the plague mask. "No, I'm afraid not. But he's busy flying this thing and we have him quite outnumbered." She peeked beneath a table. Nothing there. She opened a trunk. Empty.

"The inventor?" Her voice was the merest squeak.

"Well, I'm not sure where he is at the moment, but I'm sure he'll be absolutely livid at the theft of his ship, so you can bet he'll show up eventually. Even if he has to charter an Omnibus." The thought made her smile. Dross hated public transportation, especially the flying kind. "At least Dross is the devil we know." She sighed, and opened the top of a window seat. "There you are!"

Poor China was crumpled into a heap, her crinoline mashed and her new tights torn. Her ear was missing again (the glue Ree had used must not have had proper time to dry) and her black, inky eyes were even wider than usual. Still, she extended her china hand to Ree and allowed herself to be lifted up out of her hiding place.

"Do you really think so?" she whispered.

Ree wasn't sure what the question had been referring to, but she nodded briskly. "Of course." She dropped the lid to the seat and propped her knee up on the bench it made. She pulled aside the curtains with a sneeze. Dross needed to dust, but that was hardly shocking. He did have an inexpensive cleaning robot but it wasn't capable of climbing the stairs. It couldn't do much besides sweep the floor with its mechanical broom foot, and water the occasional plant, and sometimes it got those two chores mixed up. Ree looked outside. They were very high up, and the Bavarian Alps were too close for comfort. *Was Cullen trying to go Up Top*, she wondered? Or were they floating aimlessly? Well, they were going to wrap the airship around the mountain if he didn't steer properly. Snow was beginning to fall, and night was too.

"Are you feeling quite well?" Ree turned her attention back to China. She recalled what Nikolai had said about her not coming with him earlier because she wasn't acting like herself, or like she'd had a part removed or something. Wasn't that what he had said? Perhaps that same switch that Ree herself had flipped without knowing it – the one that Dross had said had left China in Demonstration Mode.

China lifted her hand with a jerky motion and rubbed her face. Ree winced as some of the paint from her eyes smudged. It gave her a raccoon effect. Not that Ree had ever seen a real raccoon before, but she had seen pictures once. They seemed like sweet pets. Not like cats, which as everyone knew, were unpredictable beings and prone to violence.

"Here." Ree dug into the depths of her trouser pocket and found her handkerchief. She wiped China's face gently. Why was her paint flaking and smearing? The whole thing was odd. China was falling apart.

Ree pocketed the handkerchief again and smiled brightly. "There! Like a new woman. Shall we go down?"

China nodded, but it was in several motions, like her head hurt or wasn't fastened on correctly. Ree tried not to frown.

Going down the stairwell with a clockwork doll who seemed to be running on faulty batteries was a more difficult dance than teaching Hoffman to dance. Ree was panting at the bottom. There was definitely something wrong with China. Batteries maybe, but Ree had had very little experience with those, and they weren't favored by Drosselmeier. He was a purist when it came to clockwork. There might be a gear stuck somewhere, or was there something lodged in her cerebral compartment? A loose screw maybe? She wanted to examine her, help her, but there were so many things to do. How can one organize priorities when one's life is being so dreadfully difficult and bizarre?

Nikolai was perched over the owl in the soup pot, looking at it warily, and Cullen was nowhere to be found. Ree wondered if he was having trouble in the butler's pantry, but since the workship seemed to be flying adequately enough at the moment, she rather thought she wouldn't check.

"Nikolai, help me, please." Ree brushed a wayward lock of hair out of her face. It was the white streak; it always seemed to be the most rebellious of her strands. "I want to get China over to the table."

He obliged and together they lifted up the clockwork doll onto the same table that Ree had had her on before, when she glued on the ear (evidently not very well) and tinted her hair and patched up her skirt. China seemed relieved or exhausted or both, and though her pools of ink for eyes didn't change, Ree got the impression she had closed them. Perhaps even fallen asleep. Ree glanced worriedly at Nikolai. He shrugged. Thanks goodness whatever was happening to China wasn't happening to Nikolai. At least not yet.

Before Ree could gently roll China over to check on the mechanism switch on her back, since that seemed the prudent place to start, there was the sound of both a door flying open and another window shattering. Ree whirled. The door opening so theatrically was only Cullen, exiting the butler's pantry, covered in soot. The window however ...

"For golly's sake!" Ree blurted out, channeling Georgie's earlier proclamation. "How many owls are going to ambush us?"

It wasn't another owl though. Whatever it was had arrived in a heap of petticoats, a mass of black curls, large wood and metal wings, and a whole lot of glitter.

Fritz's faery.

* * *

"Sylvie." The faery offered her hand to Ree, after picking herself off the floor and pulling some glass out of her hair. "Sorry to drop in like this."

"Um, that's quite all right. Are you sure you're not harmed?" Ree took the hand and shook it, the same way she had seen her father do with his business associates. Normally when she met new people she curtsied. But it seemed out of place to curtsy, and besides, Sylvie had made the gesture first.

"No, right as rain. Actually, it looked as though someone had already made an opening there. I just enlarged it." Sylvie chuckled and brushed her skirts off. A few more pieces of glass and a puff of glitter drifted to the floor.

What had Georgie called the Faeries? Hired thugs? Ree raised a red brow. Sylvie didn't look the part. But then again...mermaids shouldn't be dangerous and reindeer shouldn't fall in love with her brother and elves shouldn't be stuffed for mantle decoration. The thought of Fritz gave Ree pause.

"Is my brother with you? I mean, obviously not. But did he send you after us?"

"No, I thought I'd surprise him. He seemed upset at you leaving so suddenly, if his kicking and hollering was any indication. And I thought, well, I have wings. Might as well use them."

"Oh." Ree's mind was blank. How exactly did Sylvie expect to help? As rescuers went, she didn't seem entirely suited to the task.

"It's as though people are volunteering to be kidnapped now," Cullen interjected, a little sullenly. He went back into the butler's pantry.

"What, are you running low on rope to tie us up with?" Nikolai shot back as the door slammed. "Why don't we just land and we can all get off if we're in your way?"

Ree waited for the response, but there was none from behind the door. It actually wasn't a bad question. Why did Cullen want Nikolai and Ree there in the first place? If he simply wanted the use of the workship, what were the passengers for? He must need Nikolai for something. But she couldn't imagine what.

"Well, I'm not leaving all my work in his hands, even if he did drop us somewhere," Ree pointed out. "I don't think this workship should be left with him in charge. There are all sorts of dangerous things in here. Chemicals and motors and weaponry and...well, all sorts of things you wouldn't want in the hands of a madman."

Ree turned her attention back to Sylvie. "What was your aim in coming here? Here, let me turn that off." The wings had begun to hum in a grating sort of way, as if they were stuck in a position. Ree turned Sylvie around and helped her take the wings off. Now she was no faery at all; just an ordinary girl with a perky, upturned nose, freckles, and funny looking shoes.

Ree inspected the wings as Sylvie chattered about wanting to get to know Fritz's little sister. The wings really were a remarkable device. They seemed to be powered by some sort of cylindrical aluminum engine. There was a small window in the cylinder and floating in it was a viscous pink liquid. There was glitter in the liquid as well. Well, a girl needed to accessorize, Ree theorized.

"But while I can't exactly fly off with all of you," Sylvie went on, and Ree realized she hadn't heard a word the faery had said, "I can take a message down below. At least I can if we haven't drifted too high. I'm a bit winded, to tell the truth. The wings sort of fizzled out of power at the end there and I had to flap my arms." Sylvie fanned herself and then dropped down on a chair. "Hullo!" she greeted China cheerfully. "Is she well?" This was directed to Ree, as China had not responded.

"No, she isn't." Ree rubbed her head. She was getting a massive headache. She'd give anything for a cup of tea. Well, why not? She grabbed the kettle from the cupboard beneath Sylvie's feet and was elated to know by the weight of it that it still had water inside.

"Robot?"

"Hm?" Ree had lost the thread of the conversation. Again. She was preoccupied with knowing the only place to heat the kettle was in the butler's pantry, where Cullen was. She wasn't sure she wanted a cup that badly.

"The dolly? Is she a robot? She's awfully good."

"Oh, well, yes. Not entirely. I don't know exactly. She's not for sale though. She's my friend." She shot Sylvie a suspicious look.

Sylvie put her hands up in the air. "Don't bite my head off, honey. I don't have any use for robots. I do know some that do, though. She'd fetch a nice price, I expect."

Ree didn't like the mercenary look in the pretty blue eyes all of a sudden. Maybe Sylvie really was a hired thug. She never did find out who Dross' mysterious buyer was at Sea Level. All things considering, Ree wished she'd never burst through that broken window. Add to that the fact that it was letting in snow, and that settled it. Tea was an absolute necessity. First though, Ree pocketed a curved blade with a filigree handle that was lying nearby. It looked rather dangerous, at least as far as eating utensils went. The only action it had seen was slicing Dross' pickled eggs.

"I'm going to heat some water," Ree said, making eye contact with Nikolai. She hoped he was as suspicious and wary of Sylvie as she was. The last thing she needed was to come back in the room and find China gone. Those faery wings didn't look sturdy enough to fly two, but stranger things had happened. They had already, after all.

Chapter Nineteen
A Truce over Tea

"Oh, there you are," Ree said, as she entered the butler's pantry and spied Drosselmeier's robotic butler propped up against a wall. She didn't trust it to make the tea, but it could probably handle the chore of passing it out to everyone.

"Me?" Cullen sounded surprised, please even.

"What? No, not you. I'm only here to heat some water," she responded, stiffly. "Excuse me, please." Awkwardly, they did a little shuffling around one another.

"I suppose you don't know how to fly this thing?" He muttered.

"Why?" Ree busied herself and made a loud show of banging things as she settled the kettle on the hottest part of the engine block. She sighed, and turned to face Cullen. She really didn't know what to make of him. He seemed to be part fearsome villain, and part baffling annoyance. And why did he wear that mask, the dusty top hat, the old brown coat, and the white gloves? Oh, well. They were past pleasantries and being polite at this point in the kidnapping. "Why on earth do you wear that mask?"

Cullen was silent for a moment. He stared at her and for the first time, Ree had the courage to stare back, right into his eyes behind the circular rims of the mask. They were sad looking eyes, gray in color, but not a steel gray. It was the sort of gray that brought to mind the ocean, or a foggy day.

Finally, he spoke. "Maybe I get sick easily. It's a doctor's mask."

"You're a doctor?" Ree was skeptical to say the least, and she let it show in her voice.

"No, not really. But doctors use these types of masks to ward off sickness and plague."

"Yes, I know. I've studied my history, thank you. They filled them with herbs and flowers so they didn't need to smell the stink of the dead."

"Yes. And to be near the contaminated without catching their diseases."

Ree continued to study him, her hands on her hips. The kettle began to boil and whistle. They both ignored it. "There are no dead bodies here."

"As far as you know."

Ree wasn't sure but she thought he snorted. She hoped he inhaled a rosehip. "What's that supposed to mean?"

"Only that you don't know your dear godfather as well as you think you do."

Ree glared. "I've worked that out on my own, thanks. But you do? Know him, I mean?"

Cullen shrugged that disconcerting shrug of his once more; the one where it appeared as though his bony skeleton would shake off his brown coat. He was a like a human raven, albeit a brown and nearly starved one. "I know of men like him, let's say. Ask Nikolai if you don't believe me."

"I'd like to, but each time I try we get interrupted by you actually. First, your awful rats, and second, well, your awful rats." She glared as she accused him.

"That second time wasn't me." He put his hands up in surrender, as if she were pointing Fritz's gun at him. "I told you; the controlling device was stolen from me."

Ree was cynical. "By whom? My godfather?"

"I doubt it. Sea Level's market is a haven for thieves and pickpockets. I should have known better than to have them there anyway."

"Well, you were certainly the one in charge in my parlor that night."

"Yes. Yes, I was."

"Why?" Ree was curious. She couldn't quite believe she was talking so freely with this man, this enemy. But if he was agreeable to communicate, she might get more answers. She hoped Nikolai was doing something helpful out there, while she was distracting their kidnapper.

"I told you, more or less. Herr Drosselmeier and I are old acquaintances, as are I and Nikolai. But if I told you why I was really there that night with my rats, you'd never believe me. You'll have to come to your own conclusions." He turned back to the engine and dismissed her.

"Oh, no you don't!" Ree was exasperated, and she had heard that excuse from adults before. 'Work it out yourself,' and such nonsense. Why couldn't grownups simply communicate and speak to children the way they did with one another? Why did they have to leave them to figure life out on their own? If a guest came to supper, would her father tell them to find the roast beef themselves? Exasperating. "Just tell me and we can get on with our lives!"

Cullen sighed. She couldn't hear it behind his mask, but she could tell by the way his shoulders rose and slumped. It was an action she had seen often enough in Louise when Ree was making her crazy about something. Usually though Lou followed the sighing with a smart slap across the top of Ree's head. Ree was grateful Cullen kept his hands to himself.

"I'll tell you this. I assumed Drosselmeier would be there that night, and that was mainly why I was there. I planned to destroy him, or at least to show him for what he truly is, and I'm not sorry."

"Well, he wasn't there, and you caused horrific calamity. Did you know two people died because of you?"

"First of all, he was there. You just didn't know where to look." Cullen's voice was glum. "I'm sorry about the deaths, by the way. I know you don't believe me, but I am. Murder was most definitely not part of my plan. As distracting and scary as my rats are, they aren't truly murderous. Most of their poison is diluted with lady's hand cream."

Ree nibbled on her lower lip. She moved the kettle, which she didn't want to boil dry. She was halfway to believing Cullen –there was a certain level of sincerity in his voice - but she undoubtedly wasn't going to admit it. There had to be more to this story, if she could get him to keep talking. On the other hand, the longer they spoke, the further the workship drifted. For goodness sake, they were going to end up in India if they didn't get on a course eventually. Honestly, she had expected Dross to arrive by now, by hell or by a chartered omnibus. Where was he? And where was Fritz? Some big brother he was turning out to be. Ree decided never to let him live this un-rescue of his little sister down. Leaving a faery to do his work. Indeed.

"What don't I know about my godfather? I assure you, I am not his most fervent fan or devotee any longer." Or even his apprentice. I quit as of today.

"Herr Drosselmeier's heart used to be in the right place." Cullen said, slowly. He reached for the kettle and then set beside it two chipped mugs. "Tea?"

Ree rummaged in a drawer and produced some out of date Oolong from a dented tin. They would have to drink it plain; Ree knew better than to search for milk or lemon or even sugar. Dross had a one track mind when working in the laboratory, and he never remembered to shop for sundries. Normally, she inhaled the bitter dregs of his dreadful tea readily enough, but that was when she was working as well, and fully distracted by the tasks at hand.

"And then what happened?" she pressed Cullen, pouring the water into the mugs.

"He got...ahead of himself. Greedy. He was discovering things that had no business being discovered, much less exploited." Cullen took his mug. Ree wondered, a bit frantically and hysterically, how he was going to sip it with that unpleasant mask still in place. How did he eat? No small wonder he was so thin. Cullen continued. "He realized how rich he could become, and even more than that, he realized how brilliant he was becoming. I think it was actually more about that, the notoriety, the fame, the accolades, than the money. At least, initially. But dealings done in the dark produce debts, I'm afraid. It was necessary for him to reap the rewards of his discoveries, monetarily speaking."

"His discoveries of what precisely?" Ree blew on her tea, though it really was only lukewarm at this point. She took a swallow and shuddered at the taste. Hoffman would have whisked it out of her hands in horror and replaced it with something more suiting to a lady of her quality. Hoffman. She found herself missing the butler. She glanced over at Dross' poor substitute. It was a squat little thing, and it had a cobweb spun over its head. A spider wandered across his chest, up its head, and into a place unspeakable. She had a feeling the robotic butler had buttled his last.

"Merging the dead and the undead," Cullen replied, flatly. "To put it bluntly."

Ree gulped, though there was no tea in her mouth. She set her mug down. "Do you mean to tell me, he's...the body parts of Nikolai...I knew that he wasn't strictly mechanical, but...he is made from the dead?" Her heart felt as though it were breaking in a million splinters. Dissolving at her feet. She felt ill. There had to be some mistake. Not Dross. Not her eccentric, loving, gift wielding godfather. And not Nikolai. Not her newfound, brave, nutcracker friend.

"Not Nikolai, no. He's...original. Made long ago, and from his own body. Though I hear he was nearly dead when Drosselmeier intervened. But, no, his parts are his own. At least, I think so."

Ree felt a huge rush of relief that threatened to bow her knees. She gulped her terrible tea as though it were a strength giving tonic. "And China?" She wasn't sure she truly wanted to know.

"I don't really know anything about her. Drosselmeier acquired her in Europe, I believe. Excuse me." To her surprise, Cullen lifted his hands to remove his mask. She nearly held her breath with anticipation. Would he be deformed somehow? Have no face, like her earlier imaginings? Cullen seemed to sense her staring and paused. She hurriedly poured another cup of tea and stared at it instead. She was born of better breeding than that.

Staring. Mama would have boxed her ears for such low class behavior. Ree stared into her tea as a substitute and atonement, her face burning.

"Didn't you ever wonder where your godfather went? He spends more time in the air, or at Sea Level, where – let's be honest – it's easier and more productive to be a criminal. Did you truly think he was only sightseeing or on holiday?"

"No. However, I thought he might be mixed up in piracy." Ree spoke honestly, and she finished the last bits of her sludge-like tea and finally looked at Cullen. Exasperatedly, he had taken off his mask and his hat, but he had also turned to face the window. All she could see was the back of his head. Black waves. Nice hair for a rogue.

Cullen laughed. Without his mask on, it was a pleasant enough sound for a scoundrel to make. "He is, but not as one of them. They're the ones he owes money to. And it's never a good idea to make yourself a debtor to a sky pirate."

"I can imagine. No wonder he's been spending more time Up Top. We're in a No Fly Zone without a special Permit." Ree pursed her lips, thinking. "But I suppose his fascinations and discoveries force him to leave at times." It did make a sort of sense. She was disenchanted with herself for believing Cullen so readily, especially at the expense of her godfather, but it made sense. "When did he start mixing mechanicals with bodies?" She shuddered at her own query, but needed to know the answer.

"He became very secretive, so I don't know precisely. He sold a prototype at market and as soon as that happened, he had demands for many more. A veritable undead army." This time it was Cullen who shuddered. "It's disgusting what people will pay good money for. At first, his blending of prosthetics and people was groundbreaking. He was even saving lives!" Cullen became more animated, throwing his hands up in the air as he spoke. "He could make the lame walk again with his robotic legs, he could make arms and even individual fingers that could grasp fine things. He saved Nikolai's life, you know. His jaw and lower face was shattered by a close range bullet. He would have died. He couldn't eat or drink.

Drosselmeier fixed him. And in the process, he made Nikolai feel indebted."

Ree remembered the way China and Nikolai had been forced to dance at her party, and she felt ashamed.

"Even then, the old inventor could have redeemed himself. But he got greedy. He realized he could reanimate limbs from the dead and use them in his automatons. That's when I knew I had to do something to stop him. For all I knew, your whole family was in on it. Everyone Up Top. That's why I wasn't particularly concerned who got stuck in the crosshairs in the parlor. So to speak. I admit I should have researched the situation a little better."

"Nikolai and you were fighting." Ree remembered how they had thrown one another around and looked as though they were killing each other that night.

"He wasn't listening to reason. I was only fighting back."

"But why you? What are you to Dross?"

"Oh, I thought you knew." Cullen finally turned around. "I'm his nephew.

Chapter Twenty
Visitors, and a Proposal

Ree was neither prepared for that revelation or for seeing Cullen for the first time. His gray eyes were even more visible and defined now that the mask was gone, and his hair was black and shiny. She could see the resemblance to his infamous uncle, as well. Dross had been a handsome boy, according to Mrs. Stahlbaum, who had known him for years and years and years. And Cullen was rather attractive, Ree had to concede, even if he appeared half starved. Those were not the surprising things that dropped Ree's stomach down to her feet though. No, it was his age. He couldn't be any older than she, maybe one or two years at most. She gaped.

"You're just a boy!"

Cullen scowled. "I'm old enough. I could be a soldier if I wanted to."

"Well, that seems a nobler career than mask wearing anti-hero, you must admit. And do you have to put that thing back on?" She wondered if he wore it to protect himself from contamination, like he intimated, or if he didn't like his startling likeness to Drosselmeier.

"I guess not. I'm a bit asthmatic. Drosselmeier taught me to breathe eucalyptus leaves during an attack. Also, I wanted a disguise." His cheeks flushed a little, but maybe it was the steam from the tea.

"You didn't explain how you knew Nikolai. You said – or perhaps it was he who said, I don't recall exactly – that you two have a history together."

Cullen looked uneasy. "Yes, well, he isn't fond of me. I was there when Drosselmeier saved him."

"That doesn't seem a good enough reason for him to dislike you and mistrust you."

"I was also there when he was shot in the first place." Cullen pinched the bridge of his straight nose and looked up at the ceiling of the butler's pantry. "Because I'm sort of the one who shot him." Ree stared. "Accidentally! I swear. He's not very forgiving."

"I can understand holding a grudge if you've had your face blown off," Ree conceded.

"Yes, well. That's a good point. But I think he's mainly mistrustful of me because he knows what Drosselmeier is up to and he thinks I'm in league with him. You see, for a bit, I was kind of Drosselmeier's apprentice."

It was Ree's turn to scowl. "Excuse me, but I'm his apprentice."

"Maybe Up Top you are, but we've already established he does his best work down below. You're the Updweller version of me." He smiled. Ree would have been insulted, but she found herself being somewhat dazzled by his smile. "I was at Miss Ginger's as a boy, but I flunked out. I'm a terrible liar, first off. Hence, the mask again. My face gives me away. So Drosselmeier took me in, since he was my uncle and everything. Let me stay in his Sea Level house and keep it for him. After a bit, he realized I had a bent towards science and magic. So I became his apprentice. But trust me," and his smile faded, "You wouldn't want my job. He had me digging graves. Here comes another reason for the mask. Have you ever smelled a dead body? No. I suppose you haven't. Anyway, at first, I talked myself into believing it was for the good of mankind. But all along I knew better. My mother taught me better than to play God."

"I wish Dross' mother had." Ree felt heavy, like her heart was weighing her down. She had a notion she was going to sink this workship with all the rocks that were taking up residence in her stomach.

"We should check on China and the others." Cullen gestured towards the door. "And then, if you're agreeable, we should come up with some sort of a plan. If you're with me, that is." He looked away, suddenly shy. "If you believe my story."

Ree cocked her head, her white strand of hair falling right over her left eye. "I suppose I do. But you'll have to convince Nikolai. And Fritz, if he ever shows up. And my Angels." She wasn't sure why she threw them in, except that she missed Georgie. She hoped she hadn't seen the last of them. Plus, she wanted to meet Miss Ginger at some point. "Is the workship all right on its course? I mean, you seemed a bit overwhelmed with the flying. I don't want to crash or wander into a No Fly Zone."

"I've put it on Hover Mode and we've cleared the Bavarian Alps, so I think we're okay for the moment." Cullen opened the door and gestured for Ree to go first.

She did.

And saw the first floor of the workship entirely inhabited by sky pirates.

* * *

Poor China –as if she were even any kind of threat – was trussed up with her own diamond patterned stockings. Nikolai was tied to a chair with the rope that held the anchor, and he looked extremely angry. Sylvie – minus the wings – was tethered to another chair, and even the broken owl had been captured. The lid had been put on the soup pot, and it was rocking around violently as if the bird were trying to escape.

Ree swallowed down her yelp of shock, and her feet were rooted to the floor. From behind her, she heard Cullen's intake of breath. He was taken aback as well. At least he wasn't in league with the pirates then. Ree's trust in him went up one more notch.

The pirates themselves were a colorful bunch. Five of them, and each more eccentric looking than the one before. Their ages were indeterminate and all had scruffy whiskers – except for one who had an extremely impressive handlebar mustache instead - peculiar top hats with binoculars attached, belts with all sorts of what could be tools but might be instruments of torture, assorted scars in various degrees of awfulness, and layers of clothing that made them look a bit like bears in overcoats. One smoked a pipe that reminded Ree of Dross' spearmint steam pipe, and one had his large legs up on the table. His boots alone came up to Ree's hips. That particular gentleman was nearest the soup pot and he leaned forward and gave it a rap every few moments to quiet down the injured and irate owl.

144

Another pirate, who appeared to be the leader, took a step forward, towards Cullen and Ree.

"I thought there were others! Your timing is impeccable. Welcome to our party, little lady. My good sir." He bowed theatrically at them. "The nutcracker man here, he said no one else was on board, but my fine fellow, said I, my fine fellow, we saw what we saw, and what we saw was two more pass by the light of the window. Didn't I say that, Ambrose?"

The one with the mustache nodded. "You did say that, sir. I remember it like it were fifteen minutes ago, sir."

"You see, my sweet travelers," the captain continued, "I make it my job to keep an eye on these air currents, I do. It's a vocation. A calling, if you will." He paused for effect, but no one interjected, so he went on. "I pride myself on knowing what's flying around these parts, madam. I really do. I am an artist of sorts. An artist of the sky I am."

The other pirates nodded solemnly. "Tis true," Ambrose agreed. "He paints real pretty, too. Bought one of his canvases for me mum, I did. She didn't like it much, but she don't have real good taste."

Ree wasn't sure what to say, where to look, or what to do. Nikolai was glaring at her, and she took that to mean he was angry that she and Cullen hadn't stayed put where perhaps they could have done something, on the sly. As if the two of them could have crept out and snuck up on all five pirates. Ree's patience with Nikolai and his expectations went down a notch.

"Sit down, sit down, I insist! God forbid we all sit comfortably while a lady such as yourself stands! Never let it be so." The captain gestured to the nearest chair, which held the pirate with the large legs and the tall boots. The captain knocked him down to the floor and pulled the chair out for Ree.

"Um, thank you. I think I'll stand."

"Nonsense, my dove! I really must assert my invitation."

That's the politest way to say you must obey me I've ever heard, Ree thought. Mama would have been impressed.

She found herself stepping over the man on the floor and took the seat. Cullen followed her, though there was not another chair. She found it somewhat sweet, as if he wanted to stay near her, but perhaps he only wanted to distance himself from the nearest pirate, who was picking his yellow teeth with a very small but very sharp ax. Ree swallowed hard.

"I'm Fennimore Trapper, the Captain of this air, and the Captain of The Suddenly Surrendered. She's the jolliest airship this side of Arabia, if you don't mind me saying so." Fennimore bowed again. "Now that we've got our pleasantries out of the way, sweetling, I imagine you're wondering why we've dropped by so suddenly?"

"I assume so you can rob, maim, and possibly murder us in unholy ways?" Ree guessed.

Fennimore looked appalled. "Madam! You wound me! First of all, I never rob, maim, or murder ladies of quality. At least not often. Very, very rarely. Only when I'm under extreme duress. This is a highly stressful career, madam. You have no idea what I go through."

"I suppose not." Ree glanced at Cullen, who shrugged.

"Ah, so understanding. Such manners, such empathy. You may be the one for me, my dove. No, no, you make me think of matrimony more than murder. I have no interest in harming you. But I am intent on acquiring my anchor back. It's an antique. It belonged to me grandmother; a pirate first-rate. First-rate and first-mate! Hah! A little pirate humor there. Aye, my grammy, the infamous legend and myth! You've heard of her I expect? Imogene Sea? She was a corker, she was. A moment of silence, please, for my grammy, boys."

The other pirates removed their hats and placed them over their hearts, or where they would be, had they any. Ree felt as though she were stuck inside some sort of dreadful play with Louise in the lead role. She found herself wondering if someone was about to start singing. Still she bowed

146

her head along with everyone else. Good breeding and education demanded it. Especially if there had been a proposal involved, and she rather thought there had been. Of sorts.

"Amen!" said Fennimore, reverently. The rest of the pirates echoed him. "So you see, heart of my heart, we are only here to take back what belongs to us. No need to be alarmed."

"The anchor, Mr. Trapper?"

"The anchor. And your godfather, too, of course. He owes me his very soul at this point, so I've come to collect. Oh, and the ship, too. Lost it to me in a card game, I'm afraid." Fennimore leaned in closer to Ree and whispered, "Gambler. Your godfather has a problem. You should speak to him about it should the opportunity present itself. But don't let it worry you – your family is my family and we all have our skeletons in the closets, so to speak. Ha! Skeletons in the closet! That reminds me, Ambrose, I need to clean out my closet this weekend."

"How did you know he's my godfather?" Ree leaned backwards. The captain's breath smelled of anchovies, and...peppermint? "And what do you mean, you're taking him and the ship?"

"Well, just what I said, naturally! I always mean what I say, do I not, boys?" He turned to the others.

They nodded in agreement. "A veritable man of his word is Cap'n Fen," said one the pirates. This one had a Scottish kilt instead of trousers.

"Why, thank you, Seamus! Very kind of you to say, very kind. Such a good crew I have." Fennimore wiped a tear out of the corner of his eye. "Very supportive. So important in employees. Would die for me, wouldn't you, boys?"

They nodded again.

"Do you want me to prove it, dear heart?" He leaned even closer to Ree. She could feel Cullen stiffen at her side.

"I don't think so."

"I could make one of them jump, you know," Fennimore confided. "They would. Any one of 'em. Would it impress you to see that? Right out that broken window, say?"

"Of course not!" Ree was horrified. "Don't be ridiculous!"

Fennimore straightened up. "Well, you don't haveta get uppity."

"What do you intend to do with us?" Cullen demanded.

Fennimore waved the question away. He wore fingerless gloves and his nails were dirty. She squirmed. A plan. They needed a plan. And quickly. Before the captain lost patience and made them all walk out the window. Or marry him.

"I hadn't made up my mind yet." The captain took out what probably used to be a snowy white handkerchief and began to polish his binoculars. "Any suggestions?"

"Yes, you can set us free in a nice safe place." It was Sylvie, who up till now had been surprisingly quiet for one normally so chatty.

"Not you, pet!" Fennimore chuckled. "I was asking my crew."

"We could force 'em to join us?" suggested Seamus. "Been gettin' a little lonely lately." He leered at Ree most unapologetically. She made the rudest face possible and wished she could spit further than...well, dribble down her own chin was the best she could do when Fritz tried to teach her years ago.

"Drop 'em in the Sahara and watch 'em sizzle from above?" said Ambrose.

"Ransom 'em for lots and lots of money?" suggested the nameless one.

"Eat 'em?" suggested the other nameless one. They looked like twins now that Ree looked at them squarely.

148

Captain Fennimore beamed. "Excellent proposals, all of them, boys! I like your spirit, and your creativity. You've been paying attention in class."

"My brother, Fritz, is a general, sir!" Ree nearly shouted this information. "And he is looking for us this very moment. Add to that, he knows where we are!" This revelation hardly made sense with the first part of her boast, but she hoped they hadn't picked up on that discrepancy. "You will have the rage and the fury of the whole Up Top militia descend upon you, posthaste, if you do not let us go."

Instead of being properly chastened and fearful, Fennimore Trapper threw his large head back and laughed so hard his top hat and binoculars fell off. "A battle!" he cried. "Bless my soul, and what a battle it will be!"

This was not the reaction Ree had been hoping for.

Chapter Twenty-one
The Girls Join the Fight

The twin pirates were so excited at the promise of a proper battle, they ran around like lunatics in the airship, preparing. Ree watched them, not sure whether to laugh or cry. They were dangerous to be sure, but they were also slightly comical; like Fritz and his friends used to be when they played silly games as boys. Still though, she was sure their swords worked well enough, and their aim would be true. Fennimore watched them indulgently and then whispered to Ree that they weren't quite right in the head, but they meant well.

"They've both taken one too many tumbles out of The Suddenly Surrendered," the captain confided. Ree groaned.

Seamus kept making kissing faces at her, and it was making her blood boil. The two twins she learned were named Jedidiah and Obadiah, and now they were in the process of turning out all the gas lamps. By smashing them. It was getting darker with each lamp extinguished. It was now real and truly night outside the airship.

"Element of surprise, see?" Captain Fennimore had told her. "Makes it much more satisfying to jump out at the enemy in the dark when they least expect it." He practiced his jump then; with fists at the ready and a ferocious look upon his whiskered face. He landed, and shook the whole dirigible. The soup pot clattered to the floor and Ree took the occasion to scoop up the traumatized owl. She tucked it firmly beneath her elbow and cooed softly to it. It hooted wildly and frantically, and tried to beat its injured wings against her. The scarf had come undone and Ree quickly wound it around the bird again.

"Can you at least untie your prisoners?" Ree asked. "Lest they get caught in the battle? There's nowhere for them to escape to. And they might even be in your way. In the way of your fighting, I mean. You don't want to trip. I'm not sure the twins' brain can take another accident." Personally, she thought whatever they were using for brains might be chocolate soufflé at this point.

Fennimore thought for a moment. "I suppose you're correct, my dearest. You're more than just a pretty face, you are. I can see you're a right educated lady. Of course, your young men there might decide to join the fight..." He thought for another moment, stroking his whiskers. "But that'll make it fair! No one ever accused me of fighting an unfair fight. Go ahead, untie your comrades, madam."

Ree had wondered why Nikolai had been completely silent this whole time, and when she reached him and began to unwind the rope that bound him, she discovered the reason for his muteness. His metal jaw had become unhinged at one side. "Oh dear!" she murmured, taking his face in her hands. "You must be in pain. Hold still."

Ree fumbled in her hair. The key pins she used to put her hair up that morning (had it only been that morning?) were yanked out, and she used the pinning end as an impromptu screwdriver to insert into Nikolai's jaw. With a pop, it moved back into place, and he opened and closed his mouth several times.

"Thank you," he said, stiffly. Was he sore from the injury or was he put out at her sudden friendship with Cullen? Goodness, but she had so much to do. Why was there never time for proper conversation? It seemed lately that she was too busy running for her life or escaping from kidnapping to set things right with her friends. The Up Top Ree would have laughed at the thought. There was always time for tea and talking in the Stahlbaum household. After all, that was all one did when one was a rich young lady of quality, if one wasn't reciting poetry or sewing a fine seam. Of course, no one was trying to kill her there. That was likely the difference.

Now free, Nikolai untied China, who remained lifeless looking. He looked questioningly at Ree, who shrugged helplessly. Finding out what it was that was ailing the clockwork doll was something else they had to do if they got out of this alive. Cullen was freeing Sylvie while the pirates were finding hiding places. The captain was perched atop the tall bookshelf that held Dross' collection of apothecary jars. He had his knees bent up to his scruffy chin and he would have looked amusing if he hadn't looked so fierce. The last light went out with a smash and with the tinkling of broken glass.

All was dark. Suddenly, Ree could hear Fritz's voice from just beneath the dirigible. He was here. The battle would happen like Fennimore had hoped it would. Ree grabbed Sylvie by the hand, and girl and faery made for the stairs just as the door in the floor burst open.

"The owl!" Ree gasped, and turned back. She leapt through the air and snatched the owl where she had laid it at Nikolai's feet when she was doctoring his jaw, then made it back to the darkened stairwell just in time.

"Oof!" said Sylvie, as they collided.

"Sorry. Go, go!"

"Go? I'm not going anywhere! I'm fighting these dirty beasts! Let me by, woman! Don't choose now to tempt me with your lady charms! I won't be seduced when there's a battle afoot!" It wasn't Sylvie. It was Seamus.

"Oh hell's bells! Move it!" Ree pushed hastily by the man, and took the stairs two at a time. "Sylvie?" she hissed.

"Up here!" She was already at the top. Ree could dimly see her figure peering over the bannister.

The cries from below were bloodcurdling. She wasn't sure what any of them were saying but it sounded a lot like blustering threats, shouts, thumping and banging and clanging, insults, and what sounded like a Scottish war cry. She wasn't surprised that Cullen and Nikolai hadn't followed the girls up the stairs – they could handle themselves, she hoped – but she did worry for China. Ree wasn't sure she would be able to even take the strain. With any luck, the soldiers and the pirates would simply ignore her as they fought. She seemed so fragile since her capture.

"Should we join them, do you think?" Sylvie asked, in a manner that didn't match the offer. She wasn't itching to join the battle, but was game if Ree was.

Ree Stahlbaum wasn't about to be outdone in courage by a glittery faery. She'd never live it down; Fritz wouldn't let her. "I think we should have a plan first," she suggested. "If we just enter the fray, as they say, we'll be toast."

"Faery on toast is a delicacy Up Top, isn't it?"

Ree was aghast. "Of course it isn't! What do you take me for, a cannibal? That's utterly nauseating."

"Well, excuse me, Miss Fancybritches." Sylvie was insulted that Ree was insulted. "That's the reputation of you Updwellers, just so you know. Faery eaters and reindeer killers."

"I'll have you know, that's an utter lie, and you shouldn't pay attention to gossip."

Sylvie sighed. "Gossip is what makes life interesting. Gossip is information and information is what pays the bills."

Ree lowered her brows as she regarded the faery. "Yes, someone told me you might be a hired thug."

It was dark, but Ree knew Sylvie smiled. "You shouldn't pay attention to gossip."

In answer, Ree screamed. It wasn't because of Sylvie's infuriating response – though that wouldn't have been too out of place – but because a body had just hurled itself through space near the vicinity of her head. Whomever it was, ducked and rolled by. Ree didn't know whether to kick it back down the stairs as an enemy or help it to back to standing as an ally. Why did the twins have to smash all the lighting? She wanted to smash them.

Whoever it was continued to roll, flipped, and rolled all the way back down the stairwell. Ree couldn't help wincing at the sound the body made as it bounced down each stair. She hoped it wasn't Nikolai; she wasn't certain his faulty metal parts could take much manhandling without coming apart. And then there was Cullen, who was likely no match against the big, burly pirates. Ree took a deep breath, and then let it out slowly. Unless Fritz had brought his whole army of girl soldiers (and how would he have had time to collect them from Up Top?) they were more than likely doomed from the start. She hoped it wasn't just Fritz, Nikolai, and Cullen against the five pirates. She smoothed the feathers of the owl and bit her lip. Then she put down the owl and felt her way around the room. She bumped into furniture and stubbed her toes quite a few times before she found what she was looking for.

"Psst! Sylvie! Over here!"

Ree heard Sylvie make her way close to her. She hit a wardrobe and stifled an exclamation. "What I wouldn't give for my wings," she muttered, finally reaching Ree's side. "Well, what is it? What's your plan, faery eater?"

"There's a length of rope here, I noticed it earlier." Ree began to unwind it. She ignored the insult. Mama would have been pleased.

"So? What, do you think we can just wander down and start tying up all the bad guys?"

"Don't be dimwitted." So much for pleasing Mama. "Here, hold this for a second." Ree moved to the window, which was visible by the light of the moon. She fumbled with the latch and then threw it open. A cold gust of air hit her in the face.

"This won't reach to the ground. Not even close." Sylvie was skeptical. "I don't fancy swinging around in space until my arms give out."

"It doesn't have to reach to the ground. Just to the first floor."

Sylvie was still confused. "If you want to get to the first floor, take the stairs. Me, I'm happy right where I am, at least till I know who's winning down there." They both flinched as an especially loud tussle from below ended in more glass breaking. Ree was grateful for her sturdy boots.

"The element of surprise, remember?" Ree began tying one end of the rope to the sturdiest and most convenient piece of furniture she could see, or rather feel. She thought it was a writing desk, but it was a good heavy one; it should support their weight.

"So, we crash through another window?" Sylvie grimaced. "I'm not sure I can take that again. I didn't want to mention it before, but that hurt. And I tore my skirt. Plus, we don't have weapons. So after we surprise them, as you so eloquently put it, then what? We stand there and look ridiculous?"

"Of course not. We *do* have weapons," Ree argued. She tugged hard on the rope and noted that it seemed quite secure. The snow blew in and was already accumulating in her hair. She wished for the hundredth time for her bowler hat. Now she'd even lost the key pins from her hair. She was losing herself, piece by piece.

"Like what?"

"Self-respect, education, virtue, and good breeding," Ree answered, primly. "Never underestimate the power of those things."

Sylvie was baffled. "You're daffy, Updweller."

Ree laughed. "And if those don't get us anywhere, we'll use these." She produced the small knife with the wicked blade she had secreted in her pocket earlier and pressed the handle into Sylvie's hand. For herself, she had plans to come swinging in right near the cabinet with the apothecary jars. Weaponry she might not know much about, but as far as science and chemistry went...she was fairly sure she could blow up the pirates and their ship should the need arise. Or at least bluff convincingly. At the very least, create a diversion for her friends to make use of. Maybe some magical looking puffs of smoke, or an eye watering aroma that would cause a small panic.

"Coming?" Ree wound the rope around her hand and put a foot up on the ledge of the windowsill.

Sylvie only hesitated a few seconds, then she nodded briskly. "Right behind you, Updweller," she said.

Chapter Twenty-two
Ceasefire

Ree had always been a decent climber, and having experience with Dross' devil of a rope ladder helped matters as well. She shimmied down the rope fairly quickly, telling herself not to look down. It became a chant of sorts, don't look down, don't look down, for golly's sake, don't look down. Sylvie was only a couple feet above her. Both girls planted their feet firmly against the side of the airship and leaned backwards, as though they were climbing down a mountainside. It wouldn't do to swing or bounce; the very idea made Ree feel seasick. The rope burned her hands and she wished she'd brought her gloves. Mama had been right. A lady should never be without her gloves.

Although this was probably not the reason why.

Don't look down, don't look down, for golly's sake, don't look down...

Just then, Sylvie lost her grip and faltered on the rope. She slid down quickly and only Ree's head prevented her from slipping further. She was nearly perched on Ree, who tightened her grip and tried not to shout. Obviously, the faery would regain her footing without being hollered at, and they still needed that element of surprise that Fennimore was going on about if they wanted to stand a chance against the pirates.

Their balance regained, Ree continued. The snow was getting in her eyes, making it even harder to see than the night would have allowed anyway, but she dared not take her hands off the rope to brush her face. Her hair whipped around her and her heart was in her mouth. Finally, the broken window of the first floor. Ree grasped the shutter and took a deep breath.

Before she could launch herself through however, someone else came out with a mighty roar.

"Aye, I'll go down fighting but haunt ye I will!" Seamus' large body vaulted through the cold night air and plummeted down.

Ree gasped and steadied herself as she watched him fall. He seemed to stay suspended in the air for the just the tiniest second – she even had the frantic notion that he saw her and locked eyes with her – and then he was gone into the dark. She swallowed and looked up at Sylvie, whose brown eyes were wide but otherwise unaffected as she looked down at Ree.

"Well," she said in a practical voice, "One down, four to go."

The words may have been cold, but they were entirely sensible. Ree had to agree with the context, if not the sentiment.

"One," she mouthed up to Sylvie, "Two, THREE!"

And she was through the broken window. She had hoped to land squarely on her feet like she knew raccoons did, but she flew end over tea kettle in a painful manner, and landed sprawled on the floor. *Ladies do not sprawl, Marie!* She could hear Louise now. She didn't recall a time when her head had been so filled with her relative's wishes and voices. It was mildly upsetting.

Sylvie came through the window, and landed much more gracefully. The rope flapped and bounced against the window frame. No one in the chaotic room seemed to notice the girls' arrivals, a fact that both pleased and annoyed Ree. She moved quickly to one side and grabbed the first two jars she could get her hands on. She knew from experience that one was Oil of Vitriol and the other was merely the blue paint she had used to color China's hair; but no one else would know. The paint could be something lethal for all they would discern about it, and she planned to use their ignorance. Besides, the Oil of Vitriol could cause enough harm. She remembered the rats.

To her surprise, Sylvie had jumped right into the action. Ree was elated to see her brother still alive, and not only alive, but invigorated and looking very much the hero as he battled with both Ambrose and one of the twins. He'd probably be a bear to live with after he dispensed of sky pirates, she figured. Nikolai too, looked well enough, though his prosthetic arm was hanging at an odd angle and he seemed to be using it as a weapon instead of using it to hold a weapon. The arm was hitting and punching at Captain

Fennimore, who was grinning like a crazy person, even as blood ran down his face. That left Cullen with the other twin, Ree reasoned, but they were nowhere to be found. Ree tried not to think about them falling to their deaths as Seamus had. What if they had wrestled out onto the porch? She had told Dross to knock down that thing months ago. Rickety and unsafe even on the ground; and who would want a porch on a flying machine anyway? You'd be out admiring the view one moment and be blown clear to Egypt the next.

Sylvie leaped onto the back of the twin fighting with Fritz, her little knife between her teeth. Fritz hollered a cry of approval and turned all his murderous rage upon Ambrose. Just then, a huge mess of boots and clothing and arms and legs came flying down the stairwell. Cullen and the other twin; Ree thought this one was Obadiah. Cullen got up hastily enough, staggering, but Obadiah lay motionless where he had come to an abrupt and painful stop. Two down, three to go, she thought.

"Stop!" Ree shouted. It had no effect. The battle raged around her. "Stop!" she cried, louder, her throat scratching with the effort. She'd not had much practice in yelling at the top of her lungs, a total recipe for punishment in the Stahlbaum household. She'd yelled at Fritz once or twice, but got her ears boxed for it. And anyone who has had their ears boxed by a mechanical nanny knows the effect. "I said, STOP!"

The last one did it. Everyone froze and looked at her. Fourteen eyes stared at her as if she had escaped from the lunatic asylum. Ree cleared her pained throat and held up the jars of fluid. "So help me God, I will drop these both at our feet and the chemical reaction will fry what's left of your brains if you do not surrender right now." Since she didn't need to yell now that she had their attention, she settled for speaking through gritted teeth.

"She's right," Cullen interjected. "Vitriol and Sulfuric Acid will kill us all."

It was hardly Sulfuric Acid, but Ree had a feeling he knew that and knew of her plan to bluff her way out of this mess.

"You'd hardly fry us all, would you, my intended?" Fennimore didn't look taken in, though he hadn't raised his weapon again to Nikolai. It hung at his side, a polished sword. "I believe you were raised better than that. What would my mother-in-law-to-be say?"

"My mother would pinch the underside of your flabby arms for attacking her children, that's what she'd do. Until you begged for mercy."

Fennimore considered. "Sounds like my own mother, God rest her thievin' heart. That spot of flesh right below the armpit but right above the elbow?" He shuddered. "I can still feel it. But my childhood recollections won't digress my actions, my dear! Your jars don't scare me. And Fennimore Trapper never surrenders."

"They scare me a little," whimpered Jedidiah. He stared at his expired twin in misery. His sword hung at his side like a broken arm. Sylvie was still on his back, though he didn't really seem to notice. Every few moments he gave a halfhearted shrug that jiggled her a bit but didn't unseat her. She still had the knife blade between her teeth and Ree wondered if she had the courage to use it. She wasn't sure she would. Knifing someone would be a bloody and intimate way to dispatch of anyone. She'd rather poison them, should it come to that. *Sorry Mama. I know, morbid of me.*

"I propose a ceasefire," Ree continued, her hands poised over the lid of the Oil of Vitriol.

"A what now? You can't be serious!" Fennimore was not looking enthused. This was nearly as bad as surrender in his book. He almost looked like he wanted to cry. His beard quivered.

"A ceasefire. No more harm done, we shake hands, you take your grammy's anchor, and be on your way. You take your men - what's left of them – and we'll take ours. We'll pretend this nasty episode never happened. And if Herr Drosselmeier truly owes you money, I will personally see to it that he sets up a payment plan...*with* interest." It was the worst idea Ree had ever heard, and Fennimore look entirely unimpressed until she got to the ending.

"Interest, eh?" He stroked his whiskers, and fluffed his beard back up, since it had begun to droop during the fighting. "What kind of interest? 40%?"

"I think 25% is more than fair, Mr. Trapper."

"35%."

"30%."

"30% and due on the first of each month until it's paid in full. Plus, we get one of them special tickets to let us fly Up Top."

"Certainly not!" Ree frowned. That preposterous suggestion firmly uprooted Worst Idea Ever Heard, and its predecessor, Making Deals with Sky Pirates slid down to Number Two.

"Just once a year maybe? During Christmas time? You have such nice street decorations up there. We could check our weapons at the gates?"

Ree sighed. "Oh, all right. I'll see what I can do." She figured she had a year before Christmas anyway.

Fennimore beamed and thrust his burly hand with the fancy fingerless gloves at Fritz. To Ree's shock, her brother took it readily, clapped his other hand on the pirate's shoulder, smiled his big goofy grin, and offered to buy the next round of cider the next time they were at Sea Level.

"You are not going to the Scurvy Dog, Fritz!" Ree objected. "Especially with sky pirates. Mama would be outraged."

Fritz ignored his sister. "Is anyone sailing this thing?" he muttered, as a bump in the air caused them all to jostle around and find their footing.

"It's on Hover Mode." She watched as Fennimore picked up the antique anchor and tucked it in his arms like a newborn babe. "Probably just an air pocket or a gust of wind."

"Gentlemen," the captain addressed what was still standing of his crew, "Pick up our fallen comrade and let us make haste. Our ship, too, is hovering nearby and you know what happens when we leave the cook in charge. My intended," he clicked his booted heels together and bowed toward Ree, "Miss," this was to Sylvie, "If you would be so good as to dismount my man there, we will be on our way. Sirs," now he bowed to both Cullen and Fritz, "An admirable battle. I do thank you! Let us hope we meet again, under similar circumstances very soon!"

Speechless, Ree could only watch (gaping slightly) as the pirate crew opened the door in the flooring and left via the rope swing. She could only assume they had some sort of dirigible below, unless of course they were hovering directly above The Suddenly Surrendered. Then she supposed they could simply drop. In that case, perhaps Seamus had survived his fall? Ree doubted it.

Fritz bolted the door closed after them and then proceeded to block the broken window. "I'm about done with uninvited guests," he said. "Now, where is that blasted godfather of yours?"

"I haven't the foggiest notion. But now that we know Cullen isn't trying to kidnap us or kill us, I think we should turn back."

"To Sea Level?" asked Sylvie eagerly.

Nikolai didn't appear too happy with the suggestion. He frowned, or would have was his brass jaw capable. Ree knew his frown by his eyes. She couldn't blame him for not being pleased.

"Well, we can't fly around forever, and I don't really think we should go back Up Top without finding and stopping Drosselmeier. He could be in the act of making more like you, and not that you aren't wonderful," she flushed, "But I think we can all admit he is going too far."

Cullen agreed. "I've started this thing, and I want to see it through. Of course, you're not all obligated to come with me. It may be dangerous, even deadly. I can't make promises for your safety and wellbeing."

"That sounds like a challenge if I ever heard one," Sylvie commented, mildly.

"It does indeed," Fritz nodded.

Nikolai crossed his arms. "It's settled then. We go back. But first, Ree, I think we'd best pay attention to China. She looks worse."

All heads swiveled towards the clockwork doll, who had been motionless throughout the entire fight. Her missing ear was a sorrowful sight, and her smudged paint on her face looked like badly applied cosmetics. She was even paler than usual which was saying something. Sprawled on the table where they had placed her so carefully before, she looked worse than she had all day. She looked dead.

Chapter Twenty-three
Pickled Eggs, and a Very Ill Doll

"Sylvie, can you find some candles, please?" Ree was all business as she set about examining China. They were all used to the dark now, but it would hardly do for a thorough going-over.

Cullen cleared his throat. "By the way, I don't think we should risk flying this monstrosity at night. All in favor of hovering here till morning?"

"Aye, as long as you find something to eat in this contraption," Fritz agreed. "I'm starving."

"I'll whip something up for you!" Sylvie offered, brightly. She was still enamored with the soldier obviously. She went through the cupboards quickly, looking for candles, and slamming the doors shut when she found none.

"Make mine faeries on toast," Ree muttered. Then, louder, "Forget it, Sylvie. I'll find the candles, you...cook something." Her stomach rumbled in response. Those coconut meringues were a long time ago. She was absolutely famished. "But I don't know what you'll find. Dross forgets to eat when he's working in the laboratory, and he doesn't exactly keep a stocked kitchen."

"I'll find something!" Sylvie sang, and flitted off.

After searching through the cupboards that Sylvie had already been rummaging through, Ree finally found a supply of candles and flint in the bottom drawer of the apothecary shelves. She lit them all and surrounded China with them. It made for a gaudy and melancholic tableau, as if the doll were dressed and laid out in death while her companions said their goodbyes. Ree swallowed down the imagery and got to work. The shadows flickered over China's still face.

"Perhaps she is run down," Nikolai murmured, coming close to Ree and China.

"Of course she is. We all are." Ree smoothed her unruly hair back and blew the white strand out of her face. "I feel as though I could sleep for days and days."

"No, I mean literally run down. Maybe the key ...?"

"Oh. Yes. That's a brilliant suggestion, actually. Dross claimed it was strictly for show, but I'm not sure his word should be trusted. Do you know where it is?" Ree looked around the dimly lit room. She couldn't even recall the last time she saw it. When she mended China's ear the first time? Or before that?

"Here, in the box." Nikolai moved towards his former prison. He reached behind the box and pulled the key off its hook.

Ree gently rolled the doll over onto her stomach. Her head lolled to one side and her black, empty eyes stared into space. "All right, honey," she said in as bright a voice as she could muster, "Let's see what a little winding up will do, shall we?"

Nikolai handed her the heavy ornate key and Ree unbuttoned the back of China's fanciful dress. The slot in her back was small, but still horribly out of place in such smooth skin. Or porcelain. Ree wasn't sure what anything was made of any longer. Nikolai's prosthetics and metal attachments were more clear and bulky and obvious to the naked eye. China...China seemed at once all doll and all girl.

"I hate this part, I really do." Ree clenched her teeth as she inserted the key between China's shoulder blades. She twisted. With each spiral she watched China's limpid eyes, looking for some sort of change. She didn't realize she was holding her breath until she let it out in one big whoosh when China's body shifted and her hand reached out off the table towards Nikolai.

"You're safe, China, it's all right." Nikolai clasped her hand and kissed her fingers gently.

Ree felt a peculiar twinge in her stomach at the sight. She wondered what Nikolai's lips felt like. Would they be cold like metal often was? She shook off the silly notion and spoke to China.

"Hello there, Sleeping Beauty. How do you feel?"

China moved her head, just a fraction of an inch. "Feel...groggy. I think that's the word."

"It is. And you are. But no matter. Can you eat something? I mean," Ree blushed again, "Do you two eat? I mean, of course you do!" she laughed nervously. "You must. Don't you?"

Nikolai raised a brow at her. "I do."

"Perfect timing then!" Sylvie came swinging in through the butler's pantry doors. "Dinner is served!"

Dinner consisted of pickled eggs, stale toast (sans faery), more bad tea, a jar of strawberry jelly with bits of mold around the edges, dried pieces of chipped beef, and a container of sugar cookies that Ree was pretty sure Melisande had baked three weeks before and sent home with the inventor. Still, as hungry as they were, every bite was devoured. Everyone but China ate heartily – she had fallen asleep again. Halfway through the meal, Nikolai got up to put a blanket over her. Ree felt that funny feeling in her stomach again, but told herself it was the pickled eggs.

It was only three hours to sunrise, and with bellies full and danger averted – or at least, delayed – the motley crew of airship sailors fell asleep.

* * *

In the morning, Ree was the first to awake. Even Nikolai was sleeping deeply, and Fritz was snoring. Cullen looked cold, and no small wonder, he was so underfed or at least appeared to be. Sylvie had slept with her mechanical wings strapped to her back. Ree had to admit that it was nice of her to stay; she could have flown off to wherever it was her home was at any point last night. China looked the same, but she did appear to be breathing. At least, her chest rose and fell gently and there was a soft whirring sound coming from her chest cavity. It occurred to Ree that she hadn't heard the music box playing in a while. Could that be part of what was ailing her? A broken music box?

The sound of a bird calling drifted through the broken window. With a start, Ree remembered the owl. Had she left the poor thing upstairs last night, cold and hungry? She felt terrible. She'd never had a pet and wasn't used to the responsibility.

But when she reached the room at the top of the stairs, the owl was gone. A breeze wafted through the open window that she and Sylvie had gone out the night before, and Ree stood there for a moment, looking down. The bird must have flown off sometime during the night. She was happy he had mended his bent wing well enough to fly, but she would miss his soft feathers and his wise eyes. She went back downstairs.

Cullen was awake now, and he smiled at Ree as he stretched. She was getting quite used to him without the plague mask now, and she hoped he'd left it behind for good. Perhaps part of the reason he wore it was to disguise himself from his uncle, as he worked behind his back to bring his demise. Then again, who knew why boys did anything? Ree smiled back.

"Shall we figure out how to fly this ship back to Sea Level?" he asked. "We ate all the food we could find last night so I guess we won't be breaking our fast anytime soon."

"Well, if we bring an end to this nasty business, I'll buy us all a proper supper. You look like you could eat a horse."

He grinned. "I grew seven inches these past six months, that's why. My weight hasn't caught up with my height yet, that's all. Give me a bit. I'll fill out yet. You won't be able to keep your eyes off me, I 'spect." He puffed his skinny chest out.

Ree rolled her eyes. "That remains to be seen. Wake the others. It might be a bumpy flight. Don't tell them, but I honestly have no idea how to fly."

"You cannot be any worse than your godfather," he answered.

* * *

Cullen came to eat his words. Ree was good at keeping a steady course, but going up or down or turning gave her some trouble. Sylvie was airsick in less than an hour, Nikolai was tense, and Fritz was shouting directions at her.

"Shove off, Fritz!" Ree exploded. "I'm doing the best I can. It's not like driving one of your stupid mechanical horses."

"I just don't want to die like this, is all," he answered. "I'm young. I have prospects. Goals. You, on the other hand ..."

"Oh, shove off," she said again. "If you want to be helpful, tell me how in the world you managed to get here, on a floating ship?"

Fritz put on his best modest face, which made him look as though he had a toothache. "Met a friend of Sylvie. Girl named Gelsey. Lent me her wings."

"Well, that's highly irregular."

Fritz stared at her. "Let us hope so anyway."

They made it to Sea Level by the skin of their teeth, the workship no worse for wear. Ree could see the crossroads where they had first met the Russian tinkers. The sleigh was gone. She should have guessed as much. She wouldn't put it past the Angels to be the ones who'd stolen it. Remembering Georgie, Ree smiled. She would be happy to see that little urchin.

Ree still worried for China. She had woken up enough to change positions, claiming a stitch in her side. She wouldn't have minded opening up her compartments again, check on the music box mechanism among other things, but she felt suddenly inadequate. If she opened the heart compartment, what would she find? A beating heart, or a windup one? Would there be a brain, a real one, inside her porcelain head? Once upon a time, was China a real girl? Had Dross saved her the way he had saved

Nikolai? Or was she some sort of robotic hybrid made from scratch? Or was she simply a clockwork doll? Ree knew these questions had no good answers. She still couldn't bear the thought of Dross being diabolical enough to dig up graves and use the findings to build himself an undead army for profit. And yet. She was beginning to trust Cullen's fog gray eyes more and more in spite of herself.

"Where should we land?" Ree asked Nikolai, who had come into the butler's pantry.

"Or we could find something to use as an anchor and then we wouldn't have to land," he replied instead of answering her question.

"And what do we do once we go ashore?"

"And how do we find Herr Drosselmeier?"

"And are you ever going to make up with Cullen?"

"And are you ever going to mind your own business?"

They stared at one another, then Nikolai chuckled and Ree swatted him lightly on the metal arm. "How's the jaw, by the way?" she asked.

He clacked it up and down a few times. "Right as it will ever be."

"I do think he's sorry."

"Who?"

"You know who. Cullen."

"He's caused a lot of trouble for us. You don't have to stand up for him. He can fight his own battles."

"I believe Fritz said the same about you."

"So? I can."

168

"Said the man who needed my hair pin if he was ever going to talk or eat again."

"Said the girl who should be home practicing her pianoforte and accepting suitors."

"All right, all right! You win." Ree actually laughed. "Now stop distracting me. I need to land this thing without killing anyone, innocent bystanders notwithstanding." She bit her lower lip and began the descent.

Nikolai looked a little green and excused himself. "I'll just go warn – er, I mean, tell the others to prepare."

Landing turned out to be much easier than steering, and they made it to the ground with little to no injury. Sylvie had bumped against the table and bruised her shin, but Ree hardly thought that was her fault. They were in the clearing near the crossroads. When they exited the workship, Ree could spy the funny sign with all the divertissements listed. She carefully locked the door behind them even though she knew it was a little silly due to the broken window, and said a little prayer for China, still inside.

"Well?" she said, expectantly. "Anyone have a plan?"

"Miss Ree! Miss Ree!"

Ree whirled. It was Georgie, running to her from across the clearing. She had two other Angels with her. Georgie reached her and knocked her over with the force of her embrace.

"I thought you was dead fer sure!" she said, beaming from atop Ree. "When we saw the sky pirates were after you, we knew your numbers were up!"

"Them? Pshaw. They weren't anything to be worried about. But Georgie – let me up please, there's a good girl – have you seen the man I told you about yesterday? The one with the rat walking cane?"

Georgie stood and offered her hand to help Ree up. The others were standing around, awkwardly.

"Goodness, where are my manners?" Ree brushed off her trousers. "Georgie, Pork Chop, and uh-"

"Anastasia," said the new one. She stuck out a grubby hand to Ree and simultaneously took out the cigar she'd been smoking. "Nice to meetcha. It's been innerestin' since you all got here. Real innerestin'."

Sylvie they already knew, so Nikolai and Cullen introduced themselves. Fritz ignored the Angels and began walking towards market.

"Ree?" It was China. She had unlocked the door and was standing on wobbly legs on the porch. "You aren't leaving me, are you? Nikolai?"

Nikolai moved to her side, taking the four porch steps as one. "Are you well?" he asked, brushing her china hair as though it were capable of falling in her face or becoming mussed. It should have been a silly gesture to watch, but it wasn't. Her black eyes seemed dull. He peered at her, frowning.

"Can I come, too? I want to come, too."

Nikolai looked at Ree. She gave a little shrug. Worse come to worse, she supposed one of the boys could carry her if she got too weak. Likely, that would be the least of their problems anyway.

Chapter Twenty-four
Miss Ginger's School

"Look, I think we should stash the blue haired one at Miss Ginger's," said Georgie in a whisper.

They were nearly to town, but it was taking twice as long with China's odd shuffling. Fritz was so far ahead of them that they'd lost sight of his red head.

"She'll only hold us back," Georgie continued. "No offense to your friend."

"No, you're right." Ree rubbed her forehead. She felt a headache coming on.

"And it ain't that us Angels wouldn't follow you to our graves, miss, but uh, what exxackly is the plan here? I get the whole stop the madman scientist inventor fella, but how are we gonna accomplish it?"

"That's a really good question for a street urchin," Sylvie chimed in, joining them.

"Go away, elf." Georgie looked daggers.

"I'm not an elf. I'm a faery, and you know it."

"Your shoes say elf." Georgie stuck her tongue out at Sylvie.

"My shoes are going to be up your-"

"Look!" Ree interrupted. "We don't have time for squabbling. Georgie's right. We need a plan, and so far the only one I can come up with is destroying Dross' work. Namely, his laboratories. Especially the Sea Level one. Is that right, Cullen? You said he does his darkest work there?"

Cullen nodded. "I didn't see much to worry me about the workship, though I suppose we could destroy that one as well if need be. That might take the wind out of his sails, at least temporarily. But, Ree," he leaned in closer and began to talk in hushed tones, "I don't feel really good about letting these children be in danger." He looked over at Anastasia, who flicked her cigar his direction. "As rough and tumble as they may be," he paused to brush ash out of his hair and glared at the Angel, "I've caused enough deaths. I can't take any more on my head."

"You ain't the boss of us, mister." It was Pork Chop. He had the same blond curls as Georgie, but chubbier cheeks and a top hat that was several sizes too large for him. He stuck his thumbs in his suspenders and stared at Cullen stubbornly. "We go where we want to."

China stumbled, for the third time in as many minutes, and without a word, Nikolai stooped and swept her off her feet. They continued walking for a moment in silence. Ree wondered if there were something in the laboratory that would help the doll. Winding her with the key had helped somewhat, but she seemed to be breaking down.

"How will we destroy it?" Sylvie crinkled up her button nose.

"It's a scientific laboratory," Ree pointed out. "It's as flammable as they come, believe me."

"So, we...burn it down?"

"Precisely." Ree forced a note of cheer into her voice. In her heart, she was sick to be contemplating such a thing. All that work...all those supplies...experiments...books and recipes and notes...for someone with a chemist's soul, it was a hard pill to swallow. Still, it had to be done. There was no other way, short of bringing Dross to justice. And how would they accomplish that? He was the Justice of the Peace Up Top. How could this scraggly band of children and mechanicals win against him in a court of law? She could just picture it. The Angels would be all dressed up in their best dirty outfits, there'd be a doll on the witness stand, and Drosselmeier would sit there laughing at them all. He'd pat them on their heads and retire to the den for a nice glass of sherry with Dr. Stahlbaum.

"If we're to do that, tonight's the perfect night for it," Cullen said. They were nearing the town square now. Several people, the Chinese acrobats that Ree remembered among them, stared at the bunch. "Here." He nodded his head sideways, and they stepped into an alley. "Tonight's the Waltz. Everyone will be there, Drosselmeier included. Unless of course, he's too busy plotting revenge for me stealing his ship. But he's normally there, and I think we can count on it."

Ree sank down to the alley floor to rest her legs and think a minute.

"We can hide out at Miss Ginger's until sunset," he continued.

"It'll be a miracle if we get there with no one noticing," Ree said, rubbing her neck this time. The throbbing had moved down to her spine. She glanced over at China and Nikolai. They tended to draw attention.

"Ah, don't worry 'bout it. Everyone dresses strange and acts even stranger here at Sea Level, especially during the Waltz. They'll blend right in." Sylvie waved her hand.

"If you say so." Ree was doubtful. A large nutcracker man with metal parts and a life size china doll with blue hair were bound to stand out, even in the most eclectic of groups. Just because she was used to them and didn't see their peculiarities didn't mean others would be so kind. She remembered seeing them for the first time in the Grand Parlor. She'd nearly screamed. She flushed, remembering. How long ago that seemed. How much she'd changed.

"We've lost Fritz." She was thinking it, but accidentally spoke aloud.

"Want me to find him?" Of course it was Sylvie.

"If you like. Maybe it's best that we split up. We should know where Dross is before we make any kind of move anyway. You do know your way around best. You know where to find us if you need us. We'll be at Miss Ginger's School for GIFTED Young Criminals."

Sylvie saluted and disappeared. Ree was somewhat happy to see her go. It wasn't that she didn't like the faery – not exactly – but fewer people made her head feel less crowded. If Sylvie was with Fritz, she'd be safe enough, and that'd be two less people for Ree to feel responsible for. She wasn't sure how she became in charge of this strange and fantastical operation, only that she was. Probably it was when she offered to blow Dross' laboratories into smithereens. Or when she halted the pirate battle. Or when she entered the Grand Parlor at midnight and got involved with an army of rats.

"Shall we?" Cullen offered his arm, gentleman style. It didn't seem to come quite naturally, but Ree appreciated the gesture and took his elbow. Anastasia had elected herself as look-out and was peering around the corner of the darkened alley. Ree could see the puff of her cigar ring around her head like a halo. Sea Level had such odd children.

Nikolai lifted China up again, who was snuggled up against his chest, and when Anastasia gave a thumbs up sign, they left the safety of the alley.

"I feel as if I'm walking in a peculiar and outlandish parade," Ree whispered. "I only wish I had a parasol to twirl."

Cullen grinned. It made him look very boyish and lit up his gray eyes. "Don't feel self-conscious. Everyone is watching the acrobats at the moment, anyway." He nodded towards the Chinese troupe, who were in the midst of the square, presumably doing all sorts of feats and tricks. Ree couldn't quite see; there was quite a crowd gathered, and they were at the back.

"Well, thank goodness for distractions," she said, relieved.

"Sea Level is nothing if not full of distractions. It's a land of enchantment if I ever saw one."

Ree remembered the reindeer and the mermaids. "It's like a faery tale. But scarier."

"Faery tales are very scary," Cullen disagreed. "If they aren't, you've been reading the wrong ones. Whatever do they teach you Up Top anyway?"

Ree sighed. "Most of our stories have tea parties and beautiful dresses and other shallow things. So, nothing useful, I'm afraid. There's even a lack of faeries in our faery tales."

"I wouldn't go so far as to say you've learned nothing useful. You've been excellent so far in your adventuring. Not at all namby-pamby like I thought you'd be at first." He looked off in the distance as though distracted by something or other, but Ree knew he was simply and suddenly embarrassed.

"Well, thank you. You aren't at all what I expected at first either. What was that?" This was directed at Nikolai, who had been silent until now and made a sort of grunting sound.

"Nothing," he replied. "My jaw was sore."

Cullen glanced over at Ree again. "You mean, back when you thought I was an evil scoundrel?"

"Exactly. And by the way, do you expect to get your rats back?" Ree shuddered at the thought. She couldn't help it. She never wanted to see another rodent again; mechanical or otherwise.

"I probably should try at least. Don't want them running amok, wreaking havoc throughout town. I wonder where they are right now."

"Hopefully they've been eaten by mechanical raccoons," Ree answered, feeling cheered. "Look, I think we've arrived."

Miss Ginger's School for (Gifted) Young Criminals was housed in a very large brick building. It was overgrown with ivy and moss and had a huge, elaborate wrought iron fence around it. The windows were framed with black shutters that brought to mind huge eyelashes, and the windows themselves were decorated with artwork that seemed to have been done by the children, if the level of skill was any proof. All in all, though it was shabby, it was a homey looking place. Ree thought it must be rather nice to grow up there. Lack of morals and a complete disregard for the law notwithstanding, naturally.

Anastasia swung open the gate and beckoned the group to enter. Up the crumbling stairs they went and the Angel rapped quickly on the door in a sort of melodic pattern. Ree thought it sounded like *Lady Bird, Lady Bird, Fly Away Home.* A tiny window no bigger than Ree's palm opened at a child's eye level. An eyeball peered through.

"Who's it?"

"Ya know who it is, pea brain. Let us in!" Anastasia pushed on the door. It didn't budge.

"What's the password then if yous knows so much?"

"I'm gonna whoop you!"

"Nope. That ain't it."

"Let me in or you're faery on toast, ya are!"

"That was last week's password. One more try."

Anastasia kicked the door fiercely and then hopped around with her injured foot in her hand, howling.

"That ain't it either. Come back tomorrow." The little door slammed shut.

"Now what?" Ree grimaced at the sight of Anastasia, who was now cradling her foot and shouting words that she'd never even heard Dross use when his experiments went awry.

"Stop that caterwauling this moment," said a new voice.

Everyone whirled, and Anastasia ceased her hollers.

176

This could only be Miss Ginger, Ree realized. Taller than even Nikolai and Cullen, with a red dress so expansive that she took up more room on the porch than all the others combined, Miss Ginger's hair was the same shade as her dress and was set off with a purple parasol. The gloves matched the parasol, as did the extravagant eye cosmetics. Miss Ginger was the most splendid and exaggerated woman Ree had ever laid eyes on.

Especially since she was a man.

Chapter Twenty-five
Ginger

It was the full beard that tipped Ree off first, but even without it, Miss Ginger was clearly not a female, though Ree was very impressed with the deep and graceful dip of her curtsy and the way she rapped Anastasia smartly on the head with her parasol. Those were skills normally reserved for the fairest of the sexes, but obviously Miss Ginger was an exception to the rule. And then there was her bodice, which was nearly bursting at the seams, although Ree wasn't sure with what. Ree tried to look casual, but failed miserably. She settled for polite.

They made their introductions, though the proprietress of the school already knew full well who they were.

"I have eyes everywhere, my dears," she confessed. "Come along. It is tea time, and this is no time to be loitering on lawns. It's not good for business." She tapped on the tiny window in the door.

"Who's there?" The same eyeball (at least Ree assumed it was the same) peeked out.

"Your mother was a crawdad," Miss Ginger replied as she leaned down so as to be at the same level as the peephole.

The door swung open.

"That ain't even fair," Anastasia whined. "Ya can't just change the password when I'm gone like that."

"Hush," Miss Ginger admonished. She ushered everyone through the door, which was no small feat considering that she and her oversized skirt took up most of the space. Ree had to help pull aside the hoop in her dress as Nikolai and China squeezed through. It was quite heavy, that dress. Ree thought Miss Ginger must be more concerned with appearance and fashion than she was with comfort.

The inside of the school was welcoming in decoration and style, with piles of books left around, a roaring fireplace, and plenty of seating. There was a scent of baking bread in the air, and Ree's stomach growled. She was so very hungry. She hoped there would be plenty of refreshment with the promised tea.

There were Angels scrambling about, hiding in corners, and popping out from behind doorways. Anastasia wandered off, but Pork Chop and Georgie settled in by the fire, rubbing their chilled hands together and pulling off their boots to wriggle their toes. Ree decided to join them, and Nikolai laid China on the fainting couch, where she reclined, looking uncomfortable.

Miss Ginger clapped her hands. "Tea, please!" Her voice was loud and very commanding. Ree wasn't sure from whom she was demanding the said tea, but it appeared almost instantly on a wheeled cart, pushed by an Angel in a chef's hat.

"Thank you, Flip," said Miss Ginger. "That will be all."

Flip bowed low and scampered out of the room. Georgie got the honor of pouring the tea – hardly spilling at all - and for a while there was no sound except that of sipping and stirring and chewing the piled assortment of tiny cucumber and butter sandwiches. Ree ate five before she felt revived enough to try conversation.

"Miss Ginger," she began.

"Call me Ginger, dear. We're friends now."

"Thank you, Ginger. We do so appreciate you offering us solace and a roof over our heads in our time of need."

"You mean, aiding and abetting and harboring you as criminals?" Ginger dipped her sandwich in her tea and ate it all in one bite.

Ree blinked, and Cullen flushed. "Um, yes. I suppose I do."

Ginger laughed, a boisterous chuckle. Her whiskers, perfectly groomed and clipped into a V shaped goatee, shook with merriment. "You do plan to burn down half of Sea Level, don't you?"

Cullen choked on his cucumber, and Ree pounded on his back until his coughing subsided. "Not so! I mean, some of it. A little bit of it. Hardly very much at all really. One laboratory. Maybe two."

"Yes, I thought as much." Her eyes twinkled behind her heavy layer of purple shadow.

"How did you know?" Cullen asked.

"I told you, my dear. I have eyes everywhere. I hope you have safety precautions in place." Ginger reached for another sandwich. "Arson is an art form. It's not to be trifled with if one doesn't know precisely what one is doing."

"Yes ..." Cullen seemed to want to say more, but drifted off. He was at a loss for words.

"Which is why I suggest that you take my graduates from my advanced level Incineration Arts Course. They would be invaluable to you and your plan."

"Graduates? Advanced Level? Incineration Arts?" Cullen repeated.

"Yes, dear. Please don't mimic; it's childish."

"Yes, ma'am. Miss Ginger. Ginger."

Ree decided to take over the course of the conversation. "We'd rather not be responsible for the children, you see. Their safety is, of course, our utmost priority."

Ginger chuckled again. "My dear, they would be the ones keeping you safe, not the other way around. I assure you, they are the best in the country.

And I hesitate to say this, but you don't seem to have much experience in the wayward arts."

"You mean, in a life of crime?" Ree pursed her lips. "No, at least not until recently. But we do have passion and motivation on our side. That has to count for something, don't you think?"

Ginger shook her head, her massive pile of red curls barely even wobbling. They seemed to be shellacked into place, or perhaps it was simply a wig.

"No, no. That's where you're wrong. Passion is a very bad emotion when you have a job to do," she said.

Georgie agreed. "It clouds your vision," she piped up. "Distracts you."

"Of course, your brother, General Stahlbaum, would disagree with me. His army of women have been handpicked just for their passion. And he does have a point in selecting such. They fight with fervor and emotion not typical in the male sex. Myself excluded, naturally." Another good natured chuckle that shook her beard. "I have limitless depths of passion and emotion. It's what led me into the theater actually. Perhaps you saw me in the traveling Kabuki Theater last summer? No? A pity. It was my finest work, or at least it was until I saw that Miss Ginger's here was for sale. The little tykes needed a mother, you know. Now that was a role I could sink my teeth into. Every child deserves a mother. So, naturally here I am."

There were so many questions to that paragraph of Ginger's that Ree didn't know where to start.

"However do you know my brother?" Then she answered herself. "Yes, I know. Eyes everywhere. Anyway, as we were saying." She turned to face Georgie. "Let me guess, you're one of the graduates, aren't you?"

The Angel puffed out her chest and sat up taller. "Yes, indeedy. Full marks and valedictorian, to boot."

"Why am I not surprised?" Ree hid her sigh behind another sandwich.

* * *

The Waltz was held strictly during the night time hours, beginning at the stroke of midnight (Ree remembered the last time she heard a clock strike midnight and her stomach began to ache) and evidently lasted until Winter left, at which point everyone felt the need to leave as well. Winter must be a lot like the Silberhaus family Up Top, Ree assumed. Parties were nothing without Sir and Lady Silberhaus and once they went home everyone else drifted away too.

The guests at the School made themselves at home, at Ginger's request. Once they had gone through all the refreshments, they were shown to the Boy and Girl Dormitories for – as Ginger referred to it – a bit of a siesta. Though Ree was exhausted after a fitful night's sleep in the airship, where her dreams had been peppered with sky pirates and bloody owls, she knew she would not be able to sleep or even relax without attending to China. She tiptoed back to the little room with the fireplace.

China, of course, was where Nikolai had lain her, curled up like a napping child. And Nikolai was there, too. Ree felt a pang of embarrassment that he had beaten her to China. He was likely just as tired as she. He looked up as she entered.

"She's worse. I can't even tell if she's alive," he said, flatly.

Ree was concerned for both of them. "How are you?" she asked. After all, Nikolai was made of the same stuff and by the same hands that China was for all they knew. What if he began to wind down, to die, to stumble and stammer and fall? She didn't think she could stand it.

"I'll be fine. It's just," he paused, choosing his words, "It's just China is my connection to my past somehow. I don't want to lose her. She's the closest thing to a sister I have. We share a history in a way, even if it's rather recent. Do you understand?"

Like a sister. The odd feeling in her stomach left as quickly as it had arrived. The pickled eggs had finally left her system. Ree nodded. She did understand. If she were to lose Fritz or Louise she would feel the same way.

182

They had the same memories, the same history, the same legacy, even if they drove one another crackers. It would be like a part of her died too. She bit her lip. "I'll do what I can. I think it's best that I take a look in some of her compartments. Have you heard her music lately at all?"

Nikolai frowned. "No, it's been a while now that you mention it. Perhaps that addition was damaged?"

Ree laid her hands on the smooth china surface of China's shoulder. If Dross had sewn human parts into this porcelain shell, he had done quite a job, cracks and holes notwithstanding. "It seems as though the music had come from her chest cavity. Where her heart," she stumbled over wording, "Where her heart is." Was? Should be? "I wish I had my toolbox. Or Georgie's Magnocle. Golly, I think I lost those at the same time. I shouldn't be trusted with anything."

Nikolai looked amused. "Remind me not to let you operate on me then."

The light hearted comment had a good effect on Ree's mood and confidence. She smiled and leaned over China. "Here goes," she whispered. First she checked the compartments she had already opened before. They looked the same but they weren't operating like clockwork the way they had been before. The way they should be. She pried open the chest compartment, stifling down the feeling of wooziness it brought on. She didn't realize she was holding her breath until it came out in a whoosh. She put her hand inside and drew out the contents. Not a beating heart, no. Heart shaped, yes, but a gold pocket watch. Like her own Clock Bob she wore on her skirt, but more elaborate and not round, and instead of striking the hours, it hummed a song. Now that it had left China's body, the sound was more distinct, though still faint. The music sounded scratched and was skipping its melody. It groaned to a total halt as Ree held it in her hands.

Nikolai wasn't staring at the heart the way she was. He was staring at China, and he was frowning as he spoke. "Wake up, China. Come on, wake up. Don't leave us!"

"Nikolai?" Ree said in a whisper. "Look."

Where the heart had exited, there was an insignia signed into the porcelain that said:

Made in China. #15

Chapter Twenty-six
Preparing for...Whatever

Ree placed the heart back inside her patient, and for a moment, she and Nikolai simply sat there. Staring into space. Not talking. Not discussing the implications of their discovery. China wasn't...real. Not alive. Not dead either. Just a broken toy. A toy who only had a name because of where she was made. Some factory in China. #15 in a line of dolls. No wonder China had said she would be turning sixteen. It was appallingly sad.

The disappointment Ree felt was heavy in her chest. She felt like crying, though she wasn't even sure why. Would she have been happier to find human anatomy? But that would mean that China was an unnatural creation, possibly made from cadavers. Wouldn't that be worse? Ree rubbed her forehead. She hardly knew anymore.

And Nikolai? Was he simply an automaton as well? But no. She had looked into his beautiful eyes, had heard his heart beating when he held her close to his chest. And he had memories. Memories of before Drosselmeier.

"He did save you," she said, weakly.

Nikolai turned his gaze towards her. "I know," he said. "That's the only reason I haven't killed him yet."

"So, Cullen was right?"

He scowled, and his iron jaw made a clicking sound. He didn't reply.

Ree didn't push the subject.

* * *

The siesta was over for the Angels, and just in time too, because Fritz and Sylvie appeared at the door of the School. Nikolai was in no mood for light conversation, or even heavy plotting, and he exited the room when they entered. Ree let him go.

"I've likely lost my position by now," Fritz growled at his sister, but he gave her a good natured shove on the shoulder that nearly sent her sprawling. She knew him well enough to know he wasn't truly angry. Also he was wearing his hat backwards, which made it practically impossible to glare at him.

Sylvie on the other hand, looked ill tempered. Her hair was a mess and now that Ree bothered to look, she could see the tears in her skirt that had been made when she crashed through the window in the airship. She looked as though she hadn't slept in days and if her narrowed eyes were any indication, her smitten self had gotten over Fritz. Even her glitter seemed less sparkly.

"Next time you need someone fetching your brother, you can do it yourself," she sputtered, collapsing into a chair, her skirts poofing around her like a giant mushroom. She looked like a cranky child wearing her mother's dress. She kicked off her elf shoes and glared at Ree. "Stupid man was at the Scurvy Dog's Floating Saloon the whole time."

Fritz opened his mouth as if to defend himself, but all that came out was a loud belch.

"Oh, not the cider?" Ree grimaced. That did explain the hat.

Sylvie threw her hands up. "I tried to tell him, the blithering idiot. The stuff down here is stronger than you rich folk's batches. We water it down when we export it Up Top, you know."

Ree didn't know and figured her father would be quite interested in that bit of knowledge. He wouldn't take kindly to being taken in by faeries and pirates and having his liquor diluted. "Well, wonderful. Are you going to be of any use to us at all in this condition, Fritz?"

He belched again and bowed. "At your service, kiddos. I can hold my cider well enough!" Then he promptly fell over backwards and began to snore.

Ree sighed. "Fine. We don't need him anyway." She did a quick head count. "We are already too conspicuous as it is."

Sylvie continued to glare at anyone in her sight lines. "I'll make it easier on you. Count me out. I need a bath and some grub. I've done enough good deeds for you people."

"Well, I do appreciate it," Ree said, honestly. She may not particularly like the faery all that much, but she had come in handy.

"See you around, Updweller," Sylvie answered. She stood and shook out her skirts. On her way out the door, she gave Georgie a pinch and she, in turn, stuck out her tongue.

"Now, child," Ginger announced as she herself entered the crowded parlor, "We must do something about your clothing. Why is there a snoring man on my floor?" She stopped and frowned down at Fritz.

"I'm so sorry," Ree hastened to explain. "I'm happy to pull him out by his boots into the snow if you prefer."

"That's not necessary." Ginger stepped over the soldier, hiking up her giant skirt, exposing extremely large feet in laced up boots.

"No, really. I don't mind."

"Ah. This must be the brother. I thought he looked familiar. I believe I've seen him at the market before?"

"Yes, I suppose you have. He's supposed to be defending and guarding me." Ree rolled her eyes. "But at the moment, he's a bit intoxicated."

"Cider?" Ginger pursed her red, red lips.

"Indeed."

She sighed. "I've been after those Scurvy Dog employees to stop using the bewitched apples. They don't listen. They're worse than the Angels. Besides, it has a distinct aftertaste of sprite feet."

Bewitched apples? Sprites? Ree inwardly sighed. Would there ever be an end to the strangeness at Sea Level? Next she'd be hearing of ghosts and ghouls, or perhaps dragons and unicorns. "What's wrong with my clothes?" She changed the subject, glancing down at her trousers, Clock Bob, blouse, and vest. Her hair was a disheveled mess and she wished for her hat. Somewhere or other she'd even lost her cloak. *Hell's bells, at this rate I will be nearly nude by the time I return home.* She began to giggle, but turned it into a polite cough. No need to start again with her hysterical laughing in times of stress.

"There's nothing wrong with them exactly," Ginger drawled. Her tone said otherwise. "Although I don't know why you'd choose pants over a dress. Dresses really allow for more airflow. I'm quite fond of them myself. Anyway, if you are to attend the Waltz, you must have something more suitable than men's clothing. It's very disconcerting to the eye, my dear."

"The Waltz?" Ree didn't hide her surprise. "I'm not attending the Waltz! I'm burning things down, remember? Explosions? Boom? I don't even like to waltz!" It was true. Dressing up and being social was exhausting. She'd much rather concoct potions or do sums or mix up chemicals in the name of science.

Cullen chuckled softly over from the corner, where he had appeared rather suddenly. He was always appearing places, Ree realized. Fireplaces, airships, corners. He was ridiculously light on his feet. She supposed that would come in handy, for both waltzing and sneaking. In general though, it was bothersome. "I like Ree in trousers for what it's worth."

"Yes, well, my dear, I'm afraid you haven't thought that through precisely." Ginger sat down and her enormous skirt billowed in the breeze her body leant it. She was addressing Ree. "The only way to get to your godfather's laboratory is through the Ballroom. Especially at night. You really shouldn't be flying the airship at night; it isn't safe. And besides, it's awfully noticeable. I do think your godfather would notice."

"He probably has changed all the locks by now anyway." Ree chewed on a fingernail. "I don't think stealing it this time would be as easy as the first."

"That's always the way of it," Ginger agreed. "The Ballroom is a dirigible as well and it will take you right by his laboratory in the swamp. You can get off without too much noticeability, I believe."

"A swamp? A floating Ballroom?" Ree grimaced. Would it be too much to hope for a nice, city laboratory? Apparently so. "And then what? How do get back on the Ballroom after we've...gone boom?"

"My dear, I cannot solve all your problems. What kind of a teacher would I be? I'm sure if you apply yourself, you will find a solution. Now. What size are you?" She clapped her hands loudly. "Anastasia! Take Miss Ree upstairs to the fitting rooms. Pork Chop, please escort Nikolai – wherever has he taken himself off to? – and Mr. Souris upstairs as well. And the doll? Shall I put together a wardrobe for her?" Ginger glanced over at China, who was where Ree had left her.

"China is ..." Ree didn't know what to say. "China's heart is broken. I'm not sure I can repair her. If I had my toolbox ..."

Ginger, to her credit, looked quite crestfallen. "Oh my dear, I am sorry. She seemed a lovely girl."

Ree smiled at her choice of words. Not a toy, a girl. China would have liked that. "So no, she isn't coming with us. But she'd like some pink tights if you have some, please."

*　*　*

If Ree was shocked at how well Nikolai and Cullen cleaned up, she managed to control her facial expressions admirably. She barely gaped at all at the sight of Cullen in a fashionable dark tail coat and trousers, with a double breasted vest in a luxurious looking gray brocade that brought out his eyes, and a brand new top hat. He was fiddling with an intricate tie at his throat.

"Miss Ginger called it an Ascot," he whispered to Ree. "But I think it's an instrument of torture. I can feel myself being throttled little by little." He whistled. "You look pretty good in that...that gown getup. I take it back about the trousers."

Ree ignored the compliment, not that she didn't appreciate it. It was more that she felt uncomfortable. "I don't feel the slightest bit sorry for you and your Ascot. Which sounds like an expensive Canine Robotic Companion now that I say it aloud. Anyway, I'm wearing a corset of removable whale bones. So that's not exactly made for comfort either."

"Removable?" Cullen looked intrigued, but also a bit embarrassed. Probably due to speaking of removing a lady's corset. He colored as he loosened his tie.

Ree smiled. "They double duty as weapons. I'm starting to love Ginger." She twirled a bit in her gown. It was gold with a copper colored outer corset. Her gloves were brown with gold braid, and though she still missed her hat, she had to admit that the headpiece Ginger had picked out for her set off her bright hair a little better. The miniature top hat was attached by way of a stretchable headband that Ginger had assured her would make an excellent slingshot should the need for one arise. And inside the hat were the two vials Ree needed to set the fire that would destroy Dross' lab.

Nikolai made that noise with his jaw that Ree was beginning to learn meant he had something to say but wasn't sure how to say it. She smiled at him. "You look quite dashing."

He did. His outfit was similar to Cullen's but in shades of crimson and bronze. He even had been given a walking stick of such beauty that Ree gawked. It made Dross' look small and cheap. Nikolai smiled widely and pulled it apart. Inside the stick was a gleaming sword.

Cullen glared. "All my clothes are clothes! Why don't I have anything that is secretly a weapon?"

"Don't pout," said Ginger as she stepped back and surveyed her living masterpieces. "I abhor pouting. And if it makes you feel any better, dear boy, your friend's sword came from the theater. It has a dulled edge. Strictly for fashion. It couldn't even slice a tomato."

Nikolai looked disappointed, but Cullen looked cheered. "Well, brother," he said, clapping Nikolai on the back, "If the bad guys come after us, you can Fashion Stick them instead of running them through."

"I'm not your brother," Nikolai replied through gritted teeth. "Shove off."

"Nope." Cullen grinned.

"That's enough, gentlemen," Ginger admonished. "This is no time for squabbles. Angels, are you ready? Did you forge those invitations like I asked?"

"Yes, Miss G!" Pork Chop stood at attention. He had slicked his hair back with some sort of greasy pomade that Ree could smell from across the room, but other than that, he had done little to improve his appearance.

Georgie too, looked as though she had perhaps spit upon her hands and given her face a once over, but her clothes and mop of curls were untouched. Still, they looked pleased as punch and proud as peacocks as Ginger inspected them.

"Did you brush your teeth?"

They nodded as one.

"Wash your hands?"

More nodding, but with hands slyly placed behinds their backs.

"Did you finish your homework? I believe you had two pages of lessons to catch up on due to your adventuring with our guests yesterday." She raised her red eyebrows at them.

They nodded even more fervently.

"Did you use the washroom?"

They sighed and Pork Chop flushed a bright red. "Yes, Miss Ginger! May we go now? We already summoned the Air Gondola and you know how they don't like to be kept waiting!"

"One more thing. Did you fetch the toolbox for Miss Ree?"

Ree inhaled in surprise. Pork Chop reached behind a sofa. "Yup!"

"Oh, thank you so much!" Ree accepted her beloved box and immediately began rifling through it. She pulled open compartment after hidey hole after cubby, looking for something - anything - to replace China's broken heart. She was in such a hurry that gears and gadgets and pins and tiny tools began falling to the ground.

"Let me, my dear. I have some mechanical knowledge myself, you know. There's not a lot of money in acting and mothering, so I often take odd jobs on the side. I'll tinker a bit while you're adventuring, and if luck is with us, China will be as good as new by morning. In fact, if she is looking for a home, she's welcome to stay. I could use another set of eyes for these urchins, not to mention a model for my fashion design business." Ginger reached out for the toolbox, and Ree gratefully surrendered it. "Be off with you, children. I do wish you the best of luck. Please stay close to the Angels. I fear for your safety. And have them back by daybreak, please. We have a field trip tomorrow to the Lock and Key Factory. Wouldn't want them to fall behind on their studies."

"Must be a class on breaking and entering," Cullen whispered to Ree.

"Orphans have all the luck," she replied, wistfully.

192

Chapter Twenty-seven
The Floating Ballroom

Ree had never been in an Air Gondola before and was pleased with the prospect. Or rather, she would have been had she not been so distracted and nervous with what they were about to do.

"How exactly are we going to blend in? And what if I run smack into my godfather? Does he know how much we know? And how do we know when to get off the Ballroom?" She bit her fingernails down to the quick and started in on the cuticles.

"One thing at a time," Nikolai answered. "Be calm."

"Easy for you to say," she muttered. She lifted up her skirts in her hands and was the last to step on board the Air Gondola. It was both beautiful and expensive looking, painted in jeweled, multi-colored hues with curlicues of silver and gold. At the head of it was a small, friendly looking dragon. There was a metal box with a roll of parchment paper and a fancy looking set of typewriter keys beneath that. Ree watched, fascinated, as Georgie punched in their destination on the keys.

"How'd ya spell Ballroom?" she asked, fingers poised over the ornate buttons.

Ree obliged and told her. "How does it know?" She was impressed with the device.

"It's called the Gondolier, Miss Ree. It's real smart."

"Must be like my pigeon." Ree smiled. "I hope it made it home to Mama."

"What did you tell her anyway?" Cullen asked, curious. "I've gone to Sea Level to conduct dangerous and unladylike behaviors. Be home by supper?"

Ree grimaced and sat down on one of the three seating areas. "No, more like, Helping Dross with project. I'm sure to be home in time for tea. Next Monday."

Cullen looked awed. "Good on you. I hope she lets you live whenever you do return."

"If I do return." Ree clenched her shaking hands in each other and willed herself to stop trembling. There was no reason to panic. It was a little waltzing, a little small talk, a little revenge, a little arson. Nothing to panic about at all. A child could do it. She looked around at her companions. Some of them were children, and she was barely past that stage herself. "We're doomed," she murmured.

Nikolai sat down and put his hand on her clenched ones. It was heavy – no surprise seeing as how it was his metal one. Still, it was comforting. She smiled brightly at him, and the Air Gondola left the School grounds with a lurch.

It was night but there was a moon, and there was also a fantastical looking floating lantern lamppost that was attached to the dragon head. Both guided them as they flew smoothly above the streets of Sea Level. Ree found herself calming down quite sufficiently and her heart went back to a steady rhythm. That reminded her of China; China and her clockwork heart. Now she was not only calm, she was dead steady. China deserved better than a fidgety, nervous schoolgirl who was bound to fail. Ree wouldn't fail. She was resolved now, and she unclenched her hands and sat up straighter.

A rush of wind blew her hair across her face and something else brushed against it, too. Something warm and heavy that landed with a thump in her lamp. Ree looked down in alarm. It was the owl.

"Why hello there, funny thing!" She laughed, and righted it. For what had a reputation to be a graceful bird, it had somehow landed upside down. Its wise yellow eyes looked up at her trustingly. "I was worried about you. You disappeared on me." She smoothed its ruffled feathers affectionately.

Nikolai looked over and chuckled. It was a grinding sort of noise, like China's tinkling laughter, only less like a music box and more like the sound of gears grinding against one another. Ree had a brief moment of panic. What if Nikolai turned out to be less than human as well? She didn't think she could bear it. But how do you ask politely to look inside one's cranium in order to check for a brain? Or casually suggest opening up his chest to take a peek at what should be a beating heart?

"What is with you and that bird?" Cullen asked. "He probably has mange, you know."

"I've never had a pet, and he likes me. And he doesn't have mange." She buried her nose in the owl's soft feathers. "Don't listen to him, sweet heart," she told the owl. "You need a name."

"How about Archibald?" suggested Georgie.

"Or Bacon?" That was Pork Chop's idea. Ree figured he liked names in his own moniker's genre. There was a distinct Pig theme happening. Also, she was pretty sure the hair grease he had used to slick back his mane was sausage scented. Or sausage grease.

"You could call him Mangy." Cullen snorted.

"Hush, you." Ree glared at him. The Air Gondola paused at an intersection and allowed a Steam Phaeton to go by. It was full of what appeared to be party goers. They waved cheerfully at the crew in the Gondola. Ree waved back and her nervous feeling returned to the pit of her stomach. Naming the owl took a backseat to what they were about to do.

A few minutes passed in silence, and then they arrived.

* * *

The Ballroom was immense and just as cobbled together as Drosselmeier's workship, only much more expensive and less haphazard. The workship appeared as a giant, bizarre accident, while the Ballroom was obviously designed to be a work of art. It floated along at a slow enough speed that the people and Gondolas could easily pull up alongside and enter. It was a beautiful creation to be sure. Round spheres of rooms glowed from within, bathing everything in warm and comforting radiance. There were at least ten of the round rooms and Ree thought it rather fanciful. Ball shaped rooms for a Ballroom. Quite clever really. Several of the Balls had spindly looking chimneys that puffed steam out, and brought to mind jaunty witch's hats, or sorcerer's caps. There was a very large and some-what frightening staircase that was attached to the Ballroom but ended in the sky. That seemed to be where everyone entered and exited. The stair-case was like a bridge. One could peer beneath the stairs and see only stars. There was excited chatter everywhere, and Ree watched as the members of another Air Gondola pulled alongside the stairs, and clam-bered aboard. It was a bit ungraceful, but in their defense it wasn't easy to make a moving dismount such as this one. Louise would have been ap-palled but determined to master it, Ree just knew. The women were gaudy but pretty, in dresses of fantastic pinks and purples, and the men were just as whimsical in their garments. Brightly patterned scarves and complicated Ascots seemed to be the theme. Ginger obviously had been right. Ree smoothed down the gold dress as she stood.

"All right, Sir Owl," she said. She carefully placed him on her shoulder. "Behave."

He gave an agreeable and serious sort of hoot in response.

"Shall we?" Cullen offered his elbow, but Nikolai had already taken the other at that precise moment. Both glared at one another, with Ree and the owl in between.

She squeezed both her elbows close to her sides, effectively trapping them both, and stepped lively. Georgie and Pork Chop did an elaborate pantomime, with Pork Chop bowing and offering her his grubby arm, while Georgie pretended to nearly faint with feminine excitement before taking it. They both scampered up the staircase with no trouble at all. *Youth*, thought Ree, wondering where her own seemed to be. She felt rather old suddenly, and overly careful with each and every footfall.

There were robotic Footmen lined up on the bottom stair, dressed in bright uniforms of midnight blue with gold fringe and buttons and large hats that sat low on their eyes. One of them bowed and took charge of the Air Gondola, parking it securely in a floating dock beneath one of the ball shaped rooms. Ree was relieved. Who knew at what point they might need a quick exit, and the Gondola would be perfect for a quick escape.

They climbed the stairs and entered the Waltz. Ree's first impression was that old Mrs. Croftenspot would have fit right in, with her silly crow hat and her extravagant dress. Everyone was overdressed and that in turn made Ree feel underdressed. The owl on her shoulder, though, turned things up a notch, she thought. It looked like part of her costume. She kept both boys at her side, but Georgie and Pork Chop had already been assimilated into the crowd. She hoped against hope that the Angels knew what they were doing. They had assured her that they often attended the Waltz, either as servants for the guests or simply as uninvited hooligans. No one payed them any mind; Sea Level was used to Angels.

"Probably off acquiring snacks," she said aloud, though neither Nikolai nor Cullen seemed concerned.

Cullen did look nervous; his face was pinched and he was a bit sweaty. He coughed and then apologized for coughing. Nikolai looked fierce. He had looked that way since China's death, Ree recognized. He stood stiffly, his metal parts almost appearing softer than his flesh parts. Ree bit her lip.

A robotic butler (a Hoffman IV, complete with a burgundy tinted pompadour and a well done Grecian nose) offered to take their cloaks, and accepted their invitations. Ree held her breath as she thought of the forgeries (done by Anastasia, who was apparently the leader in that particular class), but the butler saw nothing amiss with his mechanical eyes. He bowed low and moved to the next guest, his gears whirring pleasantly. Ree felt a pang of loss and found herself missing Hoffman.

People were mingling and talking and dancing. There seemed to be no choreography to this party, and the guests moved and drifted from room to room in groups and bunches. Ree thought she recognized the disgusting taxidermist from Sea Level, and his freshly pressed and laundered clothes did nothing to improve his appearance. She also noticed the man who had sold her the coconut meringue and she gave a quick little wave his way. She didn't see Drosselmeier anywhere though, and that gave her pause. If he wasn't here, he was likely at his laboratory, and she had no real desire or inclination to blow him to smithereens along with his supplies. It would be so much easier if he was here. *This is a huge building, Marie Stahlbaum. No reason to panic. Stop panicking immediately.*

The owl began to preen on her shoulder and his claws wiggled uncomfortably into Ree's shoulder now that the cloak wasn't there to give its padding. "Hold still," she said in a strict voice.

"Shall we explore?" Cullen asked. "Ginger said it would be at least an hour float to the swamp."

She had explained that the Waltz had its course down to a science. Its route took the party goers on a full circle tour of Sea Level, including a dessert detour for "Bon-Bons at the Sea", a new and very popular addition to the Waltz. The entire thing took precisely six hours, and came to a halt at six in the morning, just in time for lazy guests to get a good afternoon's sleep. Once on, it would be difficult to get off before the appropriate time, but not impossible.

"There's a train," Ginger had told them, "It doesn't run any longer, not since the advancement of the airships and the availability of the Air Gondolas and such, but it will be directly beneath the Ballroom on the Old Seaside Highway as it docks for dessert. That will be your best chance to get off, unnoticed. If it's docked low enough, you should be able to drop right onto the train and you can walk right on top of it until you reach the cemetery."

"Why ever do we wish to go to a cemetery?" Ree had been confused. "In the middle of the night, no less?"

"Because it's by the swamp, of course." Ginger had frowned. Her goatee had positively dripped with disapproval. "Whatever do they teach you Up Top, dear? No Thievery Arts, no Lock Picking, and now no Geography either? How frightful for you."

Now, Ree felt her stomach ache return, as she contemplated the access of a cemetery so near Dross' work. Cullen had said Dross had taught him – or forced him – to dig graves. She had been hoping he'd been exaggerating that part of the story. Now she feared the worst.

"You'll know when we're close, of course?" Ree whispered to Cullen, ignoring his suggestion of exploration. "I don't want to miss our chance."

"Don't worry." His voice was brighter than he likely felt. He smiled at Ree warmly. Nikolai continued to glower.

"Well, we can't just stand here and look awkward." Ree took a deep breath and exhaled it. A woman in a huge fur coat that seemed to be made of a tiger moved past her, brushing against all of them. The owl hooted its reproach and spread its wings, knocking Ree's ear. "Come along. We should find the Angels and if we locate some refreshments along the way, I suppose it wouldn't be a sin to try them. After all," and she gave a mischievous grin at the owl on her shoulder, "We were invited."

Chapter Twenty-eight
The Waltz

They accomplished both – finding the Angels and finding refreshments – in one fell swoop. Georgie and Pork Chop were halfway through plates of decadent foods and they beamed at Ree, their teeth full of sticky caramels. Georgie waved a peppermint stick at them.

"Try these! They're to die for, miss." She snapped off half of hers and flourished it towards them.

"Where are all the vegetables?" Ree put on her best stern and older voice, but all she got in return was a tongue from Georgie and a snort from Pork Chop.

"Life's too short for spinach, miss. That's what I always say," Pork Chop said, wisely, choosing another Cinnamon Cream.

Cullen and Nikolai were no help either; both were fixing plates of their own. Ree didn't feel the slightest bit like eating – her nerves were a mess of emotions in her stomach – but she forced herself to a small plate. Goodness knew, tonight would be a long one, and she didn't fancy a nighttime picnic in the cemetery if she could help it. *Please pass the butter and jam, Nikolai, and mind the grave dust, would you?*

"Let's try the Coffee and Chocolate Station!" Georgie pulled on Ree's arm, upsetting the owl. It squawked and Ree fed it a bit of bread and honey to appease it. "It has whipped cream and everything!"

"Doesn't Miss Ginger feed you?" Ree followed obediently.

"Only stuff's good fer us. Nothing innerestin'. I'm sick to death of cucumber sammies."

A lady who seemed to be someone of note swept by with an entourage of young men. Ree watched as she impressed everyone without even trying.

She was the kind of woman whom everyone wanted to be with, or be, in general. She wore a floor-length ball gown of green that had somehow been fashioned to look like a lily. Now that Ree noticed, a lot of the gowns had some sort of flower theme. There were shades of purple with trims of green that resembled pansies and vibrant red dresses whose many layers of skirts looked like rose petals. But she would bet no one else had a corset of removable whale bone daggers. Ree felt a little smug, even if her gold gown was on the simple side and didn't bear a resemblance to anything you'd find in a garden.

The Coffee and Chocolate Station was manned by an Arabian fellow in a turban and a surprising lack of a shirt. Ree wasn't sure where to focus her eyes. Everyone Up Top was fully clothed in public, no exceptions. Then again, life Up Top was beginning to feel very far away. She accepted a very strong and very small cup of coffee that smelled delicious, and Georgie and Pork Chop each chose huge mugs of hot chocolate with dollops of whipped cream. She dropped a curtsy to the Arabian man, still not quite sure where to look, which made her curtsy awkward and not nearly as low as society (or Mama) would have liked. Together, Ree and the Angels moved on.

The Waltz in the Ballroom was similar to the market; only not quite so dangerous and with a lack of what Louise would call 'the riffraff.' Everyone in the Ballroom (Angels aside) was dressed impeccably and looked extremely rich, though anyone with real money could tell it was a bit of a sham. Some of the trim on the dresses were frayed, and up close Ree could see that the men's outfits were slightly cobbled together, with sleeves that were either too long or too short, and one man had mismatched shoes. Still though, it seemed you had to be at least somewhat important in Sea Level society to be here, and Ree wondered how long it would be before they were found out. She had a feeling being a Stahlbaum meant next to nothing here.

And what if they wandered right into the person who had commissioned Drosselmeier to purchase Nikolai? Ree gulped as she sipped her coffee and the brew scalded her throat. She hadn't thought that bit through. She looked around for Nikolai, all the while acting like she wasn't.

There was Cullen, still munching his refreshments (well, he had grown six inches, she remembered. That much growing was apt to build up quite the appetite). He popped a stuffed mushroom in his mouth and winked at Ree. She frowned in return. Where was Nikolai?

Just then, a hand shot out from behind a Chinese silk screen divider. Ree swallowed a scream and the owl dug its talons into her shoulder as it hung on for dear life. The hand reached around her waist and yanked her behind the screen.

She fell right into Nikolai's arms. "Stop doing that!" she hissed, righting herself.

"What? I've never pulled you behind a screen before."

"Close enough you have! Hell's bells, you nearly scared me to death. Owch, get down, birdy." Ree carefully tried to pry the owl's nails off her pink and scratched shoulder.

"Well, I was trying to get your attention from back here but you seemed lost in thought. So I went with brute force." Nikolai's eyes sparkled.

Ree was glad to see the old Nikolai back, but she still glared at him. "A simple 'psst!' would have done the trick. Now, what's so important?"

"I just got a serious once over and a scanning from that robotic butler, that's what. I think he's onto us."

"Drat. I thought our invitations convinced him." She grimaced.

"Well, the invitations might have, but whoever gives them out certainly knows there weren't any put aside for Miss Ginger's School for Thieves."

"*Gifted* Criminals." Ree drummed her fingers on her corset thoughtfully. "So you're saying the host is suspicious and put the butler on our scent?"

"Not host. Hostess."

"Oh?"

202

"Didn't you know? This is Winter's Ballroom and her Waltz," Nikolai explained.

"Oh yes, I think Faith – or was it Hope? – may have mentioned something about Winter and the Waltz in the same breath. I didn't realize she was our hostess here however."

"Well, try not to look surprised. We're posing as invited guests, remember?" Nikolai looked as uneasy as Ree felt.

"Which one is Winter?" Ree peered out from behind the screen. The owl hopped back up on her shoulder as if he wanted to see too. "The one in the green dress?"

"Her? No, that's not her. The one in white."

"Mm, that makes more sense. White." Ree scanned the crowd eagerly. Winter had seemed like such a faery tale character, and she was quite curious to meet her, or to see her at least from a safe enough distance that she wouldn't be chastised for crashing a party. Father would be so annoyed at such behavior from his youngest child. Showing up uninvited to a party was the lowest form of the most crass behavior ever imaginable.

"Should we warn the Angels?" She could see them. They'd moved on from sipping hot chocolate to sampling marzipan from a tray held by a robotic maid. They were too far away to get their attention without yelling.

"They can take care of themselves."

"I suppose. What about Cullen?" There he was, back at the original refreshment table. He seemed to be in conversation with a young lady in a sparkling silver gown. Ree frowned.

"I'm not risking my neck for him."

Ree sighed and rolled her eyes. Boys were so irritating. She really wasn't quite sure what Louise saw in them honestly. Besides how nice they looked in their best dress coats anyway. And how wonderfully Nikolai's eyes sparkled when he was feeling merry. And what a lovely shade of glossy black Cullen's head of hair was. She shook off her thoughts and turned back to spying for Winter.

"Oh, I think I see her!" Ree's voice turned to a whisper. "Oh golly, she's very stunning. Almost like the reindeer girls. I mean, without the antlers."

Winter was coming down one of the staircases that connected the Ballrooms. She glided like a ghost, and she was pale as one too. Her hair was white and hung to her knees in two tight braids. Her dress was white and lined in ermine fur. She had white feathers in her braids and white pearl jewelry. White diamonds shone at her throat, in her ears, and even in her nose. She was accompanied by a group of girls; all of them dressed in white as well, though their hair varied from shades of browns to blacks and reds. Some wore tiaras of diamonds or strands of pearls around their head, winding like crowns. There were streaks of liquid diamonds (could it be?) on their faces, smeared like paint. It made Sylvie's glitter seem crass in comparison. There was what seemed to be sparkling snow on their shoulders and hair. Ree wondered why it didn't melt. As they approached closer, she could see ice on their eyelashes, in perfect, beautiful droplets.

"They say she's enchanted them. Froze them that way, so they stay young." Cullen's voice was casual as he slipped behind the screen.

Ree yelped. "Why do you have to walk so softly?"

"Sorry. Mushroom?"

She glowered, but accepted the mushroom. It was stuffed with cheese, a favorite of Ree's. "Froze them? That's impossible." Her scientific mind was skeptical.

Cullen shrugged. "That's what they say."

"Is she...good?" Ree swallowed the mushroom.

"What do you mean?"

"Is she...on our side?"

Nikolai chuckled his grinding laugh. "What side is that exactly?"

"The good side!" Ree was insulted.

"The side that has crashed this party and is about to blow up a laboratory? That side?"

"I don't think you're very funny. Golly, here comes that big nosed Hoffman. Be quiet."

They huddled together behind the screen, silent until the robot glided past, whirring busily.

"The new model is pretty efficient," Ree whispered. "My Hoffman would have been having hysterics over the lack of pastry and people tracking in too much snow by now."

"Updwellers and their robots," Nikolai said.

"Sea Levelers and their eccentricities," Ree retorted.

"Come on," Cullen interrupted. "Let's find the kids and get off this thing. We've got to be nearly to the train by now."

"Do you think so?" Ree felt anxious. "I've never dropped out of a moving aircraft before. At least not onto a train. That goes to a swamp. By a cemetery."

"You're not chicken, are you?" Cullen demanded. "Because I only invited you on this adventure because I thought you'd be fit for the job."

"Don't be insulting. Of course I'm not chicken," she hissed. "I'm simply being reasonable. I keep remembering Ambrose falling out of the workship. Or was it Seamus? Well, it hardly matters."

"It matters to the one who didn't get splattered," Cullen pointed out. "Come on. Everyone's staring at the Snow Queen. That probably means they're docking for Bon-Bons at the Sea. Now's our chance to get the Angels."

They moved swiftly, without another word. The owl clung tightly to Ree's shoulder (which was getting rather sore) and they headed back the way they had come. The Angels were easy enough to spot. They were the dirty urchins stuffing their faces with marzipan. Ree collared Georgie easily enough, and Nikolai picked up Pork Chop like a sack of potatoes and slung him under his metal elbow. To their credit, the Angels didn't make a peep. Of course, Ree could imagine Miss Ginger picking them up this way when it was time for bed. She could probably fit two or three over her massive shoulders.

They continued out of the round room, the way they had come. Down a flight of stairs Ree barely remembered climbing, into another round room. This one had fewer people. Most everyone obviously wanted to be where their enigmatic hostess was. Then around a corner. Through a door. Into another round room. Had they really wandered so far? Ree must have been distracted or lost in thought at the time.

Finally, they were at the bottom room. Out that door and they'd be on the giant floating staircase to nowhere.

It wasn't the most comforting thought, but it was all Ree had.

Chapter Twenty-nine
The Train to the Cemetery

Sure enough, as they stood on the floating staircase, the wind blowing gently, a light flurry of snow starting to fall, the footmen nowhere to be found, they could see the winding railway cars beneath them.

Awfully far beneath them. Ree took a deep breath. The owl hooted and lifted off her shoulder, flying off into the night.

"Show off," she muttered. The Ballroom was no longer moving, but it did sway alarmingly.

"It's not as far as it looks," Nikolai assured her. "I'm sure we'll be fine."

"Yes, I'm sure we will be. Mama wouldn't stand for me dying this way. It simply isn't done. I'll should die like all the other aristocrats do, either from boredom or old age. Possibly tuberculosis like Great Aunt Marigold always threatens, if I'm feeling dramatic." She held out both her hands, one to Pork Chop and one to Georgie.

"Don't be nervous, miss!" Pork Chop squeezed her hand. "I've jumped further than this puny leap, I have. I'll catch ya."

"Perfect." She gave her best and brightest smile, though she felt like throwing up.

"I'll go first," Nikolai interjected, but before he could make good on his promise, Cullen leaped off the bottom stair with a whoop.

He landed like a rolling hedgehog, tumbling on the railway car and nearly spilling off the other side. Ree's heart skipped a full beat. Nikolai was not to be outdone and with a growl of annoyance, he too threw himself off the Ballroom premises. He landed with a bit more grace, but a lot more noise. He crashed like a hippo. An iron hippo.

But, on the bright side, they'd survived. If they could do it, so could Ree. That had basically been a mantra all her life – especially when it came to boys - and she wasn't about to change her creed now.

"One," she nodded at Pork Chop, "Two, THREE!"

Their landing was a bit haphazard as Georgie had gone on THREE, and Pork Chop and Ree had waited until after THREE, which caused something of a domino effect, and also some wrists and elbows popping. The landing was not at all ladylike, and Ree would have scrambled to cover her ankles had she any breath. Which she did not. She felt like she had been hit by the train, not vice versa.

She lay still and groaned loudly. Finally, with what energy she had left, she managed to roll her head to one side and spied all the boys, plus Georgie, looking at her with concern.

"Okay, Miss Ree?" Georgie knelt beside her. "Next time you should duck and roll. Or at least land on your bottom half. Not your head."

"Yes, capital advice, Georgie. I'll remember that next time." Ree rubbed her throbbing head. Her cute little headpiece had not survived. Gone the way of her toolbox, the Magnocle, her cloak, and her key pins. She tucked her feet beneath her and attempted to stand. The train wasn't moving – hadn't moved in years and years if rust and decay were any judge – but it was still frightening to be on top of it. The wind had really whipped itself into a frenzy and now the snow was falling steadily. But that wasn't what scared Ree.

It was the cemetery.

They were close enough that all they had to do was walk along the cars for a short bit and they'd be there. There with the white tombstones and the crosses that shone eerily in the moonlight and the disturbed soil that had likely been dug through by Cullen himself. There, with the decaying flowers left behind by mourners and the listing gate that wouldn't keep anyone (or anything) out or in. She could see the moon glinting off the headstones from here. They tilted at angles and were full of shadows. She shivered.

Faery tales Up Top weren't scary, and neither were ghost tales. But this was Sea Level. Who knew what they'd find in such a desolate spot?

"Where's the swamp?" she asked, as they began to pick their way carefully towards the cemetery. Their footfalls seemed loud in the silence of the night, though the sound of the waves crashing nearby was audible. Ree longed to see the ocean, but now was not the time. Besides, it was probably full of mermaids, she realized. The desire to see the ocean subsided quickly.

"The cemetery is basically right on edge of it," Cullen answered. "A few more years and the whole thing will likely sink."

"Whatever is a swamp doing here anywhere?" Ree mused. She opened her arms to the side for balance.

"It's not really a swamp, I guess. More of an ocean overspill. A little cove."

"Oh." Ree was relieved. "I was picturing alligators and crocodiles and snakes like we saw at the Botanical Gardens."

"Nope, no alligators or crocodiles," Cullen answered, cheerily. "Maybe sharks."

"You're joking, aren't you?"

"Of course he's joking, and this is no time for it." Once again, Nikolai was on edge. Ree supposed he had a right to be. They had a job to do and it wasn't pretty and it wasn't a time for teasing or making light of it. Lives could be at stake. Then again, it didn't hurt anyone to lighten the atmosphere.

The atmosphere of people long dead, and blowing things up.

The owl swooped down just then and he began to lead the way, flying and gliding ahead of them.

"Cheeky little thing," Ree said, affectionately.

"I hate that bird," Nikolai muttered.

As they approached the cemetery, Ree could see the outline of what had to be Drosselmeier's laboratory. Only he would have such an eccentric old building to work his magic and conduct his experiments in. If it weren't so spooky looking and in such a crazy location, she would have been jealous of Cullen for getting to spend time in it. As it was, even in the distance and in the dark, it looked as though a strong gust of wind would blow it over. It leaned dramatically to the left. It was dark as a tomb inside; Ree hoped that meant no one was at home.

Two nearly grown men, one young lady, and two urchins stood in line at the last railway car and surveyed the scene. The cemetery was old and tattered and sprawling. Indeed, several of the tombstones had sunk right into the sand of the swamp, and the rest weren't far behind. The moonlight glinted off the marble of the markers. The laboratory loomed like a monster, the headstones its rotting teeth that had fallen out of its own head.

"Home sweet evil laboratory!" Cullen said. "Shall we?"

He climbed down first, and offered his hand to Ree. The Angels declined assistance and scuttled down like crabs. Pork Chop promptly hid behind a grave and Ree pretended not to notice until he jumped out and made a menacing face. She yelped obediently, but her heart wasn't in it. Her heart was in her throat.

"What are we doing?" she murmured. "The rest of you will be at Sea Level's mercy if we're caught. I on the other hand, will be at the mercy of Drosselmeier himself Up Top. He'll likely sentence me to one hundred years of hard labor, or one hundred years of needlepoint. He does know what would be a fitting punishment." She rubbed her cold arms with her cold hands.

"Come on," Cullen was impatient. Of course he had been here before, so he had no curiosity to get in his way. "Let's get this over with. Who knows how long the Ballroom will be docked?"

They all looked up, into the night sky. The Ballroom was still hovering where they had left it, but how long did it take party guests to eat a few Bon-Bons? Ree willed her feet to move along faster. She picked up her skirts. They were sinking into the sand, and her toes were beginning to feel wet.

"Maybe we should have just waited until the lab sunk into the sea?" she suggested. "I don't think it will take too long."

"He could have a veritable army made by then," Cullen responded. "You don't understand. These graves?" He gestured around. "Most of them are empty."

Ree swallowed. "Lovely." With new resolve, she made it first to the door.

Locked.

"I don't suppose you have keys?" she asked Cullen.

He snarled. "Dross started to lose trust in me after I kept accidentally/on-purpose misplacing body parts. He had the locks changed. Sorry."

"Don't worry about it," Nikolai answered. He approached the door and slammed his iron fist into it. It crumpled like a fallen soufflé. He grinned, and they all followed suit.

Georgie and Pork Chop went first; not because they were supposed to, but because they moved the fastest. Ree went next, worried for her young charges' safety, and Cullen and Nikolai came last. The Angels lit the miniature lanterns that Ginger had insisted they take and held them high.

The shadows of what was in the old house were less scary than what they illuminated. "Oh, goody," Ree whispered, "I was hoping this adventure wouldn't come to an end without some jars of questionable specimens and/or dead bodies." She turned and came face to face with a stranger and screamed.

"It's only an automaton!" Cullen assured her. "Don't be so jumpy or you'll never get past the first level."

"Why do we have to get past the first level at all?" Ree sighed. "Let's just burn the whole thing down."

"We need to do the 'sponsible thing, miss," Pork Chop interjected. "First we make sure the place is empty 'fore we light it up. It's called integrity. It's the integral thing to do."

Ree hid her smile and turned her back on the automaton. "What if there are more like Nikolai?" It seemed strange to rescue any robots – even ones like China, with factory marks and signatures in their empty chests – but if there were human experiments?

"I told you, they're already dead." Cullen's voice was flat. He didn't want to be here anymore than the rest of them did, Ree understood. Well, the Angels maybe wanted to be here. They seemed to be having a good old time. Georgie picked up a jar of something pale and white. They were slender and extended out of the jar like flowers. They were decidedly not flowers however.

"Ladyfingers?" she asked, giggling.

"Focus, Georgie," Ree said, sternly. "Come along. We're only making sure my godfather isn't here, nor anyone else...human. And then we'll do what we came for."

"Boom?" she asked, eagerly.

"Yes, boom. And be back in time for Bon-Bons if we play our cards right."

"We don't play cards, Miss Ree." Her voice was righteous with indignation. "Miss Ginger says it's a sin."

"Oh for golly's sake, shut up and stay close." Ree had had enough conversation. "Put down that coffin lid this instant, Pork Chop! Don't be so impertinent. Nikolai and Cullen, check the rooms in this level. Children, we're going upstairs."

Silently, she was obeyed. Once again, Mama would be proud.

Ladyfingers aside.

Chapter Thirty
Boom

Pork Chop, Georgie, and Ree had nearly made it up the stairs before someone screamed. It was Ree, and it was the second time she had done so since they'd entered the house. She made a mental note to give herself a good talking to about overreacting once her heartbeat went down to a normal rate. It was only the owl that had scared them. He must have come in through the chimney.

It flew past them with a loud squawking sound, and then turned around and came back towards them, squawking again. Ree clapped her hands over her ears and scowled at the bird. "Stop that right now! You sound more like a rooster than you do a majestic owl. You should be ashamed of yourself." The owl ignored her and continued to make noise and swoop back and forth, up and down the stairs. Ree looked at Pork Chop, who shrugged.

"Got me, Miss," he said, unhelpfully. "I flunked right outta Animal Psychology. I think he's just gone crackers maybe."

"Or he's trying to tell me something," Ree mused. The owl was really going mad though; it hit a wall and flopped back in the air, then somersaulted, righted itself, and began its maniacal course of flight once more.

"Looks like he's been in the cider," Georgie theorized. "I've seen faeries who moved like that. Why, just last week I had to spatula off the remains of a-"

"Yes, yes, I know. You told me." Ree gave a gentle push to the Angel, who took a few more steps up. She was finally at the second floor.

Or was. The owl made a beeline for Georgie, and knocked her right off her feet. She tumbled down four stairs, right past Ree and into Pork Chop.

"Shove off, clumsy!" Pork Chop pushed her, and poor Georgie finished tumbling down the rest of the stairs.

"That's about enough out of you," Ree told her bird, firmly. She scooped it up and anchored it beneath the crook of her elbow, pressed against her rib cage. "This corset is a lethal weapon, I'll have you know, and I'm about to skewer you. Marinated Owl on a Stick. I bet they'd be all the rage at the market. Are you all right, Georgie?"

"Right as rain, miss," came the cheerful reply. "But if you don't mind, I'm gonna stay down here with the severed limbs and pickled digits. Seems safer than travelin' with that dumb fowl, don'tchaknow."

"Stay close to Nikolai then. Come on, Pork Chop."

They reached the second floor without incident, since the deranged bird was under control. It did struggle under Ree's arm though, and it took quite a bit of her concentration to ignore it. Pets were not as wonderful and easy as she had first believed them to be. She was beginning to regret taking one on.

The second floor was much like the first. Pork Chop's little lantern showed a table that appeared to be laid out for operating or assembling, boxes of gears and gadgets and clock parts, metal hands and feet, disassembled robotic torsos, and also a smallish bed with a reading lamp. Even in the light of day, it would have been described by anyone as ghoulish, and that was without the small collection of shrunken heads on a shelf. *This must have been Cullen's room*, Ree thought. Or Dross' himself, though she rather thought he'd have a bedroom more elaborate. Perhaps behind that door.

The door that Sylvie was standing in front of.

* * *

"Sylvie?" Ree was confused, and it showed in her voice. "Whatever are you doing here?"

"Don't be daft, miss," Pork Chop's voice was low. "I don't think she's here for a social call or nuttin'."

Ree stared at the faery. Sylvie looked much the same as she had earlier that afternoon. When she had basically rescued Fritz from drinking himself into oblivion. Hadn't she?

"You came to help, after all?" Ree guessed.

Sylvie cocked her head. "Pork Chop is right. You shouldn't be so daft. Aren't you supposed to be an educated lady?"

"Yes, well, I was brought up to be polite. Just what are you doing in my godfather's house precisely?"

Sylvie smiled. It was not a nice smile. It would have chilled Ree to the bone had she not been so annoyed. "I'm after your nutcracker man. I paid dearly for him, and he wasn't delivered in a timely fashion."

"So you really are a hired thug?" Ree was incredulous. "I knew it!" She stomped her foot for emphasis.

"Of course not, don't be insulting. I work for myself. I like being my own boss. A girl has to look out for herself, don't you know? After all, we aren't all born into royalty like you, your highness," she said, glaring at Ree.

"I really am going to smear you on toast," Ree promised. "And then I'm going to serve you Up Top at my next dinner party. Faery pate."

"Oh, please. You wouldn't want to get your hands dirty, Updweller. Now, Nikolai and I are leaving together, and then I don't much care what you do. Burn the whole thing down if you like. I would have made my move earlier, and shown my hand, but you'd gone and surrounded yourself with help. Everyone from your irritable brother to that giant woman. Oh well. A few down," she echoed herself from that night with the sky pirates, "A few more to go."

"Ree?" It was a call from downstairs. Cullen. "Everything all right up there? We're clear down here. We'd better light this thing and get out of here before Drosselmeier comes back."

Sylvie snorted a decidedly unladylike – or unfaerylike – snort. "You all are dumber than rocks." She picked up a nearby jar of what looked like teeth and shook them like dice.

Ree wanted to smack her. "Just how do you plan to overpower us anyway? There's one of you, and three of us." The owl pecked her through her dress and Ree thumped it impatiently.

"There's five of us, miss." Pork Chop looked wounded.

"Yes, I meant five, sorry." She tousled his hair with the hand that wasn't holding the owl.

Sylvie had put back the teeth and was busy brushing off her glitter, of all things to be doing. Ree watched in fascinated alarm as it swirled around her. She shook out her skirts and her hair too. Sparkling glitter that billowed and churned into...something else. Something sinister. It flew around Sylvie with force, blowing her raven hair and her skirts. She smiled once again, through the chaos the glitter was causing. Sylvie began to move towards the stairs.

"Stop her!" Ree was talking to herself more than anyone, but Pork Chop took her at her word. He reached out with both hands, then hissed, and pulled them back to his own body. Sylvie continued past them and began to move down the stairway like a sparkling phantom.

"What happened?" Ree ignored the exit of the faery for the moment and attended to the Angel, who was cradling his hands.

"It burns," he whimpered. "It's like putting your hands through glass knives."

His hands were covered in splinters and tiny shards of twinkling glitter that were dulled by the blood they were causing. Ree dropped the owl out of the nearest window and slammed it shut. Then she grabbed the coverlet from the bed, which was the nearest piece of clothing she could see in the dim light of the lantern. She wrapped up Pork Chop's hands, with a kiss on each palm for good measure, causing him to blush profusely. "Better?" she whispered.

He gulped. "Better, miss. Now what?"

"Follow her...and well...follow her. We'll start with that part. I'll let you know the rest of the plan after I come up with it." First things were first, and she yanked out a dagger from her corset. It took a moment, and Pork Chop watched with alarm as she struggled.

"You okay, miss?"

"Hell's bells, this is going to take some practice. Perfectly adequate, thank you. Are you able to hold a weapon?"

"Only with my toes." He glanced down at his wrapped hands, which roughly the size of Nikolai's metal one now, and completely lacking in any dexterity. "I'm of no use now." He was crestfallen. "You should just leave me here. I'll go down with the ship, miss. It's best that way."

"Don't be ridiculous. You're needed now more than ever." Ree spoke briskly, in her no nonsense voice. It wouldn't do for Pork Chop to pity himself at the moment. There were things that needed to be done. "First of all, unless Cullen is immune to faery glitter, or whatever that stuff really is, Sylvie and Nikolai are likely about to start flying over our heads. Though where she thinks she's going with him, I don't have the foggiest notion." The thought of the small faery carrying the rather bulky Nikolai was alternately amusing and annoying. "All in all, this doesn't change the plan."

"Boom?" Pork Chop's spirits were instantly lifted.

"Quite," agreed Ree. "Boom indeed."

"Ree!" It was Cullen, and he was shouting up the stairs.

"Yes, yes, I know all about it," Ree sighed as she and the Angel began to move towards the first floor once again.

"She's taking him, Miss Ree!" Georgie piped up, as they entered the room. She was jumping up and down with frenzied excitement. Cullen was on the floor. He seemed dazed and there was a cloud of sparkling glitter just coming to rest on the floor next to him. His head was bleeding a bit.

"They're on the roof. I should have stopped her! Done something!" He smacked himself in the forehead, and then, standing on unsteady legs, he picked up a glass vase full of skeleton bones, and threw it where it smashed against the floor.

"That's hardly helpful," Ree pointed out, stepping over the shattered glass. She tuned her ears to what sounded like a scuffle on the roof. "There isn't anything you could have done unless you had some sort of shield against that ungodly glitter. Stop fretting. And stop bleeding while you're at it. Use your Ascot for something useful."

Cullen stopped pacing and looked at her under hooded eyes. "Fretting? I'm not fretting. I'm ..."

"Pitching a fit?" Georgie supplied.

He turned his glare towards her. "Stay out of it, pipsqueak." He yanked his Ascot loose and dabbed at his head with it.

"All right, all right." Ree began the complicated process of returning her dagger to her corset, gave up, and pocketed it instead. She might need it later and it would be better if it were accessible. "Now, I've lost my hat, which means I've lost my vials as well. I suppose it doesn't really matter since this place is nothing but a tinderbox of chemicals and flammable ingredients. We could probably just toss Pork Chop's lantern at a wall and walk away. But just to be on the safe side ..." Ree picked up an apothecary jar of fluid off a bookshelf. "Dross organizes his potions here in the same manner he does on the airship. That is to say, not in a practical way at all. What is this? Hair pomade?" She showed it to Cullen.

He squinted at it. "I think it's wallpaper paste."

"Oh, for golly's sake." Ree rolled her eyes. "Sometimes I honestly don't know if he's an evil genius or just an elderly eccentric. This one?" She chose another and sniffed it experimentally. "Beef gravy. Lovely."

"Here," Cullen pulled down a larger jar off the top shelf. "Lamp oil. Highly flammable. We can douse the whole first floor."

Ree shrugged. "Old fashioned and not as scientific or ironic as I would have hoped, but it will do the trick." There was a tremendous thump from the roof. Ree peered out the nearest window and craned her head to look. She couldn't see Nikolai or Sylvie, but what she did see when she looked up made her smile.

"We don't wanna be here when it blows, miss," Pork Chop told her. "We'd best make a trail. A lighter in effect. Leave it to me and Georgie. That's what we're here for. Although you will give the nutcracker man time to get off the roof, won't you?" He was anxious. He was also staring in horrified fascination at a small crystal bowl filled with fingernail clippings.

"Naturally. Just do your part." Ree pulled her head back in. She made a motion with her head to Cullen. He came over and stuck his head out the window as well. And grinned.

Georgie was already scampering up a shelf to reach the curtains. They were trimmed up top in a gaudy fringe, and Ree understood immediately what she was thinking. It would make a perfect rope trail once it was soaked in the oil. She poured the oil in a steady but thin trickle and began to walk around the room. "Sorry," she murmured to the coffin, "But you are already dead, so I'm sure you understand." Whomever was inside stayed silent. Thank goodness.

"Cullen? Grab that tinderbox over by the fire. And please tell me it isn't empty." Ree had made her own matches before, using sticks and sulphur, but she didn't relish taking the time to do it again. It was about time something went easy in this adventure she'd found herself in.

Chapter Thirty-one
Suddenly Surrendered

The fringe from the curtains had been cut down and soaked in the oil. There was a trail of the stuff leading from a puddle in the center of the laboratory all the way outside, winding through the cemetery, and ending where the group of arsonists stood. There had indeed been a few long stick matches left in the tinderbox, and Cullen held it expectantly. Ree assumed the lamp oil would be enough to burn the whole place down, but just to be sure, they had tossed most of the remains of the apothecary jars into the puddle before they left. It had caused an awful stink and was already starting to smoke and steam even without the aid of fire.

They were all – Cullen, Georgie, and poor Pork Chop with the cut up hands – staring at Ree. How she became the leader of this ragtag crew of outlaws she wasn't sure, but she took the responsibility and liked the way it felt for the most part. She could have done without the sinking feeling in the pit of her stomach, and the remains of pickled egg that kept threatening to come back up, and also the looming feeling of pressure, but still. Ree felt ready as she'd ever be to commit a crime and get away with it.

The owl was perched on a headstone and kept letting out mournful hooting cries until Pork Chop threatened it with a rock. Ree couldn't help but glance at the inscription of the headstone in the light of Georgie's lantern.

Here lies Benjamin Moses
His kneecaps, arms, and toeses
The rest were eaten by mermaids fair
Stay away kiddies, from the sea folk's lair
RIP

Ree walked back to the group.

"Ready?" she asked.

In answer, Cullen lit the match. He did it quickly, with no hesitation at all, but Ree could tell his hands were shaking. He lowered the match to the ground, where the oil soaked fringe lay. Ree held her breath, hoping the curtain trim wasn't already too wet from the sand and snow to catch fire, but catch fire it did, and in a blaze of wonderful light. It spread quickly, racing back to the ramshackle laboratory. The owl hooted loudly and flew off in a huff. Cullen and Ree and the Angels held their breath as the flame reached the house.

BOOM!

Georgie and Pork Chop immediately began to cheer, and Ree couldn't help but to join in the celebration. They jumped up and down like lunatics, and Pork Chop pumped his arms so hard the makeshift bandage flew off. Cullen was grinning, but he calmed the others down.

"Shhh! You're going to get the attention of the Ballroom!" he admonished.

"You mean if the fireball and explosion didn't get it first?" Ree laughed, brushing the hair out of her eyes. She hooked her arm through his, and they watched as the lab burned, sending off sparks into the night sky. "This is a prettier sight than Up Top's fireworks display."

Cullen looked at her, curious. "That's a strange thing to say."

Ree felt embarrassed. She moved her hand off his elbow. "I'm sorry. I know it was your home. That was crass of me. I do apologize."

He waved away the explanation and tucked her arm back in his firmly. "No, not that. I mean, it's peculiar how you belong here at Sea Level. How you don't seem to fit in in the world you live in Up Top. Most people down here would give anything to live up there. You aren't most people. I like that."

Ree could feel herself flushing. It was peculiar. Part of her never wanted to go back home, except of course for not wanting to worry her family and wanting them with her. But even Jessa and Hoffman felt far away. A life from another lifetime. This life here at Sea Level, this enchanted life, with its strange divertissements and danger and adventure was all more suited to Ree than was a life of tea and etiquette and the occasional dabbling in mechanics when she was allowed. But what did that mean? And what did that make her? Mama would never understand.

"All right, miss," Pork Chop interjected into Ree's thoughts, "That went real nice and all, but we'd best be getting on with Phase Two. It's integral." He had his tongue stuck between his teeth and was winding the cloth back on his hands. Or trying to anyway.

"Ahoy, my dearly intended!" A shout from above. Ree would have recognized Captain Fennimore's booming voice anywhere. She saw the dim outline of his very self-hanging from a window. His whiskers blew carefree in the night breeze. "Ahoy to you, I say! We have a couple prisoners here you might want to take a look at! Identify, so to speak."

"Ahoy yourself!" she called up. "Can we come up?"

She couldn't see through the gloom of the night, but she had the distinct feeling the captain was beaming by the jovial tone in his next words. "I thought you'd never ask!"

"Ginger will kill me for exposing you to sky pirates." Ree turned to look at the Angels.

"Nah, we don't even haveta tell her." They spoke as one.

I've said that a few times in my life, thought Ree.

"Can you lower something for us to climb? And also, do you give us the assurance you won't, um, murder us?" Ree shouted.

There was a shocked silence from The Suddenly Surrendered. Then, "You wound me, madam. You truly do."

They watched from the railway car as a hatch opened in the ship. A crazy looking ladder unfolded itself with wooden rungs. It looked slightly sturdier than Dross' ramshackle rope ladder, but not by much. It seemed to have a life of its own as well; the rungs were like legs stuck out at crooked angles, and it was unfolding itself like a yawning, stretching cat.

Also, it didn't quite reach to the ground, but swung chaotically at eye level. "Well," Ree said, "If we're going up to our deaths, I'll go first. Cullen, a hand if you please."

He cupped his hands together for Ree to step on. It was a messy, swinging feat, but Ree accomplished the ladder and disappeared inside the hatch in a matter of minutes, Georgie and Pork chop scrambling below her.

* * *

"You do know I'll be telling Mama and Father about this latest escapade of yours," Fritz said, conversationally, as Ree's head popped up carefully through the hatch in the floor. He was puffing on a cigar, reminding Ree of Anastasia, and he had his boots up on a blue fainting couch. He looked quite comfortable. Sylvie, on the other hand, didn't look comfortable at all. She was tied up, bound and gagged and Ree was pleased as punch to see the gag. She'd had enough of Sylvie's obnoxious voice to last the rest of her natural life. If looks could kill, they'd all be dead. Sylvie's wings were smashed to smithereens on the floor, sticky with pink goo and glitter.

Nikolai wasn't trussed up, but he was under the watchful gaze of Fennimore Trapper.

"What are you doing here?" Ree demanded of Fritz, breathless from her climb. She reached a hand down to help Georgie. "You're supposed to be...drunk."

"I was." Fritz scowled. "Remind me to smear that faery on toast later. Kept pouring me drink after drink; acting like she was matching me, but I think she was pouring it over her shoulder or something. You could have warned me about her." Sylvie made an impolite noise from behind her gag.

"Would you have listened?" Ree leaned down on the pirate's floor and stuck her head through the hatch. Pork Chop was struggling a bit with the ladder with his sore hands. She hooked her hands beneath his armpits and tugged. Together, they wiggled their way up, and Cullen was right behind.

"That doesn't explain what you're doing here. Oh, The Scurvy Dog Pirate Saloon," Ree answered herself. "Let me guess, you were having drinks with the pirates and one thing led to another?"

Captain Fennimore could stay silent no longer. He crossed the room, planted his large mitts on each side of Ree's face, and kissed her on each cheek with a loud smack. "My dear, you are as lovely and intelligent as ever I remember!"

"Hey, knock that off," Cullen shoved the big man off Ree.

"Look," Ree was simultaneously flattered by Cullen's jealousy and irritated by Fennimore's exuberance. "Let's keep calm heads, shall we? We need to figure out some things here. Like, what to do with her." Ree gestured towards the faery betrayer. "And where we can go that Nikolai will be safe. And also, I seem to be consorting with pirates ..." That last observation was mostly for herself. The circumstances had finally caught up with her. Was she any safer up here with Fennimore and his crew than she was down there with an irate faery and an exploding laboratory? Had she gone from the frying pan right into the fire? It had seemed like a good idea at the time. There was an inscription for her own headstone if ever she'd heard one.

Ree finally took the time to look around the ship. There was Jedidiah (or was it Obadiah? She couldn't remember which was alive and which was dead). Whichever twin it was was sprawled on the upper bunk of a set of hammock beds. He appeared to be reading – Ree squinted – a copy of a dog-eared children's book. Seamus (or was it Ambrose?) was doing pushups in the corner. The ship itself was fabulously decorated, in a manner that was so colorful and bright and full of trinkets and knickknacks and oddities, that Ree thought Ginger would have felt at home. It was a bit dirty though; there was spoiled food here and there, and piles of laundry. There was a distinct smell too. Ree couldn't place what it was. Sweat...and blood? Feet? She wasn't sure.

There was also a cat. A huge orange thing with long hair. It was sharing the fainting couch with Fritz, but in terms of who was taking up more room, it was hard to say. Fritz kept moving over to give the feline more room, who would occasionally give a little hiss.

"This is Lady Marmalade," said the captain, fondly.

"Er, nice to meet you," Ree replied. She'd never seen a cat before, besides the one that had frightened her at the market. It looked tame enough. For a smallish lion anyway. "What do you plan on doing with her?" Sylvie kicked against her bonds in reply.

Fennimore's already dark countenance blackened even further. "I hate faeries," he said. "Nasty things. Flying into my ship. Cornering the market on crime down there. Sticking their pointy noses where they don't belong. And their glitter? Don't get me started on that wretched invention. Did you know they shed and the birds of the forest peck at it and it kills them? I have a fondness for the birds, you know. So, I thank you, my dove, for delivering Miss Bird Murderer to me. This particular faery and I have quite a history you might say. If you don't mind, I'd like to keep her."

Ree raised a red eyebrow at this. "Keep her? Whatever for?" She couldn't imagine and wasn't sure she wanted to.

"I think I've got a solution." It was a new voice. No, not new precisely: Ree would know it anywhere. She whirled.

It was Drosselmeier.

Chapter Thirty-two
Rescues and Reunions

Ree's heart didn't know how to react to hear the presence of her godfather. She removed the whale bone dagger from her pocket and pointed it towards Drosselmeier with a fierce expression on her face.

Fennimore placed both hands over his heart. "My dove, at this moment in history you are the very picture of everything I've ever wanted in a woman."

Ree ignored him. "When did you - how did you - what ARE you?" she finally settled on a question for her godfather.

The inventor smiled weakly. He appeared to have aged in the last few days, although honestly, Ree could sympathize with that feeling. She felt much older too. He shrugged, then winced as if something hurt. He rubbed his elbow, grimacing as though it hurt.

"Well, I'm not sure what I am. A man who has made many mistakes, first off."

Nikolai glared at him, as did Cullen. Sylvie pouted from behind her bonds. Ree kept her distance. Fennimore nodded sagely at Dross, as if in agreement.

"It's important for us old men to admit to our shortcomings," he said. "We must strive to better ourselves, pirates and gamblers alike."

"Er, yes," Dross agreed. "I got in over my head, I'm afraid. Cullen was right to try to stop me, although he probably should have gotten his facts straight first. I knew I was wrong then, though I wouldn't admit it, and of course I fully know it now. I thought I was doing good in this broken world. I thought I was advancing science, granting new life. I had given people back their limbs, fixed their broken parts. It was so much like building automatons. Soon enough the two began to blend together. When I began to owe money to the pirates here," Drosselmeier nodded towards

Fennimore, who raised the glass of ale he had just poured from a portable bar, "I started to panic."

Fennimore took a swig of ale and nodded in a solemn manner. "That's the usual reaction. Appreciate the compliment."

"Add to that," Dross continued, "Sylvie came to me and said she had a buyer. For Nikolai, and for more like him. For anything I could make, really. I boasted. Stupid cider. Started blathering that I could raise the dead, in essence. It was all nonsense really. But she took me seriously and her money was...well, I needed the advancement. I didn't realize she was working on her own plans and I probably wouldn't have taken her so seriously if I'd known. I wouldn't have been intimidated by a faery, but I assumed her employer was someone to be reckoned with." A spot of pink appeared on his cheekbones, as if embarrassed that he had been taken in and bullied by a faery.

A robotic maid entered the room. She was rather scantily dressed, even for a mechanical. Fennimore beamed. "Meet Stella! I thought you might be hungry."

Feeling a little dazed, Ree joined everyone else. Stella had delivered quite a lot of refreshments, and the Angels especially were overjoyed.

Pork Chop was digging into a large platter of chicken drumsticks. He was covered in sauce. The pantry aboard The Suddenly Surrendered was obviously much better stocked than the one aboard the workship.

"I do think we should get the children back," she mentioned to whomever was listening. Pork Chop shook his head, and Georgie began to wail.

"But Miss Ree, we ain't heard the rest of the story! And we can stay out late, we can truly! Bedtime is real flexible. It's one of the perks of being an orphan."

Ree dipped a cheese biscuit in a cup of tea and looked around her. The moment seemed to be frozen in time, just for a second or two.

Dross continued his tale. "I wasn't sure who Sylvie was working for, who exactly was trying to raise an army, and she wouldn't tell me. The captain here was after me and getting closer every day." Fennimore tried to look modest. "Cullen was starting to hate me. I was in too deep. I knew I was going to need help to undo all the damage I had caused. That's where you came in, my dear." He smiled sheepishly at Ree. "Honestly, you were the only person alive who had any love for me at all. I had a feeling if I waved a golden carrot, you'd follow it."

"Well, you could have stepped in and told us all that before now," Georgie was cross with him. She had no patience with anyone who kept coffins in the parlor. She'd said as much earlier. It was worse than playing cards.

"You wouldn't have believed me," Dross pointed out, ruefully. "You were all set to murder me once you'd realized what I'd done. And Cullen had already run away."

"It was you who took the rats after all, wasn't it?" Cullen paused in his devouring of apricot cake to ask. "In the Aquarium?"

"Well, if I'd told you once, I'd told you a thousand times not to leave the controlling device lying around. You always were a messy child." He pulled a feather out of his hair and flicked it to the floor. Ree narrowed her eyes.

"How did it go so far, godfather?" she asked. "So much sorrow, so much...death. Whatever were you thinking?" She wanted to add, *you should be ashamed of yourself*, but looking at his contrite face, she knew he already was. The feather had floated to the ground, soft and gray. It reminded Ree of the owl. But, no. How silly... Ree shook her head to clear it of its melodramatic wanderings, or the aftereffects of the wound fever.

Nikolai had been rather silent until now. "He did save my life," he said simply. "Once upon a time."

They were all quiet for a moment, pondering that.

"You mean, after I shot you?" Cullen grinned.

Ree gave him a warning look. "That doesn't mean he had the right to own you," she pointed out to Nikolai.

Suddenly, Sylvie gave a lurch. They all glanced at her. She tumbled to the floor in a heap of petticoats.

"Yes, yes, what to do about her?" Fennimore rubbed his whiskers in a thoughtful manner. "You see, old man," this was directed to Drosselmeier, "I believe we can call it square - those pesky debts of yours - if you help with one thing."

"I'm one step ahead of you, Captain." Dross lifted his rat walking stick. For one awful moment, Ree thought he meant to bludgeon Sylvie to death. She had no love at all for the wicked faery, but she'd prefer not to have to spatula her remains off the pirate's flooring. Instead, he unscrewed the top of the cane and pulled the rat head off. He leveled the cane at Sylvie. Her eyes were wide with terror. "Your ship could use a figurehead, could it not?"

Fennimore gave a shout of agreement. "Ho, she could! She could indeed!"

Ree watched in amazement. A beam like liquid lightning came shooting out of his cane. The moment it touched Sylvie, she froze solid. Like a block of wood. A block of wood shaped like a lovely faery.

"How on earth did you-" she began.

It was Dross' turn to look modest. "Who do you think sold her her glitter in the first place? I have a lot of potions and such that you have yet to learn about, my dear. I am the greatest inventor in the world." He rubbed his elbow again, and winked his one good eye.

Ree couldn't help a small smile. She was floating in a sky pirate's dragon-shaped ship in the wee hours of the morning. She was sort of engaged to the captain, although she assumed her father could get her out of that (not being an orphan also had its perks). She had better friends now than she'd ever had in her life, although she would never admit such a thing to Jessa. She was quite fond of not one, but two boys who might just be men the next time they met. She had met a woman who wasn't a woman, violent mermaids, and killer faeries. Well, just one killer faery, but still. She had dangled dangerously out of not one, but two, dirigibles, and she was wearing a corset made of daggers. She'd made and lost a very good friend in China and she would never forget her. She hoped Ginger had remembered the pink stockings. And she'd reconciled with her godfather, who if he wasn't a full-on scoundrel, was at least a humbled sinner.

"I think I'm retired now." The inventor raised his hands in surrender. "I've learned my lesson, children, No more playing with lives any longer, I promise. It'll be back to strictly clocks and gadgets and robots for me. Maybe a little piracy. You know, for when life gets boring. And for you," he looked at Ree with a twinkle in his eye, "It will be Latin, Arithmetic, and sewing a fine seam."

Ree groaned. "Don't threaten me," she said.

The End.

About the author

Melyssa Williams is a mom, sister, daughter, wife, friend, ballet teacher, ex-contemporary dancer and ballerina, and writer, who resides in Southern Oregon. She was homeschooled back in the day when it was slightly odd and eccentric, which came in handy when she decided to be an author. She drinks coffee too often and reads fiction at inopportune times. She has parented inner city teens and thinks she might want to sky dive, but that's about all the excitement she can handle. Other than that, she finds baking bread and sipping wine to be the most thrilling parts of life. As an excellent pen-pal back in the day, she can guarantee if you drop her a note, she will write back (and maybe send some stickers or something): http://melyssawilliams.com

CPSIA information can be obtained
at www.ICGtesting.com
Printed in the USA
LVHW081804081121
702776LV00014B/636